Catch the Moon, Mary

Wendy Waters

¶

Published by Linen Press, Edinburgh 2015

1 Newton Farm Cottages

Miller Hill

Dalkeith

Midlothian

EH22 1SA

www.linen-press.com

A CIP catalogue record for this book is available from the British Library.

Cover photograph: © Des Cannon at Anima Fotografie (500px.com/wildoscar)
Cover design: Louise Santa Ana / Zebedee Design
Typeset in Sabon by Zebedee Design, Edinburgh
Printed and bound in Great Britain by Biddles

ISBN 9780957596856

For my mother who gave me wings.

Acknowledgements

Once upon a time I wrote a story about a girl and an angel who planned to save the world with beautiful music. The story grew and evolved over the years and after many changes and much rearranging I finally felt it was ready to submit to publishers and agents. Five years of rejections later Lynn Michell saw a glimmer of something special in my story and offered to publish it. Now I must explain here that Lynn Michell is an editor with super-natural powers. After erasing bucket-loads of chaff she revealed a few exquisite ears of wheat and a beautiful heart – the story of a fallen angel and the woman who redeemed him. First and foremost I have to thank Lynn for her genius editing and her faith. And speaking of faith I want to thank Ali Watts, the publisher at Penguin whose support and belief has kept me going for seven years. Thank you, Ali. And thank you to my dear friends who encourage and sustain me – Kelly Anne Thacher, Hazel Philips, Nigel Lewis, Scott Hastie, Graeme and Deb Ratcliffe, Jonathan Moore, Amanda Pratt, Paul Horne, Jarrod Boyle Isabelle Vallen-Thorpe, Philip Sutherland and Anthony O'Neill. Thank you! And a huge thank you to my long-suffering family members, Sabina Campbell and Paul Hardiman, who slog through every new ms of mine and tell me the truth no matter how painful. Bless you! Thank you Shanon Whitelock for the music! And then there's my mother, Carmol Scammell, a fine poet and brilliant artist, who proofs every draft and always insists I write better than anyone! Thanks Mum! And lastly, the angels who delight in human endeavour and my magnificent daughter, Genevra, who taught me the meaning of love and is saving the world one rat at a time – fairly certain this is work-related. Thank you all.

OVERTURE

Thematic introduction to an opera or other large musical work

The night was a thin skin of stars and prophecy, the full moon unnaturally bright. All evening he'd felt a presence, as if someone or some*thing* was following him, but when he looked around there was no-one there. He was desperate to reach Sydney and take a rest and settle his nerves before embarking on another long, dark night on the wing.

'I am going mad, creating phantom company.' He spoke aloud just to hear another voice. 'If only I still had a lover in Florence.'

Florence, where lovely women left windows open for him and artists begged to paint him. How beautiful he was back then. How perfectly swathed in flesh. He'd posed nude for Michelangelo and Da Vinci, his wings a whisper of light at his shoulder-blades, a hundred tallow candles burnishing his summoned flesh, his sienna eyes and golden curls. In those halcyon Renaissance years he enjoyed a little respite from the quest, lingering in Florence where human genius had reached extraordinary heights in art and architecture. For almost a hundred years he cast no shadow on earth, sea or cloud. Time moved at a slow, luxurious pace and his flesh was a jacket he could don at will.

Now it stuck to his soul like sin.

'This modern world metes out time like currency,' he grumbled, pushing his tired wings through a thick band of cloud composed of Pacific Ocean sweat. 'Everybody rushing about in pursuit of nothing, producing little of lasting value. No-one stands still long enough to hear his own soul crying out for meaning. Who hears my message above the clamour of traders, bankers and malevolent pop music? I would bring enlightenment if only they listened. One receptive soul is all I need to spread the message.' He mentally leafed through his list of established facts. 'For it is a well-documented fact that change begins with one person.'

For a thousand years he had searched for that one shining soul whose faith would torch the night and redeem the day, a saint who would help him with his quest to enlighten the world and forge an indestructible bridge between heaven and earth. But the most likely candidate had rebuffed him.

Diavolo, accused Francesco of Assisi.

How could a man of such vision mistake him for the fallen angel whose hunger for power had glued him to earth? Diavolo. His hope died that day. But he kept going. His pride would not allow him to admit defeat.

It was well past midnight when he arrived in Sydney. The moon, still riding high, silvered the wind-bellied sails of the city's famous opera house and made a tinfoil crumple of the harbour. The spring day was unusually hot for the air was still warm and smelled faintly of jasmine, a scent that stabbed at his heart, reminded him of his brother, and for one optimistic moment he imagined it was Rigel who'd been trailing him through the southern hemisphere all evening, playing hide-and-seek with his hopes. But, of course, Rigel wasn't there. He was quite alone.

He flew over the inner city streets where the homeless, seemingly rising out of cracks in the pavement, rummaged the bins for food. 'Why do these people eat garbage when the fish in the sea and the fruit on the bough are given freely?'

The homeless did not answer nor did they look up. His wing shadows pulsed over them like lost faith. He flew into the Botanic Gardens and hovered over a bed of spring flowers the colour of Liquorice Allsorts.

'Just a brief rest,' he told himself as he rubbed his aching back and shrugged his tired wings. 'Then I'll continue my search for a saint, Father.' He glanced up. 'I promise.'

'Oh, shining one.' It was the flowers who spoke. 'Why have you chosen to bless us with your light? We are not tall like the trees or constant like the grass. Our season is brief and we depend on bees for survival.'

'I haven't chosen you and my light is almost out. I'm just resting above you until my body stops aching.'

'But you are the new day come to us by night,' they sighed in perfumed drifts.

'You're mistaken. You flowers who are rooted in a small patch of earth see little and know less. But happily you'll be dead before disappointment wearies you.'

The flowers folded their petals and shrank from him. A thousand years on the wing had made him cruel – a high price to pay for a fruitless quest.

The rigour of his existence suddenly flagged and, feather-weighted, he drifted down, missing a single note of music that pierced the waning night like a swan's last song. A second note followed, building upon the first, a star-bound rung. Then a third note rang out, completing a silver chord that echoed moonlight. But he missed them all. He tumbled onto the flowerbed, crushing the blooms into scent, silence and pastel light. Too miserable to apologise for snuffing out their brief lives even earlier, he lay on his back, glaring into the dark domain he'd occupied for the better part of ten centuries.

'Let me die. Take me, Mother Earth. Make a secret of me.'

He peeled a strip of graying flesh off his arm. Pallid light bled from the wound. 'In the morning the gardeners will find a pile of gray feathers and a sheath of pale skin. They will wonder what died in the night.' He looked heavenwards. 'Forgive me, Father, I can serve You no longer.'

It was then that the music, which he had missed when he drifted down, bathed him in melody, fragrant as hope, bubbly as windblown spume and bewitching as a siren's song. He sat up in the broken flower bed, listening intently, a yearning chambering in his soul.

'I must own this music that soothes my weary soul,' he whispered.

He rose up and flew into the labyrinthine sprawl of Sydney's western suburbs determined to find the source. At length his searching brought him to a small brown house in Blacktown where the music streamed through an open window gilding everything in its path including a bowl of honeyed bread on the sill. He dipped his finger into the melodic slipstream and withdrew it, silvered, as excitement prickled like sudden cold. 'Who needs a suspicious saint? I have stumbled upon a far more reliable path to salvation. For it is a well-documented fact that people listen to music where they ignore prophets. If I seed this music with divine inspiration it will save not only me but the entire world.' He shivered at the possibility. 'It will be played by the greatest musicians, my message reverberating through the ages.'

He peered into the room. A young girl lay in bed, her eyes fixed on the moon, the melody bursting from her soul like a genie from an uncorked bottle.

'A child!' He shrank back. 'This is awkward. Gifted children usually have ambitious parents.'

The music stopped abruptly and the child leapt out of bed

and ran to the window, small hands pressed to her heart. 'You came!'

'Are you addressing me?' he asked, edging forward.

'It's not enough though, is it?' She pointed to the bowl of honeyed bread. 'You're much bigger than I thought you'd be.' She started scratching her palms.

He looked at the sticky mess that was beginning to attract ants. 'Who exactly is this for?'

'The elves. Mum says they'll bring me luck if I leave honeyed bread on the window sill. I could even win money, Mum says.'

'Stupid whimsy.' He nudged the bowl aside. 'I heard your music. Tell me about it.'

The girl stared at the bowl, her chest rising and falling in panicky little breaths. 'It doesn't go there.'

'Is it your own composition or something you've heard?'

'It doesn't go there,' she repeated, voice rising in pitch.

'For goodness sake.' He shoved the bowl back in place.

She moved it a little to the right. 'There.'

'Forget the stupid bowl. Is the music yours or not?'

'It takes me away.' The child's wide, unblinking eyes fixed on his face.

'Must you stare at me, child? It's unnerving.'

She looked back at the bowl.

'Now, let's try again? This music –'

'It's green.'

'I beg your pardon?'

'The sea is green. The music took me under the sea tonight. People think it's blue but it's green. The sun turns it green because when you mix yellow and blue you get green.'

She leaned closer, lowered her voice as if she shared a great secret. 'The stars are blue. I've seen them up close. The music took me there. It takes me far away from *him*.'

'Who?'

'My father.' She shuddered.

'Child, listen carefully, I want to buy your music. Name your price.'

She shook her head. 'I can't sell it. When Daddy hurts me, the music takes me away.'

'How does he hurt you?'

She began rocking back and forth, singing. 'The sea is green not blue. The stars are blue not silver.'

'Child, look at me! How does your father hurt you?'

'With love,' she whispered, her eyes glued to his face.

'Love doesn't hurt.'

'Daddy says sometimes love hurts but the music takes me away from the pain.'

'Love *never* hurts. Your parents tell you some ridiculous things. I want that music so name your price.'

'But I need it to take me away.'

'I must warn you I am neither patient nor kind these days. In fact, I just killed some flowers.'

'Why? What did they do?'

'Nothing. Now tell me what you want more than anything else in the world. For I can deliver it.'

The sound of footsteps in the hallway made her rush back to her bed, throw herself down on top of the covers, and screw her eyes shut. The music resumed in a discordant jangle of notes, growing louder and louder until it drowned the room in a rising tide of green.

Presently a man slipped into her room and stood in the shadows. 'Are you awake, Mary?'

The visitor at the window watched and waited, cloaked and hidden in darkness.

SONATA

A piece of classical music for a solo instrument or small ensemble

James Granger pressed his back against the wall, immersing his body in shadow as he unzipped his fly. The full moon framed in the open window cast a perfect circle on his daughter's bed and in its lime-washed phosphorescence the room had an underwater look. Sliding his hand over the flea-trail of hair that led to his crotch, he gripped his member, pulled and coaxed as he traced the line of his sleeping daughter's body silhouetted in moonlight, his eyes greedily tracking the swell of her belly to the nipples studding the lace bodice of her thin cotton nightgown. Hiding in the shadows, watching the girl sleep while he masturbated gave him a delicious voyeuristic pleasure. And mostly, it was enough. However, there were nights when he needed more.

While her father tugged and strained, Mary heard tympani counterpoints to drown out his panting breath. Finally James cursed at his uncooperative penis. It was one of those nights when he needed to touch her to restore his flagging manhood. Quitting the shadows he moved towards her bed but when he passed the open window the moon spotlit him and stunned him like a deer caught in the flare of headlights. The light seemed unnaturally bright and for one crazy moment he imagined it was breathing. He took another step towards the bed, but this time he was halted by an invective of light that shot out of the moon and lodged in his gut, twisting his entrails with violent cramps. He fell to the floor, knees drawn up to his chest, his mouth open in a silent protesting scream.

Mary sat up slowly and watched her father's struggle for a few moments.

'Please don't hurt him. Just make him go away.'

'Killing him would be a more permanent solution.'

'He's not a flower.'

'Very well then. But the price for your freedom is your music. Do you agree?'

The child bowed her head, whispered, 'Yes.'

'Thank you.'

The light shut off instantly and James Granger crab-crawled out of his daughter's room, seeking sanctuary on the couch, a refuge he had taken so frequently during his marriage that the contours of his body had phantomed into the brown velveteen.

'What the fuck just happened?' he muttered as he rubbed his throbbing belly.

Mary's rescuer raised his wings. 'Does your mother know your father comes to your room?'

'No. He said it was our secret. He said he'd sell my piano if I told Mum. He said he'd sell my piano!' Her chest heaved.

'Calm down. He won't sell your piano nor will he come to your room again. Now I need to ask you something. You witnessed a small part of my power tonight. Do you believe in me?'

'Yes.' Her voice soft and awed.

'Good, because I assure you I am quite real.' He nodded at the bowl of honeyed bread. 'Don't encourage the elves. They're nasty, ungrateful creatures and they bite. Another question. Can you can play the music yet?' Suddenly the sky was rimmed with yellow flame as dawn cracked over the horizon like an egg.

'No, my hands are too small to reach all the notes on the

14

piano but Mum says when I'm sixteen I'll be able to play anything I want.'

'When will you be sixteen?'

'In five years. But what does it matter? The music belongs to you now. I sold it for my freedom.' Tears sliding over her cheeks.

'Five more years.' The dawn light was turning him to glass. Trees and clouds appeared through him. 'Ah well, I've waited this long. What's your name, child?'

'Mary Granger.'

'I once knew a woman called Mary. Her soul was blue and held light like a Florentine summer sky. Your eyes remind me of her soul.'

'Please be kind to the music. Don't kill it like you killed the flowers.'

'Fear not. I will take great care of the music.'

'I'll miss it.' Her voice was wobbly.

'You won't *lose* the music, child. It's your creation.' He leaned closer, spoke slowly and precisely. 'But now you've agreed, I own the rights to it and when your hands are big enough to play it to the world, I will use it as I please.' Now he spoke very fast. 'A binding contract, enforceable penalties, eternally bound. Don't even think about breaking it. Understood?'

She shook her head. 'Too many big words.'

'Well, you'll just have to trust me, Mary Granger.' His voice was soft and low. 'Fame and fortune will be yours in exchange for my protection. It suits me to guarantee your success for it will also guarantee mine.' He smiled rather wickedly. 'Some people would sell their souls for fame and fortune. It is a well-documented fact.'

Now the sun rose fully in an explosion of purest gold. 'I must go. From now on I'll be outside your window every night watching over you and protecting you from your father until your hands are big enough to play *our* music for the world. Goodbye now.'

'Please don't kill any more flowers.'

'I won't. But know this: everything kills to protect that which gives it life.' He was becoming a ripple in the sky. 'That's nature's way.'

Mary got out of bed and rushed to the window. 'You didn't tell me your name.'

'You'll know soon enough.' And he was gone, dissolved into sky.

She moved the bowl a fraction of an inch to the right. 'It goes here.'

INTERMEZZO

Short movement or interlude connecting
the main parts of a composition

As the years fell like dominoes, each one toppling into the next, Mary taught herself to play the melodies in her head and soon the music that was like breath filled the house.

'Mama used to play the piano after dinner.' Kathleen Granger sighed. 'Ah, but I remember our little cottage in Fingal Place, Stoneybatter, filling up with music every evening. Holy, it was.'

'I'm trying to read the paper,' James snapped.

'The race form.' Kathleen retorted. 'That's why we never have money. Wasted on horses, it is.'

'Stop nagging me, Kathy.' James slipped the form out of the paper, folded it and put it in his pocket. 'And Mary, shut that bloody racket up!'

Mary stopped playing, bowed her head and folded her hands in her lap.

'Keep playing, Mary,' said Kathleen. 'Your music takes me back to Dublin where I was happy.'

James leapt up. 'I wish you'd go back to bloody Dublin and take Mary with you. I'm going to the pub.' He thumped out, slamming the door behind him.

Kathleen poured herself a whisky. 'Sure he won't be back till he's good and drunk. Play for me, darling. Your music is all that soothes me soul these days. When Mama played, the perfume of roses filled the air. I can almost smell them now.'

The old piano stood in the corner of the living-room, a bit tired, a bit scratched, some of the felts worn and a couple of keys missed their ivory veneers, but Mary adored it. And every night, as he'd promised, her guardian appeared at her window to protect his investment.

'Are your hands any bigger yet, Mary Granger?' he asked from time to time, and, 'How was school today? Still no friends?'

'The other children call me Mad Mary because I don't understand their jokes.' She gazed at him helplessly. 'I don't know when things are funny. Does that mean I'm mad?'

'You have an orderly mind. There's no room for humour in an orderly mind.'

'Mum says it's good to laugh.'

'Universes are not built on humour, Mary Granger. Creation requires clarity and a balance that comes from order. Everything in its rightful place. All this free will and rampant growth has destroyed the delicate balance between heaven and earth.' He softened. 'Fear not, Mary, one day the same people who call you mad will call you a genius and when you're famous millions of people will want to be your friends.'

Some nights his skin was a little gray, his robes a little soiled, his feathers a little tattered and his temper a little short as if he'd been fighting. Other nights he was almost transparent as if something was suckling the life out of him. The stars glittered through him and branches and leaves formed a tessellation on his soul.

'I need music. Quickly. Something inspiring to reignite me.'

On such nights she bathed him in melody until his robes and wings gained substance and his mood brightened. Over time she discovered his moods were fickle as fortune and just as unpredictable.

18

Then there were the nights when he was radiant and in love with life. 'How divine the stars are tonight. How lovely the moon is floating between eternity and this sea of troubles. I've been to Florence. It has scarcely changed in five hundred years, Mary. That lovely city of angels still welcomes me. When you're old enough you must have a lover in Florence, Mary Granger.'

'Do *you* have a lover in Florence?'

He ignored her question. 'What do you dream of now that your father lets you sleep in peace?'

'I dream of playing a piano on a big stage with my Mum and my brother and sister sitting in the front row.'

'Hold tight to that dream. I promise you one day you will play Carnegie Hall.'

'Carnegie Hall,' she whispered, sensing something almost talismanic in the name. 'And what's your dream?'

'My dream is your dream.'

On the lid of the piano stood a framed photograph of Jennifer and Jonathan Granger – the children from James Granger's first marriage. Jonathan was dark and Jennifer fair but their eyes were the same intense blue that Mary's were, the only feature all three had inherited from their father. The photo was taken when Jennifer was seven and Jonathan was five. They were young teenagers now.

Mary had written a song for them – the three musketeers – invincible and sharing the sacred space that breathed between the notes.

FANTASIA

A musical composition or idea typified by improvisation

James slopped back his last beer. 'Can I sleep at your place tonight, Luce?'

Lucy was clearing the till. 'Again? Why don't you move in?'

'Leave Kath? Ah, Luce, it'd break her heart.'

He remembered the first time he'd clapped eyes on Kathleen Muir. Married to Caitlin, with Jennifer and Jonathan six and four, he'd swaggered into the local and noticed a new girl behind the bar. Her hair fell in long shining black coils, her eyes flashed like jet and her skin was the colour of whipped cream. The most gorgeous woman he'd ever seen. When she spoke, her voice rose in delicious lilts that lifted the ends of her sentences into invitations. She told him she was from Dublin on a working holiday and would be going back at the end of summer to marry one of the local lads.

'I wish I could have an exciting affair before I settle down for good.' She smiled at him mischievously.

'You don't mean it. Catholic girls never tumble before marriage.'

'I do mean it, Jimmie Granger. I want an affair like Rhett Butler and Scarlett O'Hara in *Gone with the Wind*.'

'And what if you got pregnant?'

'Sure I'd worry about that tomorrow.' She winked.

20

'I'll play Rhett to your Scarlett as long as I can disappear into the mist when autumn comes.'

Summer flew in a blaze of lust and when autumn came...

'Jimmie, I'm pregnant. When shall I tell Mama to fly out for our wedding?'

'Now Kath, you know I'm married.'

'But you'll divorce Caitlin.'

'But my children...'

'They'll be welcome in our home. Divorce Caitlin, Jimmie, and marry me.'

Lucy locked the till and flicked off the lights behind the bar. 'Think about it, Jim. I won't make the offer twice.'

CAVATINA

*A short simple melody performed by a
soloist that is part of a larger piece*

Mary's childhood ended in the winter of her sixteenth year. She was in the back yard pruning dormant roses, trying to coax spring blossoms and lessen the stranglehold of the briar. The wind had begun to howl, driving bruised green and black clouds across the sun. Her father's shirts danced wildly on the line and a loose window pane in the living room rattled. Mary heard her mother cry out and ran inside, still clutching the pruning shears.

'Does our marriage mean nothing to you, Jimmie?' Kathleen wailed.

'I was married when we met, Kathy.'

'What's happening?' Mary asked, tightening her grip on the shears.

'This is between your mother and me, Mary.' James looked like a man possessed. Deep lines furrowed his brow, skull shadows hollowed his cheeks, and his mouth was a slack, down-turned line. He was wearing his black travelling coat. Two battered suitcases stood by the front door.

'Your father's leaving me for a barmaid.'

'You were a barmaid yourself when we first met, Kathy.'

A sharp gust of wind dislodged the loose pane. The sound of shattering glass momentarily silenced the warring couple.

'I meant to fix that,' said James, glancing at the shards of broken glass on the carpet.

'Don't leave me, Jimmie,' Kathleen whispered.

'Ah, Kath, don't make this any harder than it already is.'

Mary looked at her father with unblinking indifference. 'Some of your shirts are still on the line. Do you want me to get them for you?'

His lip curled. 'I won't miss them any more than I'll miss you.'

Her expression did not change. 'Before you go ... where are my brother and sister?'

'Why are you asking me now?'

'Why, Jimmie?' Kathleen interrupted. 'What have I done to deserve this?'

'Ah Kath, it's been bad between us for years.'

Her breast heaved and quivered. 'I'm begging you –'

'Don't beg.' He gazed at her for a long, wavering moment. 'I have to go. Lucy's waiting for me.'

Kathleen cracked a slap across his cheek. 'There'll be no divorce!' she shouted, running from the room and shaking her head in frantic denial.

'Where are my brother and sister?' Mary repeated.

'I don't know, Mary.' A pause. 'I never meant to hurt Jennifer.' He picked up his bags and left.

Mary dropped the shears and leaned against the piano. 'What about me?'

There was no answer.

The wind whistled in through the empty window-frame and whipped at the frayed brown curtains, raising them like ragged wings. The music that coursed through Mary was underscored with the joy and privilege of freedom. At the piano, she worked the melody like a spell, hands flying over the keys, sleighting hope. The white keys pulsed light, the black keys winked like polished river stones. With her father gone Mary was free to play for as long as she pleased. She explored streams of melody with combinations of chords intricately woven as a tapestry. Some threads led nowhere, teasing as pathways in a labyrinth while others strengthened like rivers certain of the sea. On the wing he heard and followed the skein just as he had done five years earlier when he had first found her. He slipped in through the broken window and stood behind her listening intently. Every note convinced him she was ready to play for the world.

'It's time, Mary,' he said, the scent of pine and roses filling the air. 'Your hands are big enough.'

Mary stopped playing and whipped around. 'Oh, it's you. My father left Mum today. He didn't tell me where my brother and sister live.'

'I will bring your siblings to you when the time is right. You must learn to trust me, Mary Granger.' His light swelled and shadowed like breath.

'Who are you? You've never told me your name.'

The ghost of a smile. 'Who do you *think* I am?'

He looked like an angel in a Renaissance painting by Leonardo Da Vinci: shoulder-length golden curls framing a classically square-jawed, high cheek-boned face; deep-set, almond-shaped eyes the colour of old tiles. His skin was translucent with inner light and silhouetted beneath his white robe, spun from light rather than fabric, was an athletic body. Glowing wings arched from his shoulders and brushed the floor with snowy pinions. His mouth was a firm strong line.

'You look like an angel. But angels don't kill flowers. Angels don't kill anything.'

'How do you know? I've told you everything kills to protect that which gives it life. I *am* an angel.' The scent of roses and pine heightened and she sneezed. 'Bless you.'

'Thank you.' She tipped her head to one side, studying him.

'But I thought angels were gentle and kind. You look sad and angry. Is it because you miss your brother?'

'Of course it's because I miss my brother. Have you any idea what it feels like to struggle all alone in a world where no one understands you?'

A muscle worked in her jaw, flickering on and off like a faulty switch. 'Yes.'

He continued. 'Everybody is so busy with their small lives they don't hear my message. They're like ants the way they scurry about, glued to their mobile phones. I'm beginning to think they don't want to change.'

'Maybe the world's too old to change.'

He shuddered, radiating light. 'She said that, too – the other Mary. But she was wrong and you're wrong. It will change when it hears your music.' Suddenly he was not so beautiful. Striations of muddy light stained his robes and his face. 'And don't even think about changing your mind and pulling out of our pact now that your fingers can reach all the notes.'

Mary shook her head. 'I won't break my promise.'

He raised his wings, light flaring, blinding. 'Remember I protected you from your father.'

'I know.' Tears stung. 'Why are you reminding me? Why so nasty?'

'I can make those memories haunt you for the rest of your life if I choose.'

'Stop it!' She buried her face in her hands, sobbed.

'I'm sorry.' He knelt at her feet. 'Try to understand. I've lost everything I held dear: my Father's respect, my brother's love, my place in heaven. Unless I succeed in the quest I'll be alone forever.'

Her sobs subsided. 'Then you should learn to trust me, too.'

'I trust you.' He kissed her hands. 'Your music will change the world.'

'How?'

He smiled wickedly. 'I will add a little something to it that will make it irresistible and lure people as surely as the Pied Piper of Hamlin drew rats. Think of it, Mary, fame and fortune and all the friends you want.'

'But you haven't explained. What will my music actually do to people?'

'Enlighten them and bring everlasting peace to this stubborn old world. All will be well when I restore order.'

She thought for a minute. 'What do you mean by order?'

'There has to be a chain of command, Mary. People need to look up to something so bright it blinds them. Trees reach for the sun. Your music will make humanity look up to the light and when they see it they will be filled with such wonder nothing will ever trouble them again.'

'Like a drug.'

'Like salvation.' Once again darker tones muddied his light. 'There's a medical term for your condition. I don't care for labels myself but humanity loves putting people in boxes. The world won't believe in you like I do, Mary. They'll lock you up.'

She swallowed. 'You said I wasn't mad.'

'No medication *ever*, is that clear?'

The tic in her jaw started again. 'You said I wasn't mad.'

'Medication will silence the music and I will abandon you.' His eyes filled with flaming light. 'And then, Mary Granger, your father will shadow your dreams again.'

She shrank from him. 'Who are you?'

'You've already asked me that.'

She scratched her palms. 'You didn't tell me your name though.'

'No, I didn't. Artists call me angel. Lovers call me man. Some call me demon. The saint from Assisi called me Diavolo.'

'What does God call you?'

'Son.' He raised his wings again, white sails against the

26

brown spaces. 'For ten long centuries I've been shut out of heaven. I came here to spread my Father's message but they wouldn't listen. I didn't dare go home and tell Father I've failed.'

'I'm sorry. But please tell me your name.'

'I am the archangel Gabriel sent to enlighten the world.' He drew himself up to his full height, radiance ricocheting around the room, snagging on the shards of broken window. 'But it's been very resistant.' He lowered his wings and his voice. 'I have sinned, Mary.'

'How?'

'Please no more questions. Just play for me.'

Mary stared at the picture of her siblings on the lid of the piano. 'And you promise I'll meet my brother and sister?'

'Yes, yes, yes! Mary, I'm asking you to play your music to the world. I'm not asking you to sell your soul.'

'Gabriel? What will enlightenment look like?'

He closed his eyes, covered his heart with his hands. 'Everything – the furthest star, the merest wisp of vapour, the lowest arachnid, *all* – will be seen bathed in holy light.'

'That sounds beautiful.' Mary rested her hands on the keys. 'When I'm enlightened will I still hear the music?'

'Oh, didn't I explain myself properly?' His shadow lengthened across the carpet like a snake. '*You* won't be enlightened. The creator is never enlightened by her own creation. She knows it too well for' – he searched for the right word – 'surprise. Being the creator has its price, my dear. Loneliness.' He sighed. 'It is a well-documented fact.'

'But you promised me friends!'

'Not exactly friends but admirers who look to you for inspiration. I apologise if I did not make myself clear.'

Tears stung. 'But who will love me for myself?'

'Perhaps your mother. Perhaps no one. It's lonely at the top, Mary. The view is quite different. I'm sorry, my dear, even *I* cannot save you. Goodbye now. I'll be back soon. Keep practising.'

'Where are you going?'

'To tell my Father the good news.' He rose in a blaze of light. 'I won't be away long. We have work to do.'

Looking up, Mary caught a glimpse of golden sandals and firm buttocks under a belling white robe. 'What is it you can't save me from, Gabriel? *What*?'

'Yourself.' And he was gone.

Kathleen drifted into the living room, her eyes puffy and red from crying.

'Have I ever told you about the time every lad in Stoneybatter was lined up outside our front door with posies of fresh flowers for me?' She lifted her hand to receive an imaginary bouquet. 'Mama had me sitting up in the parlour like a princess and the lads courted me one by one. Afterwards she asked me which boy took me fancy. None of them did, Mary.' Her voice broke. 'Your father's the only man I've ever wanted. Some people blind you to all the others. They glow so bright you could pick 'em out in a crowded street. Yes, beloved people glow.' She stood in front of the broken window. The full moon burned through a scud of cloud. 'What stops it falling? Stars fall. What keeps the moon from falling?'

'Faith and gravity. But if it *does* fall, Mum, I'll catch it.'

A sob. 'Will you catch me, too?'

'Yes, Mum. I'm right here.' Mary put her hands on her mother's trembling shoulders. 'Mum, can I ask you something?' She paused. 'Is there something wrong with me? In my head?'

Kathleen swung around. 'Don't ever think that, darling. You're different, that's all. Some of the greatest people in this world have been different.' She looked back at the moon. 'Like Mama. She made up her own music too. Magdalene Muir could have set the world on fire but she never wanted to play outside of our cottage. After Da died, she taught piano. We never had much money but we lived graciously, ate our dinner at the table every night with real silver cutlery. Mama lit candles as if we were expecting company.'

'Maybe we can do that now – light candles and eat our dinner at the table instead of on our knees in front of television.'

'I suppose we could. Or we could move back to Dublin. Mama might take us in.'

'Let's do that.'

Kathleen ran her hand over her face. 'But how will Jimmie find me again?'

'Mum, I have something to say. I want to leave school. I'm ready to play my music to the world.'

'But darling, you're so...shy.' She sighed. 'Ah, I haven't the strength to argue right now. Very well, leave school but go to TAFE and learn something practical just in case the music doesn't take off.'

'It will change the world, Mum.'

'Sure every composer thinks so. And I'll get a job pulling beers again just until Jimmie comes home.'

ROCOCO

A musical style characterized as excessive, ornamental and trivial

James Granger left the family home in tatters: frayed edges on the rugs, long threads dangling from the curtains, paint flaking off the windows and doors, the garden a tangle of untrimmed privet and roses reverted to briar. The day after, Mary began patching and mending, starting with the broken window before moving on to trim the curtains, clip the privet, prune the roses and tidy the frayed edges of the rugs.

Kathleen watched her daughter's tireless efforts. 'You like things just so, don't you darlin'?'

'I like order.' Mary placed a vase of red roses on top of the piano next to the picture of her siblings. 'Everything has its own special place, Mum.'

'Well, the house looks better for it. Sure I never had the heart to make a lovely home when Jimmie was betraying me.'

'Can we not talk about Dad? Let me play you something. It's got unusual chords. See what you think.'

And so order was established and at the end of that term Mary left school and played the piano. Kathleen found a job pulling beers at the local. Every night Mary set the kitchen table with candles and the reproduction silver cutlery Kathleen had bought in a charity shop. After dinner, she played for them just as Magdalene Muir had done.

'I called in at TAFE on my way home from work,' said Kathleen one evening. She dropped a brochure on the table. 'I picked up a list of their courses for next term.'

Mary was removing two meals from the freezer. 'Chicken or beef?'

'Chicken. You need to decide on a course, darling. Unless you want to pull beers like me.'

'I'm going to play my music for the world.'

Kathleen tapped the brochure. 'Choose something.'

Mary closed her eyes and stabbed a fork into the list. 'This one.'

'Ah sure an' that's a fine way to choose a profession. Let's see what the fork thinks you should do with your life.'

The fork had stabbed a two year Diploma Course in Legal Services, which would qualify her as a paralegal: a secretary who could also handle simple cases.

'Well, the fork knew what it was about,' said Kathleen. 'You'll always have work, for sure people are forever getting themselves into trouble. But do you really think law is something you'll like? It's very dry.'

'It's only until my music takes off.' The microwave beeped. Mary took out the chicken dinner and put in the beef. 'Dom, dom, dom,' she sang, her right hand tapping out the melody. 'Bom, bom, dah, dah, dah, dom, dom.'

'I've always wondered if your music is like a soundtrack in a movie. Does it fit what's happening around you?'

'Dom, dom. Sometimes. But mostly it shows me other worlds, other people I'd like to meet. My brother and sister.'

'Ah, well, darling, don't go hoping for miracles there.'

Beep, beep, sang the microwave. Mary removed her meal and sat at the table. 'I'll meet them, Mum. I know I will. I bet my sister's beautiful. Not plain like me.'

'You're lovely in your own way, my girl.' She lifted her fork. '*Bon appétit,* as they say in France.'

'Dom, dah, dah,' sang Mary in between bites, the fingers of her left hand tapping out the notes on the table.

'Mary, when someone is supernaturally gifted like you, it makes me wonder, do you suppose child prodigies sign some kind of contract with heaven before birth?'

Mary felt suddenly ill and pushed her meal aside. 'Not always *before* birth.'

FARSA

Farce

'I am home, Father.'

No answer.

Gabriel tried again. Louder this time. 'Father, I'm home and I have great news.'

Not a sound or a movement or spark of light responded. It was as if heaven had ceased to exist.

'Is anyone here?' Gabriel folded his wings around him like a cloak. 'Father?'

The empire of light Gabriel had left a thousand years earlier to pursue the quest was now a bleak gray landscape stretching into infinity. The air smelled of ammonia. Gone was the signature fragrance of ambrosia.

'Are you right here in front of me? Have my sins blinded me to your light?' He reached out his hand tentatively and felt the air.

There was a sudden explosion of multi-coloured light and a vast Technicolor empire rose on the murky plain. Gabriel blinked and it was gone.

A second explosion and a new empire rose and fell. Then a succession of landscapes composed of mountains and castles and fantastic monoliths that lasted less than a moment before dissolving into nothing.

'Who's doing this?'

Laughter rang out.

'Show yourself!'

A creature composed entirely of winking lights appeared. 'Did you enjoy my little show?'

'No,' said Gabriel. 'What's the point of building empires that don't last?'

'Fun.'

'Ridiculous. Creation must have some purpose beyond mere amusement.'

'No one bothers with purpose any more. We just manipulate light for the fun of it.'

'Who are you?'

'An angel.'

'What's happened to heaven?'

'This *is* heaven,' it said, dispersing into glitter.

Gabriel looked wistfully down at earth, at the familiar terrain of mountains, seas and forests that had existed for millennia and sustained a rich diversity of life. He sought the lights of Florence, wondered if perhaps a window had been left open for him. Catching his reflection in the icy vapours of yet another dying empire he smiled at the anachronism he had apparently become.

'Have they all lost their passion for life, Father? Father?'

Silence.

He sought his reflection again. How reassuring was a narcissistic smile in this faceless wasteland where creation was a pastime rather than a purpose.

'Father, where are you? Don't you recognise your own son?'

No answer.

'Uriel? Raphael? Michael?'

Still no answer.

But there was one angel who might respond.

'Rigel! Are you here? It's me, Gabriel!'

A rumble of thunder, a crackle of light and an entity of

gigantic proportions stood before him. Gabriel shrank from the tendril-like arms, fiery torso and fierce scarlet eyes that settled unnervingly on his face. 'Rigel?'

'It's Raphael. Don't you recognise me?'

He stared at the monstrosity that had once been the most glorious angel in the Renaissance ideal. 'Has heaven turned into hell in the last thousand years?'

Raphael laughed. 'I'd forgotten how witty you are. How long have you been back?'

'A few hours in human measure. A billion lost empires in yours. Raphael, please change back while we talk. The ugly aberration you've become makes me feel most uncomfortable.'

The monster assumed his previous glorious winged human form. 'Better?'

'Much. Why do you appear as fire when you could be light?'

'Fire is more exciting.'

'But you were beautiful, Raphael. This inferno you've become is ugly. Have you lost all concept of beauty?'

'You've been away too long, my friend. But now you're back you'll soon adjust. I'm glad Rigel found you.'

'What do you mean?'

'Rigel went to earth to look for you and bring you home.'

'I haven't seen my brother in a thousand years.'

'We are all brothers and sisters here, Gabriel.' Raphael reminded him.

'I know but Rigel understands me better than any of you. That makes him my only brother. He loves me.'

Raphael laughed. 'I thought you didn't believe in love.'

'I don't. But Rigel does.'

'Yes, poor Rigel still clings to that quaint ideal.' Raphael's form flickered. 'He never stopped believing in you, even though –'

'Father stopped believing in me.'

'I wasn't going to say that, Gabriel. I was going to say even though you told Rigel that love was fodder for fools.'

'Love can't be relied upon.' Gabriel shuddered. 'When did Rigel leave?'

'A year by human measure. He went down to tell you to abandon the quest.'

Gabriel took a moment to process this. 'I don't believe you. Father wants humanity enlightened.'

'Father's gone.'

'*What*! Where?'

'We neither know nor care. The old order has fallen, Gabriel. There is no heaven or hell, reward or punishment, sanctity or sin. This is the era of free will, my friend. We do as we please whenever we please.'

'But who will absolve me of my sins now Father is gone? The guilt is killing me.'

Raphael looked at him blankly. 'I can't help you, Gabriel. We don't recognise sin in the new order.'

Gabriel shook his head in despair. 'What order? This is chaos.'

'Out of chaos comes creation, Gabriel.'

'Unsustainable worlds are not creation. They are distraction.'

'They are fun. You should try it.'

Again the air rang with the laughter of unseen company.

'Come and play with us, Gabriel. You'll soon forget your sins.'

'I must find Rigel.'

'Forget Rigel. Lighten up.'

'Light!' cried Gabriel. 'That's what I came here to tell Father. I've found a way to enlighten humanity.'

Raphael's blank eyes looked through him. 'Enlightenment is irrelevant now.'

Gabriel gazed down at earth. 'Then I should go home.'

'You are home.'

'This is not my home any more. When did Father leave?'

'Five hundred years ago by human measure.'

'During the Renaissance?' Gabriel shivered. 'But humanity was just beginning to see the light. Father's message was getting through. To some.'

'Father grew tired of waiting. He decided to create again.'

'Without me?' Gabriel shook his head in disbelief. 'He won't create an entirely new universe in seven days without me.'

'Still so boastful.'

'I had all the practical solutions: gravity, force, particles. Father imagined it but I put it together. Who's helping Him now?'

Raphael yawned. 'Father always has His followers. Move on, Gabriel. You can't cling to the past. Things change. Nothing is constant.'

'Father's light is constant. Well, it *was*.'

'Find your own light.'

'I can't. My sins shadow me. I need absolution.'

'Absolve yourself. Aren't you the great archangel Gabriel?' Raphael burst into flame and laughter, his cant echoing unto infinity. 'Save yourself, my friend.'

Gabriel, the great archangel who once spearheaded reformation in both heaven and earth, stood alone, remembering his sins.

BATTAGLIA

An instrumental piece suggesting a battle

𝄞

The sinning began with bats.

When he left heaven a thousand years ago, he flew at night because saintly human souls shone more brightly in the dark. After a hundred years of flying through perpetual night, depression and boredom took hold. To enliven the long, dark stretches he amused himself by trailing bats on their nightly hunts for shrews and mice. It began in innocence as most sins do. He wondered if he could catch a mouse when he was on the wing like the bats did and one night he swooped on a rodent. Before he had time to think he tore into the creature's living flesh. The salty warmth of blood on his tongue sent a tingling sensation down his spine and even though he felt sickened and ashamed, he could not deny the elation. The thrill of the hunt was addictive. Sinful.

Soon the taste for flesh manifested in another way. His loneliness drove him into the arms and the beds of women whose husbands had left them alone while they fought a pointless war or explored an endless ocean or scaled a dizzying height in the name of ambition. Men were always away, chasing impossible dreams and their absence gave him ample opportunity to sate his growing appetite for carnal delight. Failing to recognise the parallel between the ambitious husbands and his own quest for global enlightenment he left the women behind, offering no explanation for his abandonment.

And there was also the sin of vanity.

In Florence during the Renaissance his pride inflated with the adulation he received from artists and from the women who left windows open for him. Every night he had his pick of the fairest flowers of Florentine femininity. During the past thousand years Gabriel sinned until sinning became second nature and now he was burdened with the consequence: guilt that glued his summoned flesh to his soul and nothing but the total reformation of humanity could lighten the load.

Or so he hoped.

He looked around the lifeless gray plain of heaven.

'Father, I could have helped You fashion a new world of beauty and imagination if only you had trusted me.' A new idea occurred to him. 'But if earth is abandoned, then it can be mine. I can do as I please with it and not answer to anyone.'

Nothing moved. Nothing changed. There wasn't even an echo. Gabriel hovered in a silence as hollow as the spaces between the notes on Mary's piano. He had no idea what to do next.

Then he remembered Rigel. He crept closer to the edge of heaven where choices determine fate and, crying out his brother's name, he plunged. As he fell, spiraling into feather and flesh, a thought occurred to him.

Before he went looking for Rigel, he needed a little time in Florence.

VARIATIONS

Repetition of a theme with slight differences

&

Kathleen saw the ad in the Sydney Morning Herald. Goodman and Oldfield, a prestigious law firm situated in the heart of the city, needed a legal secretary. The preferred applicant would have a minimum of five years experience.

It had been two years since Mary graduated from TAFE and despite many interviews, she had yet to land a job.

'They'll want the very best, Mum.'

'Well, that's you, darling. Here. Read the ad.'

Mary took the paper. 'They want someone with at least five years experience.'

'Call them anyway. Tell them you're a paralegal. It's worth a shot.'

She called. The receptionist said, 'You're probably over qualified but come in anyway on Monday morning at nine.'

Late Friday afternoon, James Oldfield Jnr. perched on the edge of his partner's desk. 'What are you and Jillian up to this weekend?'

Robert Goodman didn't look up. '*I'll* be working and Jillian will be redecorating the house. Get your arse off my desk, James.'

James didn't budge. 'I'm spending the weekend with an actress, twenty-something. Gorgeous.'

'I don't want to know. Poor Lucinda.'

'My wife's no saint.' James loosened his tie. 'Listen, Robert –'

The phone rang. Robert snatched the receiver off the hook, listened for a moment. 'Yes, put him through, Judy.' A tight smile. 'Ian, what can I do for you?'

'I've gone home if he asks.' James slid off the desk and sauntered over to the window.

'James? No, sorry, you just missed him. Why?' There was a long pause. 'I see.' Robert swung around the black leather chair his father had sat in for twenty years and glared at James. 'Thank you, Ian, I understand perfectly. Thank you.' He hung up. 'Ian said you drained our expense account an hour ago.'

James pulled a Calvin Klein handkerchief out of his breast pocket. 'That's what I came to tell you, but Scrooge Turnbull got in first. Like it's any of his fucking business.' He dabbed at his forehead.

'What's wrong with you?' Robert asked slowly.

James turned away from the million dollar view. 'What do you mean?'

'We have rent to pay, an outstanding phone bill, wages, and you drain the account?'

'It's our bloody money.' He slammed his palms down on his partner's desk. 'I'm not answerable to a snoopy fucking bank manager.'

'You're answerable to me. I asked Ian to keep an eye on you.'

'You *what?*'

Now Robert slammed down his palms. 'You'll bankrupt us, James. You spend money faster than I earn it and now you've drained the fucking account!'

'I own half this firm –'

'Then do half the work.' Robert thumped the tottering pile of cases. 'Give me a bloody weekend off. What possessed you, James? You didn't even ask me first!'

'Jillian's redecorating your house again,' said James quietly. 'That costs money, doesn't it?'

'That was a gift from Mum. I wouldn't put the firm at risk.' A muscle worked in his jaw.

'Calm down Rob. You don't want to die young like your Dad. Heart disease runs in families, you know.'

'I'm giving you until midnight to get the money back into the account or I'll dissolve our partnership. I can work from home just as easily.'

'Don't do anything you'll regret, Rob.'

Robert stared at him for a long moment. 'Like drain our expense account when we have a mountain of bills to pay?'

'You and Turnbull are making a huge drama out of this. Look, I'm seeing the old man on Monday morning. I'll hit him for a loan and fix up the account then. OK?'

'No, not OK. You put the money back in tonight, cancel your weekend plans and leave your father out of it. We already owe him a fortune.'

'But Rob, I have great plans for this weekend.'

'Screw your plans.' Robert hissed.

'Screw?' He laughed. 'That *is* my plan.'

Robert took a deep breath. 'If infidelity is what you've planned for this weekend why the hell do you need so much money?'

'Ah, well, you see –' He wiped his palms on his jacket. 'I owe a bit –'

'What do you mean?'

'I have a few creditors. So what? Who doesn't?'

Robert narrowed his eyes. 'What's really going on with you, James? Drugs? Gambling?'

'Don't give me the third degree. I'm entitled to a bit of fun every now and then. You should try it.' He picked up the framed photograph of Jillian Goodman. 'Don't you ever feel like...new young flesh?'

Robert snatched back the photograph. 'You need help.'

'I don't have a problem.'

'Then start pulling your weight or we split. I mean it. I've had enough.'

'OK, OK. I'll get some help. Promise.' He nodded at the files. 'Give me the ones you can't handle. I'll cancel my weekend and return these by Monday afternoon. And since I won't be here Monday morning, I'm relying on you to check the talent and hire eye candy. No woofers.'

'For God's sake, James. I'll hire the best person for the job.' Robert shoved a fistful of files at his partner. 'Judy said a paralegal's applied.' He checked the list of applicants. 'A Mary Granger.'

'We can't afford a paralegal. Can we?'

'No. But with no experience, she might agree to start on a secretary's wage and do the work you don't do.'

'I won't let you down again, Robert.' He held his free hand up as if to caress the view. 'I don't want to lose this view.'

'I don't want to lose this view either, but it's expensive.'

Monday was clear and spring-like. Kathleen looked at the almost flawless sky while she cooked Mary a heavy breakfast.

'Eat it all, Mary. Give you strength for the interview.'

'I feel sick.' She tapped out a frantic little tune midair. 'I shouldn't have agreed to this interview. I need to practice the piano for when –' she *almost* said it.

'Darling, I'm afraid you need to earn money like everybody else. I'm coming into town with you. We'll treat ourselves to lunch after your interview.'

'Not more food,' Mary groaned. 'Should I wear make-up? Try to make myself pretty?'

'You don't need to paint your lovely young skin. Please finish your breakfast.'

'What about a bit of rouge? Do you have any rouge? Or lipstick?'

'You don't need lipstick or rouge. You're a natural beauty, Mary.'

'I'm plain, Mum.'

'I won't listen to that nonsense. Now eat.'

'Can't eat any more.'

'Leave it then. Play something on the piano to steady your nerves while I get myself ready.'

Lifting the lid of the piano was like opening a magician's box of tricks. Even though the keys displayed no hint of magic, a clever musician could conjure it. Played by themselves the notes were plain but in combination with other notes they were beautiful, magical. It was puzzling why some combinations worked better than others. For instance when Mary played C, E and G the sound was ordinary but when she added top E the effect was startling. Beautiful.

'Just one note makes the difference between plain and beautiful,' said Mary, adding F sharp to A and D and creating a new beauty. 'But why?'

She explored other combinations, noting how the addition of just one note turned a plain chord into a beautiful one. A, D and F sharp played together were divine but A, E and B flat were ugly.

So it was with human beauty. Why were some faces plain and others beautiful when the basic ingredients were the same? Her mother's face, for instance, was an A, D and F sharp combination: white skin, dark eyes and lovely bones. Beautiful. Her own face was a plain C chord: pale skin lacking the translucence of her mother's, serviceable bone-structure and her mid-brown hair was no crowning glory. Even her F sharp magnificent blue eyes could not save the chord. Unlike her mother, who still turned the occasional head, Mary passed through crowds unseen.

'I don't want a normal job with normal people who will look straight through me or worse, think me crazy.' She played a succession of chords to which she added unexpected notes that either jarred or mesmerised. Bubbles of beauty and ugliness rose, burst and fell into silence. 'I want to stay home and practise my music for my real career.'

'Time to go, sweetheart.'

Mary swung around. Her mother was wearing the dark blue frock she'd bought at a charity shop when she'd bought Mary's black work skirt and white blouse. By adding a blue velvet beret to the outfit, she'd created a stunning contrast to her creamy skin and dark curls.

'You look beautiful, Mum.' Mary smoothed her own shoulder-length mid-brown hair. 'I wish I had your looks.'

'You've got your own. Come along now.'

The city thrummed. Pedestrians hurried past and Kathleen pointed out significant landmarks on route to the offices of Goodman & Oldfield.

'That huge fig tree. When you see it you'll know there's two more blocks to go.'

'I may not get the job, Mum.'

'You'll get it. I've got a good feeling about this.' Kathleen checked her directions. 'OK, here we turn right. Remember that, Mary. Right at the big intersection. You've got to learn this new routine. Create your new map.'

'Yes, Mum.'

'How are you feeling, darling?'

'A bit sick but excited, too. The city is fast. I like the pace of its music.'

Kathleen smiled. 'This is a new beginning for you, darlin'. It's a lovely day.'

It *was* a lovely day. Sunlight splashed off the upper storey windows of towering office blocks concertinaed along the arterial grid of city roads. The pavements streamed with people and Mary's music added a subtext to every glamorous stranger. *If by some miracle I do get the job*, Mary decided, *I'll be honest about my musical aspirations. It wouldn't be fair to let Mr. Goodman think I'll stay forever.*

Just around the corner of Macquarie Street on Bridge Street was a glass and tile obelisk scraper. On the brass name plaque was Goodman & Oldfield, 10th floor.

'This is it,' whispered Kathleen. 'My, it's a tall building. Are you nervous?'

'Yes.' Mary scratched her palms. 'Where will *you* be?'

'Right here in this coffee shop,' said Kathleen, looking around. 'I'll sit at the table next to the window so you can find me easily when you come out with your good news. Go on, sweetheart. Through the glass door and up in the lift. Think of a tune and try to stay calm.'

Think of a tune. In the revolving glass doors Mary had a moment of panic about missing the exit and ending up back on the street. But there was plenty of time to make her way out.

A tune. In the lift *The Girl from Ipanema* piped out. She created a counter rhythm until the doors slid open directly into the reception area of Goodman & Oldfield – a large, gray tiled room with four black leather couches arranged around a central glass coffee table covered in world newspapers and glossy magazines. A breathtaking cityscape of the Harbour Bridge, Opera House and Kirribilli foreshore glimmered in shades of blue, green and terracotta. Three applicants were already there – black stockings, long legs, smart black suits, red lipstick, beautifully made-up eyes – supermodel types who advertised sports cars. *The kind of women who turn heads,* Mary thought. *I shouldn't have come.* She turned around and pressed the ground floor button on the lift. *Now if I can just get out of here before anybody notices me...*

'Mary Granger?' The voice was pleasant and calm.

'Yes?'

'I'm Judy. We spoke on the phone. Take a seat. Mr. Goodman won't be long.'

She took a seat facing the view. The other three women glanced at her and returned to their magazines with pictures of women just like them. Mary clutched her handbag on her knees.

'Good morning, ladies.'

He had slipped into the foyer so quietly no one noticed. The three glamorous women closed their magazines, slapped them down on the glass table and smiled brightly at the tall, handsome man.

'I'm Robert Goodman. I'll be interviewing you this morning. My partner James Oldfield Jnr. is busy and can't be here.' He smiled at each of them, then turned to Mary. 'I'll interview you first.'

'Me? I was the last to arrive.'

Robert Goodman's mouth twitched in a lopsided smile. 'Then you'll be the first one interviewed.'

In a rush to obey, Mary leapt to her feet and upturned her handbag – chapstick, TAFE diploma, notebook and two pens rolled right up to the polished toes of Robert Goodman's designer shoes.

'I'm so sorry.' Kneeling down, face burning, she collected her belongings under the stares of thinly veiled contempt from the other women. Incredibly, Robert Goodman knelt down beside her.

'I don't know how you women manage to get so much into your bags.' He picked up a scrolled page. 'Is this your TAFE diploma?'

'Yes. I brought it to show you. To prove I was –'

'A paralegal.'

'Yes. How did you know it was me?'

'I hoped it was. Follow me please, Mary.'

The hallway was lined with spectacular paintings.

'My father collected art,' said Robert, indicating the walls. 'These paintings were part of his collection. All originals – Boyd, Tucker, Drysdale and Nolan – all the Aussie greats.' He said the word *greats* through gritted teeth but covered his irritation with a smile. Halfway along the hall he opened the door to an office with the same stunning view.

'After you, Mary,' he said, stepping back.

But she didn't move. 'Who painted *that* picture?' she asked, staring at the painting across from his office.

'Sidney Nolan. Why?'

'Is it your favourite?'

He cleared his throat. 'It was my father's favourite painting.'

'So that's why it glows.'

'What do mean?'

'Beloved things glow. Beloved people, too,' she said as she met his eyes.

'I see. How fascinating. I've never noticed.' He shifted slightly under her unblinking gaze. 'Please take the seat facing the view, Mary.'

Robert Goodman squinted at the Nolan, then rubbed his forehead and shut the door firmly on his father's favourite painting.

'Now, before we –'

'I don't have any experience, Mr. Goodman. My mother said I should call anyway. She had a good feeling about the job. She's Irish.'

One corner of his mouth twitched and his hazel eyes sparkled with amusement. 'My mother's English. She gets feelings about things, too. Judy, our receptionist, warned me you had no experience. Let me look at this, then we'll talk.'

He rolled her diploma out on his desk, held it flat with his left hand fanned out like a bird's outstretched wing. Silver cufflinks flashed at his wrist. They looked expensive like the designer suit and the crisp white shirt. Mary looked down at her own cuff where a little tear showed near the buttonhole and a watermark remained where the previous owner had washed out a stain.

'Mary –'

'Yes?' She jerked up her head.

'You know you're overqualified for the position of legal secretary, Judy said she told you that on the phone. However, if you would consider taking a role here at Goodman and Oldfield, starting on a secretary's wage but acting as a paralegal, I will hire you.'

'You will?'

'I will.' He returned her diploma. 'You can tell your mother her feeling was quite correct.'

'I will! She's waiting in the coffee shop and she'll be so excited for me. This is my first job. We're going to have lunch in town.' A slight frown. 'Mr. Goodman, why do you ignore the view?'

'My father had the desk facing his favourite painting. When I took over from him I guess I just left it that way.'

'But it's your desk now. You can turn it around if you want to.'

He reached for a glass of water, took a long sip. 'It's uncanny the way you picked the Nolan out. Is there anything else you want to ask me before we discuss the job?'

On his desk was a heart-shaped frame similar to the one that held the picture of her brother and sister, but undoubtedly more expensive. It was half-turned towards her and she could see it held a photograph of a woman with short dark, fashionably cut hair. Her expression was a mixture of seduction and maternal concern as she smiled at someone beyond the lens.

'Who is in that picture?' Mary pointed.

'My wife, Jillian.' He turned the picture around so she could see. 'My other half. You will no doubt see a glow around her. She's absolutely – what was your word?'

'Beloved.'

There was a shadow where there should have been a glow and the music said this woman was very unhappy. Possibly ill.

'Is your wife ill?'

He grabbed the frame and swung it back around. 'Jillian's fine. Now Mary, as I said, you'll start on a secretary's wage but I'll increase your salary after six months if things work out well.' He coughed slightly. 'Let's see if we like each other.'

'Oh, I like you already Mr. Goodman. You helped me when I dropped my bag.'

'Thank you. Eight o'clock start. Yours is the small office next to mine.' He smiled. 'Same view.'

The silver frame wasn't at the same angle. It had been obliquely positioned to the edge of the flat screen but now the light fell across it, adding to the shadows around Jillian. The disorder jangled. Her palms itched.

'Mr. Goodman, do you mind if I just –' she leaned across the desk and moved the picture back into position. 'That's how it was before you turned it around.'

'You have an uncanny eye for detail.'

'I need things to be in their right place.' Her right hand was tapping midair. She clenched it into a fist. 'I'm sorry. I sometimes do that – play a tune. I don't always notice. I'm sorry.'

'Please don't apologise. We're all a little mad in our own ways, aren't we?'

'Are we?' Her eyes widened in alarm.

The girl had the most remarkable eyes: clear blue like a sky holding sunlight and her gaze was deep and intense. 'That was a joke, Mary.'

'I don't understand when things are funny.'

'Well, neither do I sometimes.'

'That's why I never make jokes.'

'Good to know.' He cleared his throat. 'Now, one more thing, we handle some very sensitive cases, so what goes on within these four walls stays here. OK?'

She nodded slowly. 'I'm very good at keeping secrets, Mr. Goodman.'

'I wouldn't call them secrets.' He laughed awkwardly.

'Was that a joke, too?'

'No. I'm just saying we have nothing to hide.' He let his breath out slowly. 'But we do need to be discreet to protect our clients. I don't mean we're dishonest –'

'I've been dishonest with you, Mr. Goodman.'

He flopped back in his chair. 'You have? How?'

'I have another career planned. I compose music and when it takes off I will leave here. You should know that.'

Robert laughed.

'I'm not joking, Mr. Goodman.'

'Oh, no, you never joke. I'll tell you what, when your music takes off, you may leave with my blessing. In fact, I'll buy the first ticket to your concert. Now Mary, I prefer my staff to call me Robert. Mr. Goodman makes me sound so old. Of course I *am* old compared to you.'

'I don't think you're old, Mr. ... Robert.'

'I'm in my late thirties but sometimes I feel as if I'm a hundred.' He gave a world-weary sigh. 'Do you have a good black suit?'

'Only this one.'

He took his wallet out of his breast pocket, counted five hundred dollars and handed it to her. 'Buy a nice black suit while you're in town. Get your mother to help you.'

She stared at the money in her palm. 'Do you want me to spend all this on one suit?'

'Five hundred dollars won't get you top of the range, but it's a start. Get a white blouse and some shoes as well. Here's another three hundred dollars.'

51

'I've never paid this much for clothes in my life.'

Right then as Robert handed Mary another three hundred dollars the sky outside the window appeared to burst into flame. Every crest on the harbour was a tongue of flame. The radiance resolved into a single ball of light that came to rest outside the window. Mary pressed her hands to her throat and opened her eyes wide. The angel, who had been absent for two whole years, had returned and was now gesticulating wildly behind her new employer's back, swinging his hands across his chest in a skull and crossbones gesture while Robert offered more details about the job. The music in her head began to hammer and throb.

'And you can even see Kirribilli from your office.' He half-turned to the window. 'I'll point it out for you.'

'No!' *Don't look at the view. There's an angel outside the window and the sky's on fire.* 'I noticed it earlier.'

'All right. Any other questions?'

Pretend everything is normal. Stay calm. 'When do I start?'

'Tomorrow morning. I'll meet you in reception and show you to your office.'

For one ridiculous moment, he imagined the girl was staring at something outside the tenth floor window. The impulse to turn around and check was almost overwhelming. He wound up the interview.

'Thank you for coming in, Mary. Employing you promises to be very interesting.' When he stood up, the girl too bounced to her feet, eager to depart. *Eager to get away from the vision outside.*

'You really ought to put that money away before you go back out to reception. The other women might get the wrong idea.' He laughed. 'That was a joke.'

'About those other women. Is it really fair not to give them a chance?'

'My God, you're honest! It's a good thing, of course, but

most people would be thrilled to have eliminated the competition so easily.'

'It's not fair though, is it?'

'Life isn't fair, Mary. Oh, and one more thing, my partner, James Oldfield Jnr, currently has no secretary. Could you manage a bit of extra typing just until –?'

'James? That was my father's name.' The intense gaze did not alter. 'There are three other women out there who need jobs. Why don't you hire one for James?'

'Because we can't afford to!' He instantly regretted revealing so much to the girl. 'It's just temporary. World global thing. Finances will improve. Recessions are just cycles.'

She held out the money. 'Please...'

'No, you must look the part. Success is all smoke and mirrors. Illusion. Our clients need to think we're doing well or they won't trust us.' The phone rang. 'Excuse me one moment.' He answered. 'Ian! Thank you for calling back. One moment.' He covered the phone. 'I'll see you tomorrow, Mary.' Again he spoke into the receiver. 'Monday lunchtime at the very latest.' He lowered his voice, sat back down and swung his chair to the window. 'Can you make that work?'

SOGGETTO CAVATO

A musical cryptogram, using coded symbols as a basis for an opera

The angel was pacing back and forth, fists balled, wings quivering while Mary watched from her bed.

'I told you I'd be back. Why did you get a job?'

'I have to help Mum with bills and anyway, you've been gone for two years.'

He stopped pacing. 'I told you I'd be back.'

'How was your Father?'

'I didn't see him.'

'I'm sorry.'

'I don't want your pity.' He blazed. 'I want you to leave that job because you don't have time. The music has to be note perfect before you play it for the world. I won't have my plans ruined.'

'I don't want to let Robert down.'

'Robert?' he asked slowly.

'My new boss. He chose me over three glamorous women with experience.'

He pointed a slender finger at her. 'I chose you over all the women on earth!'

She twisted the corner of the sheet. 'Where have you been for the last two years?'

He looked away. 'Florence.'

'With your lover?'

'Don't cross-examine me like a wretched lawyer.'

'I'm a paralegal.'

'In heaven they told me my brother's on earth looking for me.'

'Oh, Gabriel, that's wonderful news.' She pressed her hands together, eyes shining.

He plucked a loose feather from his wing, dropped it on the floor. 'Heaven's changed, Mary. The angels create worlds that flicker and die and they said –' he shuddered. 'They told me enlightenment was irrelevant.' He raised his chin. 'But I'll prove them wrong. I'll make a new heaven here on earth. A better one. Light is still worth worshipping. It is the only unfaltering principal in creation. Everything else alters.'

'Except love.'

He snorted. '*Love alters when it alteration finds.* Thus wrote Shakespeare and never a truer word was writ in any kingdom.'

'What about the lady with the beautiful blue soul? Didn't she love you?'

'I don't want to talk about her.'

'Where's your brother?'

'I don't know. He's probably just another face in the crowd by now. I could pass him by and not even recognise him.'

'You'll recognise him by his glow. Beloved people have a special glow.'

He shivered, lay down next to her and rested his head on her shoulder. 'He's been here for a year, Mary. Has he stopped looking for me? Maybe he's been distracted by the pleasures of the flesh. People forget their family and friends when they fall in love.'

'He's here. That's all that matters.'

He slung his arm across her. 'So, tell me more about *Robert*.'

'He's got kind eyes and lovely hands. And he gave me eight hundred dollars to buy an outfit for work! I've never had that much money in my entire life. Robert says I must look the part. Success is all smoke and mirrors, he says. Illusion. He thinks he's old but he's not. He loves his wife Jillian, calls her his other half. Isn't that romantic?'

He yawned. 'Fascinating. When something is cut in half it dies. It would be a great pity if Robert were to lose his other half.'

Mary sat up. 'What are you saying?'

Gabriel made a stabbing gesture at his heart.

'You wouldn't.'

He smiled wickedly. 'I have no reason to carve up your romantic boss, Mary. Not yet.' Clouds drifted across the moon. 'So tell me more about this paragon.'

'I don't really know any more.'

'Maybe I'll pay another visit to your office and find out for myself.'

'Please don't, Gabriel. I promise I'll leave as soon as my music takes off. I told Robert that, too.'

He pulled her back down and clung to her. 'See that you do. Everything depends on the music now.'

'Poor angel.' She stroked his forehead. 'So lonely. But soon you'll find your brother.'

'But if I never find Rigel, you're all I have, Mary.'

'Robert said –'

'Cease.' A sharp intake of breath. 'I don't want to hear Robert's name again. I won't share you with anyone.'

'All right.' She shivered.

'Rigel smells of jasmine the way I smell of pine and roses. No more talk now. Sleep.'

Moonlight silvered the angel and the girl he clung to. In the morning, he was gone. A gray feather on the floor was the only hint that he had ever been.

DISSONANCE

Harsh, discordant, lacking harmony. A chord that sounds
incomplete until it resolves itself on a harmonious chord

'I told you to hire someone glamorous!'

'Shut the door, James, and keep your voice down.'

James slammed the door. 'Why did you hire that troll?'

'God, you're rude. Mary Granger is a qualified paralegal.
And she's doing some of your work.'

'We can't afford her.'

'She's on a secretary's wage for six months. I'm busy, James.
Unless there's something else you want to discuss.'

'Dad gave us a bit extra to tide us over. It's a gift not a loan.'

'I asked you not to bother your father.'

'He offered. I also wanted to tell you I'm getting help for
my little problem.'

'Gambling? Or drugs?'

'I'd rather not say.'

A long pause. 'As long as you're on top of it, I don't need
to know. Does your father know about your problem?'

'Hell no. Why? Has he said something to you?'

'Of course not. He's too loyal.' Robert fidgeted with some
papers on his desk, avoiding eye contact. 'You don't need to
deal with this alone, James. You can talk to me if you want to.'

'Sure. Thanks.' He ran his hand through his hair. 'Are you
happy with Mary Granger?'

'Very. Why don't you introduce yourself and thank her for keeping this firm afloat.'

'I will. Soon.'

Five weeks later James Oldfield Jnr. walked into Mary's office.

'Hi there.'

'Oh, Good Morning.'

'James Oldfield Jnr. – Robert's partner.'

She stood up. 'Good Morning, Mr. Oldfield Jnr.'

'I'm sorry I haven't introduced myself before now. The time just gets away.' He closed the door, strode across to her desk, held out his hand. 'Call me James.'

She shook his hand and noticed his palm was damp.

'Please sit down, Mary, I'm not royalty.' He moved a Perspex file holder aside and perched on the edge of her desk. 'So, how are you enjoying working here?'

The holder was out of place. It belonged five centimetres to the right of the flat screen.

'I'm sorry, would you rather I sat on a chair?' Noting her discomfort, he got off her desk, pulled up a chair and plopped down. 'Better?'

'Yes, thank you.' She put the holder back in place.

'A wee bit anal, Mary?'

'A wee bit –?'

'An–al'. He separated the syllables. 'Never mind. Are you enjoying working here?'

She hesitated, unsure whether or not Mr. Oldfield Jnr. really wanted an answer. He was already looking bored, flicking some lint off his cuff.

'I am enjoying it now that it's all familiar...which trains to catch and which road to walk up. I walk up Macquarie Street and turn left at the big intersection into Bridge Street. There's a fig tree –'

'Do I make you nervous, Mary?' He leaned forward and

58

tweaked the edge of a file she was working on, moved it an inch to the right.

She stared at the out-of-place file. 'Everyone makes me nervous, Mr. Oldfie –'

'James.' Slowly, deliberately, he moved the file back into place. 'Now you can breathe again, Mary.'

She sat perfectly still and waited for him to explain why he had closed her door and was now sitting so close she could smell his aftershave. He was handsome. Blue eyes, dark hair and skin so fine it would have looked lovely on a woman.

'Why *is* that?' A cold, mean smile.

'What?'

'Why does everyone make you nervous?'

James Oldfield's exquisite eyes pinned her like a butterfly to a board and even though he was smiling, she knew he was not joking.

'Do you realise you're playing an invisible piano with your right hand?'

'I am?' She balled her fists and pressed them firmly onto her lap.

'Should you be taking something to calm you down, Mary?' Leaning so close she could feel the heat of his body. 'Some sort of medication?'

No medication ever or the music will be silenced and my father will haunt me. 'I won't take medication.'

His manner softened. 'Good for you, Mary. I won't take mine either.' He winked at her. 'Do you hear voices, too?'

She scratched her palms rhythmically, first the left, then the right, the pace increasing, alternating. 'I hear music.'

'That's different. I hear ghosts, Napoleon, angels. Don't tell Robert.'

'Angels?' she whispered, scratching, scratching.

'Sometimes.' Placing his elbows on the edge of her desk, careful not to upset anything, he leaned his chin on his fists and studied her. There were tiny gold flecks of sunlight trapped in his eyes. 'So, what have you heard about me?'

'Nothing.'

'Robert caught me having sex on my desk with my last secretary. We had to let her go, unfortunately, and that's why you've been doing my typing and handling some of my cases.' He grabbed her hands. 'Stop that fucking scratching! You're driving me nuts!'

She froze.

'Sorry. I'm sorry, Mary, that wasn't fair. Please don't be nervous. I didn't come in here to seduce you.' He laughed. 'I wouldn't dream of messing up your desk.'

She wiped her palms on her skirt. 'You wouldn't seduce *me*, Mr. Oldfield. I'm too plain to interest you.'

His eyes widened in surprise. 'Did Robert tell you that?'

'No. I worked it out for myself. You've been avoiding me. Robert said you were just busy but that's not true. It's because I'm not your type.'

His eyes were the same light-trapping shade of blue as her father's. And hers.

'Mary?'

'Yes, Mr. Oldfield.'

'James. Am I *your* type?' He dropped his hand onto her lap and caressed her itchy palms.

Leaping up she pitched against the desk, upsetting the pen holder, which tipped over, scattering five pens. The sudden disarray made her panic, her breath coming hard and fast as if she had run a race.

'This is how it was? Right?' he asked, collecting the pens and putting them back in the holder before repositioning it precisely.

'A fraction more to the right. Thank you.'

'You leapt up because I touched you, right?' Watching her carefully.

She nodded.

'It won't happen again. I promise.' His hand on his heart as he moved to her door. 'I'm glad we had this little chat. I did think you were plain at first. But now I think you have extraordinarily beautiful eyes. And Mary –'

'Yes?'

'I'll keep your secret if you keep mine.' He circled his temple with his forefinger.

When he left, she put the chair back against the wall exactly where it had been and sat down at her desk, heart pounding.

CASTRATO

Male singers who were castrated to
preserve their soprano vocal range

After a brief, restorative break in Florence he began to search in earnest and with growing need for his brother. He winged over cities, forests and oceans, bound the world in ribbons of flight. But Rigel seemed to have disappeared.

After three years of fruitless searching, he returned to Florence, took a lover and sat for new artists. But this time the glorious Tuscan city with its acceptance of angels – fallen, painted, marble or flesh – failed to satisfy him and soon he left again, abandoning his lover and leaving painters with half-finished works.

He was part way over the Pacific Ocean, on his way back to Australia and Mary, when he decided to rest. Alighting on the ocean, the summer sun burned a hole in the sky above him and cool blue pooled below him. The weight of his sorrow – his inability to find his brother, the disappearance of his Father, the chaos of heaven, the thousand year quest, Mary's job with Robert – dragged him below the surface and down to the sea bed where he lay pinned beneath fathoms of interminable blue. High above, the sun was a watery nimbus, a benchmark should he ever wish to rise again.

Hours became days. Days became weeks. Weeks stretched into months and he felt himself dissolving, becoming as sea.

Cruising sharks swam by, dead-eyed, full-bellied, and ignored him. Not even food for a shark. He felt hollow, pointless. What was his purpose now that the angels above wanted to have fun? There was still Mary's music but why bother when there would be no concert in heaven, no Father to impress, no brother to share his victory, no earthly lover to adorn his temples with a laurel wreath. His eternal life played out in movie frame visions of past glory and future desperation. Sometimes he imagined Mary's music calling to him. And once, Mary was there with him, as clear and present as a vision or a dream.

'I saw your brother walking down a city street,' she said in her musical voice. 'A man who looked just like you. He smelled of jasmine.'

But this was all an illusion founded on hope and longing. As he did in moments of despair, he thought again of that long-ago Mary – the lady at the well, silver lights in her long black hair, midnight eyes holding infinity. When he had said Goodbye, she had begged him to stay, kissed him with lips tasting of salt tears like the sea. Gently he had explained there were messages to deliver, universes to create, worship to be mantled.

'But what is any of that compared to love?' Her tears were sunlit beads on her cheeks.

'It is glory,' he said, raising his wings. 'And glory is my calling.'

In a single beat he left her – pregnant, unwed and weeping beside the well. Centuries later, a Florentine courtesan would tell him that worship was the smallest love of all, that men who settled for it were spiritually impoverished. He left her, too.

'I have left everyone who ever loved me,' he cried, bubbles of pale light shivering off him and rising to the surface. 'And when I come back looking for them they do not want to be found.'

He shrunk and shrivelled more under the weight of the sea and wished he could die of this emptiness and pain. But a merciful death was not available to immortals. The Lethe of the womb, the gentle reawakening of birth, the blissful restoration of innocence was denied to the higher orders of life. Angels, faeries, indeed all the citizens of *Otherworld* lived eternally, conscious of their sins. Unless a merciful Father redeemed them.

Time under the sea had a dreamlike quality. A year passed. The summer sun returned, piercing the blue fathoms with a brilliant, singular light that triggered a slight movement away from his submerged self-pity. He moved his water-logged weight off the sea bed and began the climb through miles of soggy hallucination, resolving to renew his search for Rigel and enlist his brother's support with the quest for enlightenment. Together they would restore order – the hierarchy that had its roots in hell but led rung by rung to his Father in heaven.

All day, held on the ocean's surface, he lay on his back while sunlight scored off residual doubt. And that night, bathed in the moon's cold luminescence, he planned his strategy. First, he would force Mary to leave her time-wasting job. Then he would search out Rigel and, with their combined gnosis, they would infuse Mary's music with divine inspiration and finally, gloriously, they would conquer the world stage by stage.

'It's a good plan,' he said, rising up, shaking the sea from his soul. 'No, it's a *great* plan.'

He flew towards Australia, the morning sun at his back.

LEITMOTIF

*A musical theme given to a particular
idea or main character in an opera*

A bowl of honeyed bread sat on the sill of her open window.

'I see you still tempt elves.' He was perched in the frame like a fantastic gargoyle.

'Gabriel?' She sat up in bed, rubbed the sleep from her eyes. 'Am I imagining you?'

'No.'

'James says –'

'Who's James?'

'My boss.'

'I thought his name was Robert.'

'James is Robert's partner. James thinks I have a similar condition to his.'

'What condition does James have?'

'He imagines ghosts and Napoleon. And angels.'

'He's mad.' Gabriel dropped into the room. 'Did James tell you you're imagining me?'

'He implied it.'

'Why do you listen to a crazy man who talks to Napoleon?'

'I have no proof that you exist, Gabriel.'

He pushed the bowl of honeyed bread into the hydrangeas. 'There's your proof.'

'The elves could have knocked that off.'

'The *elves*?' He laughed. 'Mary, you may hear what others cannot hear and see what others cannot see, but that doesn't make you mad. It makes you gifted. Like me. My imagination soars higher than others of my kind. Ignore James and his ramblings. It's time to leave your job and devote yourself to your music.'

'You think I'll obey an imaginary angel?'

His light darkened and became as shadow. 'Everything real was first imagined.' He flicked his hand at the stars framed in her window. 'Those stars existed in my imagination long before they were fashioned into stone and fire, long before my Father breathed light into them. Many of them no longer exist but their light lives on. Are they real? Are they illusion? Speculating about what is real and what is imagined will drive you mad.'

'James said –'

'*James* talks too much. Maybe it's time to deal with James' – he paused – '*and* Robert so you'll be in no doubt that I am real.'

'What do you mean?' Sweat prickling on her palms, her chest tightening.

'It's time to decide who you believe in, Mary Granger.' He raised his wings and in a single downward beat disappeared into the night.

Mary got up and went to the window. The elf dish lay on top of the hydrangeas. She hoisted herself onto the sill, reached down and retrieved it. The bread had fallen off but that wasn't as important as having the dish in its place. She set it back in the middle of the sill.

'That's better. Everything will be all right now.'

QUARTET

Four musicians who perform a piece set in four parts

Five deaths occurred in Mary's fifth year with the firm.

The first was the death of Jillian Goodman at the end of January. The stomach tumour that claimed the life of Robert Goodman's *other half* seemingly appeared overnight. Robert said that Jillian woke up one morning complaining of indigestion and that night she was in agony. He called Mary and James from the hospital and told them he'd be taking a week off because Jillian had to have some tests to find out what was wrong.

'Probably just kidney stones,' James assured his partner. 'You'll have her home by the end of the week.'

By the end of the week she was dead.

The loss of his wife broke Robert Goodman's spirit, but instead of taking time off to grieve, he pushed deeper and deeper into his work. He was in the office every day at 6am, stayed until late and went home only to sleep. If he slept. And like all overused medication, the antidotes to his agony soon failed. Within a month the pain resurged stronger and keener. He forgot to shave, forgot to eat, and finally, forgot to work. He spent his days sitting at his desk staring at Jillian's photo until it was time to go home.

While her boss grieved, Mary managed his simpler cases and prodded James into taking on his more complex ones. While

Robert floated in his sorrow, James became an ever-strengthening tide of vagueness and unreliability. Mary rowed between the two, doing her best to keep things afloat.

Midday. Again, James had just arrived at work, looking almost as dishevelled as his grieving partner.

'You missed two client appointments this morning,' said Mary, intercepting him in the hallway and trailing him to his office. 'I rescheduled them for tomorrow morning. Please be here on time. James, did you hear me?'

He dumped his briefcase on his desk and frowned at the pile of cases. 'Are these all new?'

'Yes.'

He looked at her vaguely, his eyes red-rimmed, sweat beading on his forehead and upper lip. 'How is Robert?'

'Grieving for the love of his life.'

He pressed a handkerchief to his upper lip, nodded at the files. 'Can't you take care of these?'

'No. They're too complicated for me. Please, James, I'm doing everything else.'

He slumped into his chair. 'OK, get me a coffee and I'll make a start.'

Mary lowered her voice. 'James, we need to talk.'

'About the mess we're in? What is there to say?'

'About your gambling.'

He jerked upright. 'Who told you?'

'Your father.'

'My father doesn't know,' he said slowly.

'He guessed.'

'Shit.' James dragged his hand across his mouth. 'He shouldn't have discussed my personal life with you.'

'Please don't be angry with him. He's desperately worried about you and needed someone to talk to. He wants you to get help.'

'I tried medication, Mary. It numbs me. I'm on top of it. When do you think Robert will be back on deck?'

'I don't know.' She pressed her hands together. 'Maybe if you took your medication just until Robert's able to work again.'

'It makes me feel old.'

'Please, James.'

He bowed his head. 'OK, I guess I can go without fun for a few months.'

That afternoon, Robert called her to his office. His open briefcase was stuffed with his personal belongings: his laptop, his diary, his favourite pen and the picture of Jillian in the silver heart-shaped frame.

'I'm going to England to stay with Mum. I need to get away from my empty house … empty life for a while.' Oblique rays of sunlight accentuated lines of sorrow around his mouth. Highlighted the pain in his eyes. He handed her a piece of paper. 'My mother's phone number if you need me.'

The panic started as a fluttering of wings in her belly. 'How long will you be gone?'

'I don't know.' He locked his briefcase. 'Walk me to the lift?'

She scrambled after him. 'Aren't you going to say goodbye to James?'

'No, he'll try to talk me out of it, tell me he can't manage. I have to get out of here for a while, Mary. Tell him for me please.'

'Yes.'

At the lift, he paused and looked around blindly. 'I didn't even know Jillian was ill.'

Somewhere along the hall a phone was ringing and no one was answering. It stopped for a beat then started again. 'But you knew. When I interviewed you … you asked me if Jillian was ill. How did you know, Mary?'

'I saw a shadow over her picture.'

'Like you saw a light over the Nolan. But she couldn't have been sick four years ago. The doctor said it was a very rare, fast-moving cancer.' He rubbed his forehead. 'But *you* knew. Somehow you knew.'

The music jangled, tangled. 'Did I cause her death?'

'Of course not.'

'Maybe you should have hired one of those other women, Robert.' The melody rose in pitch.

'No. Without you, this firm would have gone down the tubes. You've been heroic, Mary.' He pressed the button. 'Will you play your music for me when I come back? I'd like to hear it before the world does.'

'Why do you say that?'

'You told me, Mary. I bet you'll be right about that, too.' The lift doors slid apart and Robert stepped in, holding the door open a minute longer. 'Call me if you need anything.' Two shining metallic doors erased him.

The tenth floor was almost empty. Minute sounds echoed in walled corners: the click of a keyboard at the far end of the corridor, the hum of air-conditioning, the subliminal pulse of circuitry. Outside, the harbour sweated gold light under the burning eye of the midday sun. Her music found concert with the fibulation of the outside world.

Something moved inside the melody, a beating rhythm that grew louder and louder until there was a shrieking explosion of black feathers and crucified form – a pinned butterfly planed against the floor-to-ceiling window dividing the tenth floor from the open sky.

'Look what you've done to me!' Gabriel peeled a skeletal finger from the dividing plane and pointed it at her. 'Why didn't you leave here when I told you to?'

Mary gaped at the splayed dark angel. 'What happened to you?'

'I killed for you and now I am as death.'

'Killed?' Her heart juddered.

'Jillian Goodman. Is her death proof enough of my reality, Mary? Or do you need more?'

'What did she do to deserve your hatred?'

'Nothing.'

'Then why?' She hammered her fists against the window. 'Why?'

'She needed to die to break Robert.'

'Who are you to do such harm? To inflict such sorrow?'

'Someone you don't mess with. *Now* will you leave?'

'I can't. Robert's gone to England.'

'Screw Robert.'

She flattened her palms against the pane. 'Please, Gabriel, I have to stay until Robert comes back. Then I'll leave. I promise you. Please.'

His funereal eyes glowed sepia. 'I'm dying, Mary.'

'But you're an angel. You *can't* die.'

'I can rot.' He held up his arm and peeled off a strip of decaying flesh. 'This is how I was before I heard your music. Perhaps if you played for me again I might heal. Play for me tonight.'

'Only if you'll be patient until Robert gets back.'

'If I must.'

'Come after dinner. It's when I practice.'

'Leave the window open for me. This flesh sticks to my soul.'

'I'll make sure the window is open.'

'See that it is.' And he peeled himself – burnt feather and cankerous flesh – from the glass and winged north, black moth to the sun.

A warm hand on her shoulder.

She swung around. 'Oh, James, you scared me.'

'Everyone scares you.'

She shivered. 'I know.'

'Where's Robert?'

'He's gone to England.'

'Shit! When?'

'Just now.'

'Without telling me?' He covered his face with his hands for a long minute.

'James? Are you OK?'

'No. How the fuck am I supposed to manage?'

'With difficulty. And with my help. And only if you take your medication.'

He dropped his hands to his sides, glared at the view. 'I don't suppose he bothered to tell you when he'd be back?'

'When he feels better.'

'And how long's that going to take?' James slammed his fist against his thigh and stalked off.

FIORITURA

A highly embellished vocal line

He came – black-feathered, ragged robed, drained of light – and listened, head bowed in an attitude of transfixed humility. Note by note, the music redeemed him. His gray flesh acquired a dim phosphorescence like the moonlit sea, the smell of rotting leaves sweetened to pine and roses. An hour later, Mary played the last resonating note but did not turn around for fear of embarrassing him in his dislocated, partly-balmed state.

'Will you play again tomorrow night?' he asked.

'Yes,' she whispered.

'Leave the window open for me.'

'I will.'

'Stop encouraging elves. They bite.'

'Old habits die hard. They still might bring me luck. You never know.'

The faintest jigger of light needled the brown spaces in the room. 'I suppose there is some small destiny in luck. But elves cannot be relied upon. They have no ambition.'

'How can you talk about elves and ambition when you just murdered Jillian Goodman?'

'Jillian is free of him now,' he said casually.

She jerked her head up. 'Free of Robert? They completed each other!'

'They strangled each other. She's happy now. I am not such a monster, Mary. My world is beyond your understanding.'

'But Robert adored her. They had a perfect life together.'

A hissed intake of breath. 'Life is overrated, Mary Granger.'

'It's all we've got to live for.'

'Life is all we've got to live for?' Gurgled laughter. 'Now why haven't the sages thought of that?'

'James said –'

'Why do you listen to that fool? I'll deal with *him* next.'

'No! I played for you!' She swung around but he was gone, the curtains twitching in the wake of his flight. 'You promised to be patient if I played for you.'

'Mary? Is everything all right?' Kathleen called out.

In the hall, her mother's open door threw a trapezoid of light across the floorboards. 'Can I talk to you, Mum?'

'Of course, darling.'

'Do you ever imagine things that aren't real?'

'I imagine your father will come back to me one day. I dreamt about him last night. Do you suppose he ever dreams of me?'

'Why sure, Mum. He'll always dream of Dublin's fairest maid.'

Her chin puckered. 'Dublin's fairest maid...and still he left me.' She patted the bed. 'Sit yourself down and tell me why you cried out just now.'

Sitting on the very edge of the bed, Mary folded her hands in her lap. 'If you were the cause of something very bad, something you could have changed but didn't, would that make you guilty?'

'Well now, I suppose it depends on whether or not you wanted to cause another pain.'

'Never.'

'Is this a case you're working on?'

'No. Mum, I may have caused Jillian's death.'

'She had cancer, darling. No one causes cancer save God, and His ways are not for us to question.'

'Maybe we should question them.'

Kathleen crossed herself. 'She doesn't mean it, Lord.'

She gripped her mother's hands. 'He killed Jillian and he's going to kill again!'

Kathleen sat bolt upright. 'Mary, get a grip. What are you talking about?'

'The angel! The angel who talks to me.' Her body jerking with sobs.

'There now, cry it out. You're exhausted and confused. Angels don't kill.'

'How do you know?'

'They're God's messengers. Sure they prepare the way for great things.'

Mary drew back. 'Have you ever seen an angel, Mum? Has grandma?'

'No, but many Irish people have been visited by angels. It's a holy thing, darling.'

'He says my music will enlighten the world.'

'Well, that's very good news. But don't go taking the whole world on your shoulders. None of us was designed for such a burden save the Lord and even he died under its weight.'

CADENCE

A sequence of chords that brings an end to a phrase,
either in the middle or at the end of a composition

At eight o'clock on Monday morning James Oldfield Jnr. knocked on Mary's office door.

'Got a minute?' He waited to be invited in. The medication had worked a charm on his personality making him kinder, calmer and punctual.

She put her pen back in the holder, moved her notepad level with the phone. 'Yes.'

'I finished all those cases over the weekend. Shall I work on some of yours now?'

'Thank you, James.' She handed him the Perspex box marked *Robert*. 'You look well and happy. Are you?'

'I don't feel much to be honest. The medication numbs me.' He half-laughed. 'But at least it keeps me out of trouble. Have you had spoken to Dad recently?'

'Yesterday. I always ring your father on Sundays. He misses you. Why don't you call him?'

'I feel too guilty.'

'Your father doesn't care about the money you've borrowed.'

'Stolen more like.'

'He doesn't care. He just wants to talk to his son. I told him you're running the firm while Robert's in England.'

'Thank you, Mary. Why does life smooth the path for some

people and strew boulders for others? Dad and Rob both lost wives they adored while I'm chained to Lucinda.'

'Can't you divorce her?'

'Neither one of us wants to let go of our overpriced mansion in Rose Bay we laughingly call home. Rob crucified himself over a pile of bricks, too. Did he tell you he wanted to be an artist?'

'No.'

'His father railroaded him into law. It was either take over the family firm or be cut out of the will. No way was Rob going to lose Shalamar.'

'What's Shalamar?

'The family mansion in Vaucluse. Cedric left it to him on condition he gave up art and became a lawyer.'

'So cruel. What about Robert's mother?'

'Cedric left her nothing but Nancy has a wealthy family in England. Old money. She went back home.' He narrowed his eyes, remembering something. 'Rob told me you're a composer. What's your instrument?'

'The piano,' she murmured.

'King of instruments.' He looked out the window. The sky hung low, a gray shroud over the harbour, and here and there spears of light broke through dappling the steel-gray water. 'Rob feels Jillian's death terribly...partly because they never had kids.'

'As you said, life isn't fair.'

He turned away from the window. 'Mary? Are you all right? You look a bit peaky.'

'I've had a few late nights.'

'Take a fortnight off. I can manage. You go home and compose some music. And don't worry about my father. I'll go and see him tonight after work.' He laughed softly. 'Life is dull without my voices leading me astray but I don't want to end up like my mother.'

'What do you mean?'

He blinked rapidly. 'Has Rob not told you?'

'No.'

'Another time.' He turned to go, then paused. 'How do you battle your demons without medication?'

'I play for him and he's satisfied.'

'Ah.' James nodded. 'Is that all he wants?'

'He wants me to leave here and give myself to my music.'

'Maybe you should. Life is so brief, Mary.' Tiny fragments of light were trapped in his eyes. 'I wish I had a great talent but I'm just your average garden-variety crazy.'

'Perhaps I don't imagine him. What if he's real?'

'He's not.' He took a small packet out of his pocket. 'These little pills silence the voices. Mind you, my voices were dangerous but your imaginary friend is encouraging you to compose music. He doesn't sound too bad.'

'He's very dangerous.' She glanced out the window.

James flipped two tablets out of his packet and placed them on her desk. 'You need a break. Take these. He'll leave you alone, I promise you.'

'He said the music would be silenced if I took medication.'

'Rubbish.'

'He'll know if I do and' – gingerly picking up the tablets – 'things will get much worse.'

'Put those tablets in your bag. Think of them as a loaded gun when you need to defend yourself.'

After he left, Mary tried to get back to work, but music hammered in her head. And then came the scent of pine and roses. She checked the window again. Nothing but the view. Out in the hallway the scent was stronger, so strong it made her sneeze, and stronger still outside James' office where the door was open. He sat at his desk, studying a case file, computer screen flickering. She walked towards him.

'Mary?'

'Can you smell pine and roses?'

He sniffed and shook his head.

'He's here, James,' she whispered, her gaze darting about the room.

James left his side of the desk and went to her. 'Nobody's here but me, Mary.'

A siren wailed on the street below. There was a flash of light outside James' window. The pane shattered and blood dripped from every jagged shard.

'He's here!' she screamed, pointing at the window.

James' voice seemed to be coming from somewhere far away. 'Fight it, Mary. Fight him with everything you've got!'

Torrid music poured through the gaping hole in the pane, washing over the bloodstained shards. Red pools of melody gathered at her feet.

'I can't,' she whispered. 'He's in the music.'

'He's not. He's only in your head. He doesn't exist. Look at me!'

She looked at him. Blood ran down his cheeks like tears. 'Oh my God, he hurt you. He said he'd deal with you next. I'm so sorry.' Trembling and sobbing. 'I'm so sorry, James.'

'Mary, I'm fine.'

'But there's blood on your face and the window –' She turned to the window. It was fine too. Not shattered. Not bloodstained. 'I don't understand. It was smashed a minute ago.'

'Take the tablets tonight, Mary. Give yourself a break. Please. Come on...I'm taking you home. Take two weeks off and take two pills tonight. Savvy?'

She nodded and allowed herself to be led into the basement and into his car.

'My mother was a schizophrenic,' James said, his knuckles white as his grip on the steering wheel tightened. 'All my symptoms – spending money like there's no tomorrow, infidelity, paranoia, delusions of grandeur, hearing voices – are the same as hers. And you? The same?'

She gazed out the window at the slipstreaming suburbs. 'I have delusions of grandeur. I believe my music will enlighten the world.'

'All composers believe that.' He drove on in silence. 'My mother committed suicide when I was a kid. I'm sure that's why my father had his stroke.'

'I'm so sorry, James.'

'You never get over it completely.'

They said nothing more for a few minutes.

'Some amazingly brilliant musicians have been mentally ill,' said James.

'Really?'

'Sure. There was Mozart, Beethoven. It's a fine line, isn't it, between genius and illness?'

'Is it?' The music buzzed around her like a swarm of bees.

'I'd say you're somewhere on the high-functioning end of the spectrum. Can I ask you a personal question?'

'Yes.'

'Were you interfered with when you were a child?'

The music screamed, threatening to shatter her skull. She pressed her hands against the sides of her head and hummed loudly to drown out the mangled symphony.

A warm hand caught hold of hers. 'I'm sorry. I had no business asking you that. Let's talk about something else.'

The music settled and flowed like water over rocks bringing calm. 'You were telling me about your mother.'

James whistled. 'My God, how do you push that emotion down so quickly?'

'The music does it.'

'Right. My mother left a note saying the *angel* told her it was time to go. So she swallowed sleeping pills and –'

'Went.'

They continued in silence the rest of the way. James walked Mary to her front door, touched her cheek with the backs of his fingers. 'Please, be careful.'

She gave him a brief, wary look. 'I was going to say the same thing to you.'

'Mary? Is that you?' Kathleen hurried down the hallway, stopped dead at the sight of James. 'Oh, hello.'

James extended his hand. 'Hi, I'm James Oldfield Jnr. – Mary's boss. I brought Mary home because she's not feeling well.'

'What's wrong, darling?' asked Kathleen anxiously.

'Nothing to worry about, Mum. I'm just tired.'

'She's been carrying a heavy load with Robert away,' said James. 'I'm giving her a fortnight off. Longer if she needs it. Mary, I'll go now. Don't forget what I said about giving yourself a break.' He nodded at her handbag. 'A loaded gun if you need it.'

'What's all this about a gun?' asked Kathleen.

'Nothing, Mum. Thank you, James. I'll think about it.'

They exchanged a brief look and then James smiled at Kathleen. 'Lovely to meet you, Mrs. Granger. I can see who Mary gets her pretty smile from.'

'Oh...call me Kathleen and thank you for bringing my girl home.'

When he had gone Kathleen locked the front door.

'You never told me how handsome your boss is,' she said. 'Is he single?'

'He's married. I need to lie down.'

'Sure,' said Kathleen. 'Get yourself into bed and I'll be up directly.'

Mary was already drifting off to sleep when Kathleen came into the room and closed the window and drew the curtains.

'Mum, please leave my window open,' she said, half sitting up.

'No. The elves will have to forage elsewhere tonight. There's a fierce wind blowing and I won't have you catching your death of cold.'

'Wake me for dinner, please. I don't want to sleep through to morning. It's important.'

'What's more important than your health, darling?'

'I need to practise the piano.'

'You need to sleep. The piano can wait.' Kathleen hovered in the doorway. 'James likes you. I can tell. Pity he's married.'

'James told me his mother talked to an angel.'

'Oh, was she Irish?'

'No, she was schizophrenic.'

'The Irish talk to the little people and angels all the time and I doubt the entire population is schizophrenic.'

'She killed herself, Mum, because the angel told her to.'

Kathleen crossed herself. 'That's tragic. But you can't blame the angels. It was her own sick head telling her to do such a mischief.'

The wind rattled the pane. 'Please open my window.'

'Not tonight, darling.'

FERMATA

*A tone or rest held beyond the written
value at the discretion of the performer*

Mary woke with a raging appetite, leapt out of bed, pulled back the curtains and flung the window open. Sunlight chased shadows out of the corners of her room and the smell of dew-damp roses freshened the air. Her music found a joyful rhythm in the breath of life. In the kitchen, her mother was hunched over a mug of tea, her eyes red-rimmed.

'Mum?'

'Mama died.'

'I'm so sorry, Mum. When? Why didn't you come and get me?'

'I didn't want to wake you.'

'What do you mean? How long have I been asleep?'

'Two days and two nights. You obviously needed it.'

Mary felt blindly for the chair and sank into it. 'And my window was shut.'

'It was sudden, Mary. One minute she was well and the next minute gone.' She choked back a sob. 'The coroner found no reason for her death. It was just her time, I suppose, but I wish I'd said Goodbye.'

'This is my fault,' she whispered, pressing her hands to her throat. 'You should have woken me, Mum! I asked you to wake me for dinner! You should have!'

Outside incongruous: blue sky, treacle sunlight, fast birds and slow worms.

'What could you have done?'

'I could have played for him!' She covered her face with her hands. 'He killed her like he killed Jillian!'

'Stop it, Mary! Don't be ridiculous. It's fine to believe in angels and elves but don't give them powers they don't possess.'

Mary shook her head as if she'd missed a clue. 'I don't understand. He made no threat against Nana. Only James and Robert.'

'Mary! I said stop it!'

The phone rang.

'I'll get it, Mum.'

'No, you eat some breakfast. I'll get it.'

After a few minutes Kathleen returned to the kitchen. 'That was Mama's solicitor. She's left her house, her savings, everything she had, to you.'

'But she never even met me.'

'Probably my punishment for marrying your father. I'll be in my room for a bit. I need to be alone. Will you be all right?'

'Yes, Mum.'

Moments later, the lock on her mother's bedroom door clicked.

Mary opened the window, then went to the piano and began to play. After only eight bars the curtains ballooned and the angel plummeted through the open window. Mary twisted in her stool to face the seraph.

'Why?'

He was on his knees, part light, part clinging flesh and feather, a spill of burnished light in his eyes. 'Why what?'

'Why did you kill my grandmother?'

'I didn't kill your grandmother.'

'But she changed her will in my favour. You must be behind it.'

He twitched at his robes. 'Has she left you much?'

'Everything she had: her cottage, her savings. That's very convenient, isn't it? Now I have money, I can leave my job.'

'You said you wouldn't leave until Robert comes back. That's what we agreed.' His flesh began to bruise and weep dirty light. 'Please play for me.'

'I have tablets that will make you go away.'

'Medication?' His eyes glittering like a wolf's. 'Where did you get it?'

'James gave it to me.'

'James had no right.'

'He's my friend, which gives him the right.'

'Our agreement gives *me* sole rights.'

'I'm reneging.'

'The consequences of betrayal will be more deaths. Don't fight me, Mary.' He dragged at his night-stained robes. 'I am bound by forces you will never understand. When you imagine an entire universe you never imagine the consequences. They orchestrate to quite a different baton but still they must be dealt with. We are not here to have fun and play games like children. I must save the world. But I am already weakened by this fickle flesh, these falling feathers and failing light, I need your music to strengthen me. We had an agreement. Honour it.'

'You have killed since then.'

'Everything kills to protect that which gives it life. But I did not kill your grandmother.'

'You killed Jillian.'

'Have mercy on me, Mary. I am shut out of heaven. Shut out of life. I can't find my brother. And yet his scent haunts me. I smelled jasmine in –'

'And why were you in my office the other day? Why?'

Light flittered around him like burning moths. 'I caught a scent of him in Cremorne. I came to ask you to help me find him.'

'I know you did something to James' window. I saw it all smashed and covered in blood.'

'It was a little spell. Nothing sinister.'

'I told you never to come to my office.'

'But my brother —'

Mary sighed. 'Cremorne, you say?'

'Yes.'

'I will help you find him. But I want your promise you'll never, never kill again.'

'I swear it on all I hold sacred.' He grabbed her hand and kissed it fervently. 'Thank you, Mary Granger. Thank you.'

She pulled her hand free. 'You won't hurt James? Promise.'

'I promise. Now will you play for me?'

'Not tonight. It would be disrespectful to play the piano when Mum's grieving for Nana.'

'Maybe some music will soothe her?'

'Tomorrow night.'

He crawled to the window and climbed on to the sill. 'When the lift doors opened in your building I heard the same tune – *The Girl from Ipanema*. I hear it in Florence, too, and other places. Is it the world's anthem?'

'No, just a pop song. It's played in lifts all over the world.'

'Soon, your music will be playing in lifts all over the world.'

MODULATION

To shift to another key

Magdalene Muir's cottage in Fingal Place, Stoneybatter, Dublin
sold later that year. Mary decided that she and her mother
would move to Cremorne, the beautiful harbour-side suburb
several coves east of Kirribilli. They would leave the past behind
and start afresh. And it was in Cremorne that Gabriel had
picked up his brother's scent of jasmine. So, Mary reasoned,
if she found an earth-bound angel there, it would mean Gabriel
was real, not a voice in her head. She would explain her situation
to Rigel. Hopefully he would sympathise with her plight and
talk his brother out of killing again. The move would mean a
new routine but Cremorne was just a ferry ride into the city
and a walk up Macquarie Street to work. Not too challenging.

'But how will your father find me?' Kathleen asked when
Mary voiced her plan.

'He's not coming back.' Mary said as gently as she could.

'He might.'

'I love you, Mum, but I need to move from here.'

'Well, you'll move on your own.'

'So be it.'

GLISSANDO

Sliding between two notes

James had found a wonderful apartment on the third floor of a converted 1930s mansion in Cremorne Point. It had polished timber floors, high ceilings and wainscoting. He'd gone with Mary when the estate agent showed her round.

'Sometimes a change of space can chase phantoms away,' said James.

'What do you mean?'

They were standing in the kitchen. The estate agent had stepped outside to take a call and left them alone to wander.

'Once you leave Blacktown you may leave your unwelcome visitor behind.'

'If only it were that simple.'

'It is. Come and take a look out here.' James led her onto the small balcony adjacent to the kitchen. 'If you fill this with potted plants you'd have your own sanctuary and look,' he pointed towards Shellcove, 'you can catch glimpses of the city.'

'And if that was my room,' said Mary, indicating the adjoining bedroom through the French doors, 'I could go to sleep looking at the stars.'

'Your mother could have the other bedroom down the hall.'

'Mum's not moving.'

'Oh, well, perhaps it's time to cut the apron strings. She'll be fine and so will you. Take a good look round. I'll wait here,' he said, confident of the result.

For Mary the decision to buy rested on one thing, whether or not there was a perfect spot for her piano. She wandered into the living room. Under a leadlight window there was a recessed space where fragments of coloured light fell in dappled harmony.

'That's it,' she whispered. 'My piano belongs here.'

She went back to James.

'I want this apartment.'

'That was quick.'

'I've seen all I need to.'

James laughed. 'Do you want me to make an offer now?'

'Maybe tomorrow.' Mary played a tune midair, her fingers striking a melody half-summoning, half-retreating. 'I can't do this. Not today.'

'If not today then when? Next year? The year after?' James seized her hands and squeezed gently. 'Stop playing your music and concentrate, Mary. I know how powerful and persuasive it is but you need to be *here*. This apartment is great and at the moment you can afford it. In a year's time, who knows? Where will you put your piano?' A deft move.

'There's an alcove in the living room that's perfect.'

James smiled. 'Good girl! I'll make an offer then?'

She gripped his arm. 'Are you sure he won't find me here?'

'It'll take him a while.'

James handled the sale. He put in a low offer that was accepted, leaving Mary money to spend on her new home. She moved on a beautiful Saturday in late spring. James and Kathleen helped place her furniture exactly as she wanted it: light and shadow falling just right, every item placed just so. When the piano was delivered late in the afternoon and was placed in the alcove, Mary had a sense of arriving home after a long difficult journey. *My sacred space*, she told herself, *everything in its rightful place. Nothing can go wrong in here.* And in that moment she truly believed Gabriel would never dare to trespass.

'Play something,' said Kathleen, her cheeks flushed from their hectic day.

'Yes, please do. I've never heard your music,' James added.

'Haven't you?' Kathleen's dark eyes narrowed suspiciously. 'Really?'

'There's no piano at work.'

'Mum, I don't think playing now is a good idea.'

'Why ever not, Mary? Your young man hasn't heard it.'

James stared at Kathleen. 'What did you just call me?'

'Mum thinks you like me.'

'I *do* like you.'

'Romantically.'

'Mary's my friend, Kathleen. Nothing more,' he said quietly. 'I should go and leave you two together.' He turned to Kathleen. 'Will you be staying here for a bit? If not, I'm happy to come over and help Mary with her new routine.'

'I'll be staying. You go home to your wife, Jimmie.'

James caught his breath. 'My mother used to call me that.'

It was a beautiful new routine.

Mary woke to the sound of birdsong and after breakfast, she and her mother walked along Shellcove path to the wharf. The ferry ride into the city took fifteen minutes and from there it became the old routine: up Macquarie Street to Bridge Street, a takeaway coffee from her favourite little hole-in-the-wall café, through the revolving doors of the building, the lift to the tenth floor and into her office to enjoy the view and her coffee before getting down to work.

And after work, Kathleen met Mary in the coffee shop on the ground floor of her building and repeated the exercise in reverse. Along Bridge down Macquarie to Circular Quay, catch the Mosman ferry, get off at Cremorne Point, walk along the path paralleling Shellcove, open the back gate, take the path along the right-hand side of the building, up the stairs to the top floor, turn the key, open the door and ... home.

Mary set the kitchen table for two with silver cutlery and lit a candle while Kathleen arranged the roses they had bought at Circular Quay.

'You seem settled now.' Kathleen began.

'I know what you're going to say but please stay a bit longer.'

'I've taken too much time off work, Mary. I need to get back.'

The city lights were popping to life, the inlet reflecting ladders of gold, the birds gathering in their evening roosts to sing the closing of the day.

'You haven't played the piano all week, darling.'

'I can live without it.'

'Since when?'

'He'll find me if I play my music. That's how he found me before.'

'You mean the angel who believes in you?'

'I mean the angel who killed Jillian and Nana.'

'Stop your nonsense, Mary.'

'It's true, Mum.'

'Jillian died of natural causes and it was Mama's time. Sure you have a great gift, darlin' and wasn't it your dream to share it with the world one of these days?'

'I've changed my mind.'

'Well, change it back again. I'll be going home tomorrow. You fill your new home with music as God intended.'

Mary sat alone on her balcony. The air was so still, the night sounds – cricket song, possum snuffling, the slap-slurp of wavelets in the cove – found concert in a melody that made her fingers dance. Soon she lifted the lid of her piano and began to play. The first time since moving to Cremorne. It was like breathing out after holding her breath so long that it almost choked her.

Music poured out of her soul. But as she moved from joyful major chords into an augmented minor a shadow fell across the board and the temperature in the room dropped. She shivered and changed the tone with a frivolous arpeggio, increasing the tempo on a rising scale of radiant major chords. Higher and brighter the music soared until the room shuddered with heat and light. He was there. Breathing hard against his presence, she played on, the notes sparkling around her like glitter in a shaken snow-globe. Only when she finished, did she close the lid.

'When I first heard your music...have I've told you this already?' His voice was so soft it was little more than a breeze.

'You found me.'

'Did you really think I wouldn't?' He moved around the room like a cat exploring its new home. 'Thank you for moving to Cremorne. Perhaps you'll find my brother here.'

'If he exists.'

'As I was saying, when I first heard your music I felt as if your soul spoke directly to mine. People tire of prophets and they crucify saviours, but music, ah, they'll listen to music. But you know all this...'

She ran her hands over the lid, feeling the tiny imperfections, wincing. 'James said it would take you a while to find me.'

'So you still listen to James.'

'He's my friend.'

'I'm your friend, but let's not spoil our reunion arguing about James. You're playing again now. That's all that matters. And soon you'll find my brother.'

DECEPTIVE CADENCE

A chord progression that seems to lead to resolving
itself on the final chord, but does not

The third death occurred in summer against a backdrop of cathedral spires, obelisk scrapers and verdigris domes. The sun scorched the pavements and in the Royal Botanic Gardens hundred year old oaks and pines sweated black lace shadows on the wilting lawns.

Even at 6.30am the city streets were crowded with commuters attempting to beat the heat. After disembarking at Circular Quay, Mary entered the stream of humanity flowing along Macquarie Street before her ritual stop at Rica's. The shop was little bigger than a phone box but served the best takeaway coffee in Sydney.

'Could you make mine extra strong today, please, Rica? I didn't get much sleep last night.'

Rica winked. 'Your boyfriend keep you up, Mary?'

'I don't have a boyfriend.'

'Still? What's wrong with men? Now if I was single, I'd bring a ladder to your window.' He made her a double shot cappuccino with extra chocolate on top. 'Here you go, Bella, this'll get you through the day.'

She had stayed up late perfecting an ambitious new piece. Gabriel had come and pronounced it enchanting and called it *his* song.

'*Song for Gabriel* will be the first piece of your music to enslave the world.'

'Enslave?' Mary had frowned at him.

'I mean enlighten.' The angel was glowing again, his beauty strengthening every time she played the piano. 'When's Robert coming back?'

'He might stay in England for Christmas. By the way, James is going to find my brother and sister for me so you needn't worry about that.'

Gabriel lifted her chin with his finger. 'Have you stopped believing in me, Mary?'

'No.' She met his unblinking eyes and tried not to flinch.

'I promised you *I'd* find your brother and sister. James can stop meddling. I mean it, Mary. Ignore me at your peril.' He smiled sweetly and left.

That smile kept her awake for hours and when she finally slept it was to dream about corpses strewn on a path leading to a grand piano perched on a stage. Gabriel was hunched on the lid, a smirking satyr. Her audience grinning like fools. Happy. Obedient. Enlightened.

'Dom, dom, dah, dom, dom.' She circled her fingers round the paper cup and hummed as she hurried along the busy street, head down, free hand tracing the notes of her new melody. 'Dom, dom, dom.'

'Hey! Watch where you're going.'

She looked up into the angry face of a middle-aged man.

'Look what you've done.' He swiped at a miniscule droplet of coffee on his lapel, a single *café au lait* tear on his suit. A little bump, a tiny spill.

'I'm sorry. I didn't mean to.'

'Be more careful in future.' He huffed off, cleaving the crowd.

She stood quite still on the busy street, the stream of

commuters parting around her. 'I really didn't mean to hurt anyone.' Tears welling. 'Just a tiny spill.'

'Are you all right, dear?' A gentle female voice, kind blue eyes.

'It was an accident but he acted as if I did it on purpose.'

The lady patted her arm. 'Take a deep breath, my dear, and think of a tune. That's what I do when the world gets too much for me.' And then she was gone, absorbed into the crowd like rain at sea.

'Think of a tune? Why did you say that?' The thought vanished into silence but set her nerves jangling.

The sun splintered the harbour into jewel-rich shades of gold, blue and turquoise and ferries trailed strings of white foam.

James burst into her office. He looked terrible, wild-eyed, his hair unkempt, his face unshaven. 'Something incredible has happened, Mary.'

'What's wrong? Has somebody died? Your father?'

'Nothing's wrong. Everything's perfect.' He took a deep breath, made the announcement. 'My mother visited me last night and brought someone with her. Bet you can't imagine who?'

'Your mother is dead, James. Have you stopped taking your medication?' Mary knew without asking.

'Yes. You persuaded me, Mary. I wanted to see if I could manage without it. Like you. Fight my demons. And I'm glad I did.'

'I didn't tell you to stop taking your medication.'

'Not in so many words. You led by example. Actions speak louder than words, Mary. It's a well-documented fact.'

'It's a *what*?' she asked faintly.

He walked up to the window, flattened his palms against the glass. 'Imagine flying into all that blue.'

A mad carousel tune began to loop in her mind. 'James, people can't fly.'

He rubbed his palm up and down on the pane. 'The angel told me I could.'

'The angel?' Her breath caught in her throat. 'What angel, James?'

'The angel who came with my mother. He had a message for me, Mary.'

She opened her handbag, took out the tablets. 'Take these *now*.'

'It was like being touched by God.' He gazed at the sky. 'This is my chance to make my father proud of me.'

'Your father is already proud of you.'

'Prouder then. What I am about to do will make me special, Mary. Like you.' He hurried away.

She dialled Robert's number in England. Finally – and it felt like an eternity – he answered. 'Something's happened.'

'Mary? It's the middle of the night.'

The smash reverberated throughout the tenth floor.

'Oh God, Robert!'

Followed by another.

'Robert! Something terrible is happening...'

And another.

'Mary, what's going on? Mary!'

But she had dropped the phone.

James was crouched in the gaping window, chunks of broken glass and a sledge hammer on the floor. He must have carried the hammer up in the lift earlier that morning. Did no one see? Or wonder?

He turned to her, a zealous light in his eyes. 'I've called the press. I'm just waiting for them to arrive before I fly.'

'James, stop it! You can't fly!' Although she screamed her warning, her voice sounded small and hopeless against the expanse of summoning blue.

'And show I have no faith? No, Mary, a lack of faith has

been my problem all along. The angel explained it. Faith will make me whole. My test is flying like playing music is yours. We are alike, Mary. We have both been chosen to restore the balance between heaven and earth. You with your music and me by defying gravity.'

'He mentioned me?' She swayed against his desk.

'Oh yes, by name.'

A whirring sound.

'The news chopper. The glare of publicity! I will share my faith with the world. The angel said people need a miracle to make them look up and see the light. They'll look up now when I fly.'

James squatted in the broken window, caught between life and a fall that would be his death.

'James...come back to me. Step back down into the room. We can talk.'

'Later, Mary. After I've flown.'

The helicopter flew into sight with a cameraman harnessed in the open doorway, his lens pointed at the gaping hole in the plate glass. Sirens shrieked below and someone holding a loudspeaker pleaded with James, urging him to go back inside.

'Don't, James! Don't do it. Your father's suffered enough.' Through tears she saw James nettled in slivers of broken glass, blood dripping from cuts in his thighs and arms.

'Have faith, Mary!' And with that he plunged into interminable blue, arms flapping. Seconds later, James Oldfield Jnr. was a pink smear on Bridge Street. Sirens wailed. People screamed. A whirring helicopter documented every moment of the tragedy and made fodder for the evening news.

Gabriel flew out of the sun and hovered in the bloodstained frame. 'He shouldn't have meddled.'

OPERA SERIA

An opera with a serious classical theme

Night was closing purple curtains over the harbour by the time she got home. She opened the balcony doors, letting in the amplified night sounds and the hothouse scent of weary plants. At her piano, she played a fantastic, summoning melody, not doubting for a minute its potency.

When he came, stinking of dying roses and leaking dirty light, she was ready for him.

'Hello, Gabriel.' She picked up the tablets James had given her and cradled them in her palm.

'Now Mary, before you do something you'll regret –'

'I only regret not doing this sooner.'

'You'll silence the music.'

'I know.'

Sparks darted, burned, fell. 'You'll silence your soul.' Shadows pulsed over him like a passing flock of birds. 'Memories of your father will return.'

She took a trembling breath. 'I know.'

'You'll dream of him, and without the sound track that blocks him you'll relive all the nights he came to your bed before I protected you.'

'Dom, dom, dah, dah –' she pressed her hands to her ears and rocked back and forth.

'I won't be here to stab him with my light!' His voice and wings raised. 'Listen to me, Mary!'

The phone rang. They both fell silent and stared at it.

'Take the call,' said Gabriel.

She palmed the tablets and answered. 'Hello?'

'Am I speaking to Mary Granger?' The gruff yet hesitant voice of a woman. 'This is Jennifer Granger. Your sister.'

Mary braced herself against the piano's solid plane. Gabriel watched her.

'I've got some news.' Mary heard the suck of a cigarette. 'No idea why his landlord called me instead of you but he asked me to let you know.' A long pause. 'Our father died last night.'

Mary worked out the timings in her head. She stared at Gabriel. '*Last night*? Are you sure?'

'This isn't a joke. And I am your sister. *Half*-sister. Our father passed away last night. A heart attack, the landlord said.'

Mary remained silent.

'I don't suppose you know about me. It must be a shock. Hell, I didn't know about *you* until this morning. The old bastard must have hired a private investigator to find us.' The sound of drawn-in breath. 'He never paid me a visit, thank God. Anyway Mary, we have to organise his funeral. Do you want to meet at my place or shall we come to you?'

'*We*? Are you married?'

'No. You've a brother as well. Jonathan.'

'I'll come to you. Is that OK? What's your address?'

And so it was arranged. The three musketeers together at last.

Gabriel, who had listened to every word, flickered and dimmed. 'I kept my promise.'

She unclenched her fist, looked at the tablets. 'I can't let you kill again.' And raised her palm to her lips.

'Don't silence the music, Mary. Your sister needs it even more than you do.'

'What do you mean?'

'He raped her, too.'

She closed her fingers. Swayed.

A long uncertain silence held them and then Mary said, 'Goodbye Gabriel.'

'Wait! I'll leave. Don't destroy the music. I'll return to heaven, see if my Father's come back.' From the balcony door, he threw a sly glance over his shoulder. 'But I won't go alone. I'll kill your brother and sister and take them with me.'

'No!' Mary dropped the tablets on the floor. 'You win, Gabriel.'

'Good girl. Wise girl. Play something for me.'

She went to the piano, raised the lid and played a sad melancholy air.

Gabriel slipped back into the room and stood behind her. 'One day you will see that I am right.'

'Let me tell you something about entrapment, Gabriel,' she said over the top of the melody. 'It's the worst kind of evil.'

'What do you know of evil? You haven't witnessed the fall of empires and ideals like I have.'

'Maybe not but I know that entrapment seeps through the bars, infecting jailer and prisoner in equal measure.' She glanced over her shoulder. 'It's a well-documented fact.'

'I've never heard it. Shall I tell what I heard the night I wished my soul would bleed into the earth?'

She stared blindly at the board. 'My music.'

'I heard life – pure and simple. Its message of joy unequivocal. The meaning of words can get lost in translation but music needs no interpreter. It speaks directly to the soul. Your music told me I would create the greatest universe ever imagined. Beyond anything my Father ever conceived or achieved.' A flash of light. 'Your music completes me, Mary Granger. Let it complete you too.' He placed his hand on her head. 'Follow where it leads.'

The music led her into the world of her imagination where melody and light erased shadows and doubt. And there, deep and almost hidden, she heard the sound of a lock being slid back into place.

'There now,' said Gabriel. 'You're safe again. Don't hate me. James is happy now. He's with his mother and he's truly flying. And your father is in the place reserved for those who drain the light of others. I have locked him away in the dark where he can do no more harm. And you are –'

'Trapped.'

'Free, Mary.' Had she looked around she would have seen a creature of unparalleled beauty, reborn as light, transmogrified by music so ordered and precise it trafficked with God.

'You are doing what you were born to do, Mary Granger. How many can claim that privilege? And soon your genius will raise every soul to the light.'

'Every soul but mine.'

'Is it so bad being Mary Granger?'

A tear fell onto the back of her hand. 'It's unbearably lonely.'

'Ah, the price of creation.' He kissed the top of her head. 'You won't feel so lonely when they worship you. Forget all else but the music now. Let it be your reason for living. Until tomorrow.' He left in a whisper of wings and light.

She closed the lid of the piano and struggled to remember something. Then it came to her. The death of her father occurred on the same evening an angel visited James to whisper cruel promises of flight into his ear. It was no coincidence.

OSTINATO

A repeated phrase

It had been a triumphant day one way and another: eliminating the competition, removing the last boulder and now glimpsing a mesmerising light that threw his past thousand year tenure on the wing into bas relief against a brilliant future.

He lay on the ocean facing eternity, his robes rippling around until he resembled a sea creature, his wings pulsing below the surface, his hands dripping phosphorescence.

'Father, I am planning a New World – an enlightened world. First humanity and then every species of inquiring life on every inhabited planet, star and mote will become enraptured by light. You will be so proud of me.'

A lone gull winging homeward cawed sadly.

'I created all this,' he told the gull as he swept his hand across the milky arch of stars above. 'Everything measurable – earth, water, air, substance, distance, time – was first imagined by me. Father only added life and a spill of light.' He punched his fist into the sea-skin. 'And yet they worship *Him*!' He flung his hands heavenward as if his Father still reigned there. 'I didn't mean it, Father. I'm sorry.'

His Father once warned him about conceit. 'Gabriel, your vanity will be your undoing, son. Perhaps another messenger –'

'No, Father, please trust me. I'll make them see Your light.'

And ignore my substance he would have added had he dared.

But God chose another son and Gabriel was told to prepare the way for him.

The other son told humanity love would lead them home. Love thy neighbour. Love thine enemies. Just love. And then he gave humanity the keys to the kingdom.

All this and more you can do. He told them. What lunacy possessed him? He might as well have told them they were equal! He might as well have said *come and play with us.*

Humanity took the keys to the kingdom and crucified him.

Well, it was time to take the keys back.

LACRIMOSO

Tearful, mournful

On his first morning back in Australia, and in his own bed, Robert rolled over to wrap his arms around Jillian. She had walked through his dreams and her presence still lingered in the space between waking and sleeping but when he circled only emptiness, he woke up to reality.

'You idiot!' he told himself.

The castigation had started a month after Jillian died and now, ten months on, the self recrimination was habitual. Suffering was preferable to numbness: that living death. To sharpen his grief he sat up and looked hard at the visual assault of the room: the blue walls, green curtains, a yellow and lime-striped bedspread and a turquoise and black Akira Isogawa rug on the polished floorboards. During her final weeks, and as if suspecting her time was running out, Jillian had redecorated Shalamar. Working feverishly, she had inflicted a cacophonic décor on the house.

'Life affirming,' she had told him.

'Ugly,' he muttered now. 'I should repaint all the walls white.'

But then Jillian would be painted out of his life and his bedroom would be a tomb.

'Not yet.' He flopped back and stared at the mercifully white ceiling. 'I suppose I should get up.'

But what for? There was no work to go to, no soul mate

to talk to, no friends because he hadn't bothered to make friends, no children, no work partner. He could ring his mother but she'd just repeat her advice – leave Australia and the past behind and move to England. But he couldn't sell Shalamar.

For the first time in his life, he felt utterly alone – until he remembered that Mary had promised to play the piano for him when he got back. He checked the time: six thirty. Too early to call.

He lay there listening to the sounds of life outside: birdsong, leaf-rustle and the low hum of the earth turning. Inside the silence was broken only by the faint dull thud of his heart and the hissing sibilance of his dragged-in breath. Then a sudden crushing weight on his chest.

He lay perfectly still, his focus on his pain.

Five hours later he still lay there, staring at the ceiling. He checked the time on his bedside clock: eleven thirty.

'I could call her now.'

He sat up slowly, and in quiet desperation he dialed Mary's number.

ARIOSA

A type of solo vocal piece during an opera

Mary had been awake since dawn making a mental list of the things she mustn't do when she met Jennifer and Jonathan. She mustn't play an invisible piano, mustn't stare at them, scratch her palms, hum or get distracted by the soundtrack in her head. First impressions were so important. They set the tone of any new relationship and she wanted her siblings to trust her because they would be the three musketeers – invincible. She had to make absolutely sure Jennifer and Jonathan didn't think her crazy.

'I must try to act normally,' she told herself.

She had planned the day's routine to the minute, allowing for minor variations over which she had no control like heavy traffic or an unexpected storm. At seven a.m. she got up and showered. At seven thirty she opened her wardrobe: three black work suits, four white blouses, a casual track suit for her walks around the neighbourhood and a simple black dress – the kind you might wear to a funeral. She chose that.

At eight o'clock she forced herself to eat a heavy breakfast so she wouldn't feel hungry during the most important meeting of her life and at eight thirty she grabbed her handbag and glanced around before leaving, making sure everything was in its right place. At eight thirty-five she was down on the street waiting for the cab she'd arranged the night before.

At eight forty-seven, she gave the driver her siblings' address – 7/8 Regret Street in Newtown and then, sitting on the back seat clutching her handbag, she watched her music polish the sky and throw jeweled light on the suburban gardens.

'Dom, dom, dom, dom,' she hummed.

The driver glanced at her in the rear vision mirror.

'I'm a composer,' she told him without apology because it didn't matter if *he* thought she was crazy.

He shrugged and looked back at the road.

After crossing the Harbour Bridge the cabdriver took the Eastern Distributor. An hour later, the multilane arterial road shrunk to two single lanes of dense traffic, and, on the crowded sidewalks where dark little shops squatted under awnings, the storekeepers leaned in open doorways sipping coffee and tracking the passersby with sloe eyes, narrowed and watchful. Emerging from the throng of gray-suited pedestrians, a sudden exotic note: an Indian woman in a magnificent jade sari followed by two Muslim women in full-length black robes and headscarves with silver threads harvesting sunlight.

Her music absorbed the rhythm of the multicultural suburb, made counterpoints of the honking horns and ligatures of the bicyclists in business suits who tagged the bumper-to-bumper traffic. But when the driver turned left into a quiet little street and stopped outside an ugly red-brick block of flats fronting a pavement unrelieved by greenery or pedestrians, her music paused for breath.

'This is it,' he said, half turning. After taking the fare he smiled, displaying crooked yellow teeth. 'Good luck with the music.'

Regret Street was eerily quiet and deserted. The gutters were crammed with rubbish: yellowing newspapers, used condoms, discarded needles and, on the red brick wall of Jennifer and Jonathan's building, someone had written, "Today's fucked.

Tomorrow's fucked. Eternity's fucked!" The message was scribed in indelible black paint, the kind you spray on.

She checked her watch: five minutes to ten. Jennifer had said ten o'clock. She stepped over a pile of rubbish on the first step – chocolate bar wrappers, some square cuts of tinfoil and a broken bottle – and entered the building through a pebbled glass door jammed open with a brick. The stairwell stank of wine and garlic. Noises seeped from behind closed doors: a muffled argument, a trickle of laughter, the theme music of a daily soap, a ringing phone. But number seven was silent.

At precisely ten o'clock Mary knocked on her siblings' bright red front door. A volley of footsteps and then the door opened as far as three sets of chains allowed and someone peered at her suspiciously.

'Mary?'

'Yes.'

The chains were unbolted, the door swung open and Jennifer stood there – tall and slender, a supermodel-type in faded jeans and a simple yellow tee-shirt. Her face was completely free of make-up. Naturally beautiful with high cheekbones, full red mouth, flawless olive complexion, blonde hair tied back in a ponytail and the same brilliant blue eyes as Mary's. The only thing marring her perfection was the smudge of dark rings beneath her eyes.

'Come in.'

Mary took a step and bumped into the doorframe. Jennifer shot out a supportive hand. 'Have you had breakfast?' She didn't wait for an answer. 'Neither have I. I'll cook something for both of us. You like eggs?'

'Yes, but I've already had –'

'Take a seat.' She closed the door and secured the bolts again. 'I always lock up. You get all types in this neighbourhood.'

'I saw that awful thing someone wrote on the front wall.'

'Oh, yes, I meant to scrub that off.'

'It's indelible.'

'I'll paint over it then. I'll just let Jonathan know you're here and then I'll feed you.'

The unit was dark, a blind drawn at the window and the only light coming from a dim standard lamp in the corner. A shabby orange sofa and two matching armchairs flanked a stained coffee table. Mary sat in one of the armchairs and watched her exquisite half-sister glide across the darkened room to knock on a closed door sporting a faded full-length poster of Michael Hutchence. Underneath the rock-star's face a wreath made of baby's breath and yellow button roses hung on a nail.

'Jonathan! Mary's here.'

No answer.

'Get up, Jonathan. First warning.' She glided back across the room, flung a purple beaded curtain aside and went into a tiny kitchen that adjoined the living room.

An empty pizza box lay on the floor next to the sofa. On the coffee table, a used coffee cup stained with pink lipstick sat next to a book of Oscar Wilde's collected works. At the far end was a can of black spray paint. In front of the window a laminated orange table was stacked with serious-looking books with titles like *Plants for a City Garden* and *Horticultural Tips* and on the floor underneath were four rows of cracked teacups filled with dirt.

The sound of toast popping up, the whistle of a kettle and a long, sad moan from behind the door with Michael Hutchence on it.

'Cup of tea?' Jennifer called from the kitchen.

'Only if you're –'

'Yes or no?'

'Yes, thank you.'

'Milk and sugar?'

'Yes, thank you.'

'How *much* sugar?'

'Just one...thank you.'

Several minutes later Jennifer emerged through the purple beaded curtain carrying two mugs of tea in one hand and two plates of poached eggs on toast in the other.

'Let me help.' Mary half-stood.

'No, please don't.' A slightly abrupt edge to her voice. 'I used to be a waitress. I can carry three plates at once if I have to.'

'Like a juggler.'

'What do you mean?' she asked, placing the mugs and plates on the table.

'*Three* plates at once.'

'Waitresses don't *toss* plates. You're thinking of circuses and clowns.' She sat on the sofa and ferreted between the seat cushions, presently unearthing a packet of cigarettes. 'I think clowns have psychological problems. Who hides behind layers of preposterous make-up? Mind if I smoke?'

'Models. It's not very good for you.'

'What? Make-up? I notice you don't wear any.'

'Smoking.' Mary picked up the mug of tea and held it without drinking.

'Why would you give a damn about me?'

'You're my sister.'

'Half-sister...technically.' Jennifer lit up and dragged on her cigarette. 'Models have psychological problems too. Obsessed with their looks.' The words were released in a cloud of smoke. 'Starving to death in the name of beauty. Crazy.'

'You could be a model.'

'Did you hear what I just said?'

'You're so beautiful you wouldn't even need make-up.'

For a moment Jennifer looked almost vulnerable, then her eyes shuttered. 'So, let's discuss burying Dad. That's why you came here.'

'I came here to meet you.'

Jennifer narrowed her eyes. 'I thought you didn't know about me.'

'I didn't say that. I have a picture of you and Jonathan on top of my piano.' A pause. 'It was Dad's.'

A brief look away and then, 'I haven't had a chance to tidy up. Sorry.' She flicked her hand around the unit. There was a filament of dirt under her nails and her fingers were cracked and chafed.

'That's all right. I didn't tidy up either.' Even though she knew everything was in its exact place.

Jennifer stared at her. 'We're not at *your* place, Mary.'

'No, I just meant it's all right that you didn't tidy up. I don't mind.' She nodded at the rows of cups along the wall. 'What are the cups of dirt for?'

'My seedlings. I sell plants to the local nursery for a bit of extra money and sometimes I provide stock for my clients.'

'What sort of clients do you have?'

'Anyone who'll pay.' Jennifer half-smiled.

A pause. 'You give them seedlings as well?'

'That was a joke, Mary. I'm not a prostitute. I'm a gardener. Something wrong with the eggs?'

'No.' Mary put her mug down, cut a bite-size chunk of toast and egg and forced herself to eat more food.

'Plants are my passion.' She wielded her fork with one hand while the other held her cigarette. 'They're honest.'

'How do you know? Do you talk to them?'

'I observe them. Eat, don't talk.' Jennifer finished her meal, laid the fork at a jagged angle on her plate and leaned back on the sofa. 'In a forest, trees will kill other trees to get to the sun. Plants survive no matter what conditions they find themselves in. People, on the other hand' – she drew back on the cigarette, the tip flaring bright orange – 'refuse to try unless they get everything they want: nice house, nice clothes, nice car, nice life. Plants sink their roots into a crevice in a cliff and give thanks for a patch of sky and a drop of dew. They'll follow any twisted line to the sun. That's why there are no straight lines in nature.'

When she finished eating her second breakfast for the day Mary carefully placed her knife and fork together on the plate. Then her gaze fixed on the jagged arrangement of Jennifer's knife and fork. The urge to straighten them was irresistible.

'Is something wrong?' asked Jennifer, watching her closely.

'Do you mind if I straighten your knife and fork?' Her body pitched forward as if pulled by invisible strings.

'Be my guest.'

After straightening the cutlery Mary settled back and took a deep breath. 'Light.'

'Sorry?'

'Light travels in a straight line when it leaves the stars.'

'Well, then, apart from light, nature travels in a cruel and twisted but profoundly honest line, devouring everything in its path. There's a silent war going on around us all the time. You never hear the screams of dying plants, Mary.'

James didn't scream even when he knew his wings hadn't opened. 'Maybe they don't believe they're going to die.' She leaned forward, picked up her mug of tea, clung to it for ballast.

'We're all going to die, Mary.' She nodded at the cups filled with dirt. 'Even my babies, the chosen few I play God to. Each one of my orphans gets its own little cup, lovely friable dirt, plenty of clean water, as much sun as they can cope with. But my babies will die and there's not a goddamned thing I can do about it.' She said nothing for a few moments and then swung forward and collected both plates. 'You like things to be ordered, don't you? What kind of work do you do? Cleaning?' she asked as she disappeared into the kitchen.

'I'm a paralegal at Goodman and Oldfield.'

The beaded curtains flew open and Jennifer launched back into the room. 'Holy shit, wasn't that where the crazy guy jumped out the tenth floor window?'

112

'James wasn't crazy. He just thought he could fly.'

'And that's not crazy?' She sat down again, lit up another cigarette. 'Did you actually *see* him jump?'

'Yes.' The music thumped in her chest and the surface of her tea shivered with ripples.

'You're in shock.' She used her cigarette as a pointer, individually jabbing each word. 'I've read lots of books about how the mind works. Shock kills every healthy instinct for survival. I've seen plants die of shock. People, too. They might feel pain on the outside, but inside they're numb, dying slowly. Horror shuts you down, suppresses the bad memories until you can deal with them. But they're still there just waiting to surface. Most people never deal with them. They medicate them.'

'What with?'

'Drugs,' she glanced at the spray can briefly, 'alcohol, sex, food, *order*. You have to deal with your issues, or they'll destroy you. People are so good at denial, Mary. But denial is a long river full of crocodiles.'

'The Nile. That's clever. Was it another joke?'

'It's no laughing matter. The crocodiles are just waiting to surface.'

'What makes them come up?' Her eyes fixed on her sister's face, her palms began to itch. *Don't scratch.*

'Hunger. Air. Everything wants to live.'

They said nothing more for a long moment.

'Well,' said Jennifer suddenly, 'what shall we do about burying our father?'

Mary took a piece of paper out of her bag. 'I googled churches in Saint Leonards after you called me and –'

'How efficient you are.'

Jennifer was half-smiling and Mary wasn't sure if she was making a joke or being sarcastic. James once told her that sarcasm and humour can look very alike. 'I emailed this one and they can do the service next Thursday. Here's the address.'

113

She put the paper down on the coffee table. 'I thought ten o'clock. What do you think?'

'How much is it gonna cost us?'

'I don't mind paying.'

Jennifer tossed her head proudly. 'I'll pay our share when I sell some more seedlings.'

'You don't have to.'

'We're not a charity case, Mary.'

'I didn't mean to imply that. I'm sorry.'

'Forget it.' She swung her hand around the flat. 'We'll move out of this dump when my gardening business builds up.'

Another awkward pause.

'Is your mother as beautiful as you, Jennifer?'

'My mother's dead.' She jumped up, went to Jonathan's door, banged on it again. 'Second warning.' Then she marched into another room and came back out with a framed picture, which she handed to Mary. 'That's Mum. Her name was Caitlin Granger. She never dealt with her issues.'

Caitlin Granger was almost as stunning as Jennifer. 'She was beautiful.'

'Yeh, she was.' Jennifer picked up her cigarette and clung to it. 'What about *your* mother?'

'Oh, she's stunning, too. I'm the only ordinary one.'

Jennifer did not argue. 'I meant is your mother still alive?'

'Yes.'

'Mum died when I was fifteen. Overdose. She got on the junk after Dad left her – never got over the prick.'

'Who looked after you and Jonathan after your mother died?'

'I did. We lived on the streets for a while.' She took another long drag on the cigarette. 'Even this dump is better than that nightmare. So tell me, how did our loving father treat *you*?'

'He ignored me.' Her voice small, breathy. 'Mostly.'

'I see.' Jennifer crossed one long leg over the other. 'Our father who art in hell shut down your sexuality, too.'

114

Mary's face burned. 'No, I didn't say that.'

'How old are you, Mary?'

'Twenty-two.'

'Ever had a boyfriend?'

'No.'

'Me neither and I'm twenty-nine. Jonathan's had a few.'

'Boyfriends?'

'They never stuck around.' She swung up off the sofa, stamped across to Jonathan's door and banged on it. 'Jonathan, get out here now or I'm coming in!' A muffled groan. 'Honestly, anyone would think he was five. He's twenty-seven.' She stomped back across the room. 'So where were we? Ah, yes, we were discussing our father's sexual abuse. You've got to clear the past or it destroys the future. I painted our front door red last week and look what's happened this week – the bastard died.'

'And I came into your life.'

She fixed Mary with an intense, level gaze. 'Don't stay in denial about what that pig did to you or you'll never be free of him.'

A single violin, fragile and flickering as a candle in an open window. 'I'm not in denial.'

'Then say it and shoot the crocs.' Jennifer's eyes – blue pools of drowned wishes, tossed coins – glinted with tears. 'You've got just as many crocodiles lurking as I have.' She sagged back, slackened her visual hold. 'You should stop lying. It doesn't help.'

'I'm not lying!' Mary cried, her tea spilling on the carpet. 'I'm so sorry! That was my fault!'

'Just a tiny spill,' said Jennifer, leaning across, taking the mug from her trembling hands and placing it on the table. 'The place is a mess anyway.'

'I should have been more careful!' Scratching, scratching.

'Mary, it was an accident.'

'It was no accident. He warned me something would happen.'

'Are we still talking about our father?' Jennifer asked slowly.

Mary's eyes fixed on a point just above her sister's head. 'I begged him to get down, I pleaded with him but he'd stopped taking his medication and he didn't believe me.' Her voice rose in pitch. 'I had two of his tablets in my bag, I should have crushed them up in his coffee. Tricked him into taking them. I told him people can't fly. I said he lied to you, James. But he didn't believe me!' Her body jerked with sobs. 'I let him die!'

'He *jumped*, Mary.' Jennifer spoke slowly and clearly. 'You couldn't have saved him.'

'I could have!' The tic in her jaw flickered. 'I *should* have.'

'No! You're not responsible for the whole world.'

'Oh but I am.' Her voice was suddenly low, her eyes narrowed like a hunted animal's. 'I compose music that will save the world.'

'Music?' Jennifer slumped back. 'What do you mean?'

'It saved me when he came into my room. He said it could save you, too.'

'Who? Are we still talking about James?'

'I should have played for James when he asked me to. The music might have saved him. Let me play for you. Please.' Her hands were raised and tripping over the keys of an imaginary piano.

'When did the music start?' asked Jennifer, leaning forward and taking Mary's hands gently.

'He said you needed the music even more than I do.'

'Mary, focus. When did the music start? Think hard.'

An oboe coiled around the violins. 'It's always been playing in my head.'

'What was the exact moment?'

The oboe tightened its hold, squeezing the breath out of her. 'I can't remember.'

'*When*?' Jennifer's eyes pinning her.

'It started one night when my father came into my room.'
Staring blindly into the middle distance.

'Yes. Yes, go on. What did he do to you, Mary? Say it. I
won't judge you.'

'He was drunk.'

'He was always drunk.'

MELODRAMA

An overblown style of opera, an aberration of the classical form

He was drunk the first time he lifted her nightgown. Drunk the night he disordered her world. The day had begun with the usual routine, breakfast at seven, school at nine, her mother collecting her at three, walking home, counting the horizontal lines in the pavement, 457 from the school gate to home, afternoon tea and then sitting at the piano searching for the right notes, dinner at six o'clock, bath at six thirty and then Daddy came home, ignored her as usual, made Mummy cry as usual and then she put the elf dish on the windowsill and went to bed. As usual.

The next thing should have been morning but he came into her room and told her they would have a special secret she must never tell Mummy. If she told Mummy he would sell her piano. Then he lifted her nightgown and kissed her belly. That was all he did that night. The next time he came into her room he pushed his fingers into her, into the part that should never be touched until you were married, Mummy had said. When she cried out he kissed her and said he hadn't meant to hurt her. After that he stopped coming in for a while and she thought her world was restored to its previous order but then one night he came again and inflicted a pain so private she wished for death.

'Love hurts, he said.'

'I remember,' whispered Jennifer. 'Go on.'

Over the next two years the visits were random, disordered and impossible to measure. Her nights were tortured with uncertainty and his weight on her body was a suffocating shame that lasted fifteen minutes. This she *could* measure. Then something extraordinary happened. He was on her, in her, his face close, tiny moons caught in the corners of his eyes and suddenly she wasn't there any more. A great wave of music had lifted her out of her body and deposited her soul in another world. From then on the music came for her every time and took her to glorious places: tropical islands, desert oases, moonlit groves, once to the glacial side of the moon, another time to a coral garden under the sea where mermaids braided pearls into their green hair.

'But mostly, it took me to the stars,' she whispered. 'They're blue.'

Tears coursed down Jennifer's face. 'Come back to earth, Mary. It's time.'

'Even after the angel –' she stopped, adjusted her words. 'Even after he stopped coming into my room ...'

'He *stopped*?' asked Jennifer incredulously.

'Yes. When I was eleven. But after that he teased me whenever Mum was out of hearing, said I was crazy and plain, said my music annoyed him.'

'Pig. Did your friend James know any of this?'

'James only knew about the music.' Her gaze fixing on the beautiful woman clinging to her cigarette. 'Let me play for you and Jonathan, help drown those crocodiles.'

'Maybe you can help Jonathan but it's too late for me.' She squeezed her eyes shut, pinched the bridge of her nose. 'I have scars that will never heal.'

Mary's phone rang, a jarring insistent shrill.

'Go on. Answer it,' said Jennifer.

She checked the caller ID. 'It's my boss. I can call him back later.'

'Take it. The poor man must be in a mess.'

She answered. 'Robert?'

'I just need to talk to someone.'

'I'm with my sister. Jennifer.'

An intake of breath. 'I didn't know you had a sister. How long will you be there?'

'I'm not sure.'

'Can you please come over afterwards?' He rushed on. 'Do you remember...you promised to play for me when I got back?'

'Yes. Maybe next week.'

Jennifer mouthed the words. 'I'll make some fresh tea.'

'No. Tonight, please,' said Robert. 'I'm going crazy in this house all alone. I'm asking you to play for me. That's all.'

'All right.' *She had refused to play for James when he asked. It might have saved him. She would never refuse the music again.*

'Thank you, Mary. Do you have a pen? I'll give you my address.'

'Um,' she reached for her bag.

'What do you need?' asked Jennifer, delivering fresh tea.

'A pen and paper.'

Jennifer disappeared into the second bedroom.

'Are you and Jennifer close?' asked Robert.

A pause. 'Very.'

'Is she musical too?'

'No, she's a gardener.'

'I need a gardener.'

'Pen and paper,' said Jennifer marching back into the room.

Mary wrote the address down, folded the paper and placed it in her bag.

'Come around six. I'll cook you dinner before you play. The piano's a baby grand. It was Jillian's.' A pause. 'Could I speak to Jennifer for a moment? About the garden.'

'Hang on, Robert.' She covered the phone. 'Robert wants to speak to you about gardening at his house.'

'Sure.' She held out her hand for the phone.

'I told him we were close.'

Jennifer nodded and took the phone. 'Hi, Robert, I'm Jennifer, Mary's sister. I'm so sorry about your loss. Have you had counseling?' She listened, frowning. 'No, you *should*. Don't bury your feelings under a layer of denial or you'll have no future.' She reached for her cigarette. 'So, how big is your garden?' She raised her eyebrows. 'Wow. An acre. Wow…Sorry, what was that? Are my sister and I close?'

Mary's eyes flew open.

'We're virtually inseparable. I'm surprised she hasn't mentioned me.' She leaned across, patted Mary's knee. 'Robert I'd love to keep chatting but Mary, Jonathan and I are organising our father's funeral.' She listened again, looked down. 'Thank you, but our father was *ill* for a very long time.' She flashed a look at Mary. 'Jonathan is our brother. Now don't tell me she's never mentioned him either. I will have words with her. By the way, I charge thirty dollars an hour and' – she grinned – 'I bring my own shovel.' A pause. 'Yes, of course we'll be there for Mary. See you next Friday. You take a walk around your garden and try to stay calm. Goodbye now, Robert.' She handed the phone back.

'Friday?' asked Mary.

'Robert just invited me to James' funeral.' A warm smile, the first she had given her. 'I'll be there if that's what *you* want.'

'I'd love you to be there.' Tears stung. 'Would you and Jonathan come to my apartment for dinner this week so I can play for you? It's very important you hear my music.'

'Dinner and music?' The door with Michael Hutchence on it swung open and a skinny man in a black leather jacket and black denim jeans stood swaying. 'Well, isn't that civilised, Jenny? We'd love to. Hello Mary, I'm your brother, Jonathan.'

121

OPERA SEMISERIA

A semi-serious opera

He turned to the poster, crossed himself before ambling over to the sofa and slumping down next to Jennifer. 'How Biblical of our father to name you Mary. Are you a saint or a sinner? I'm a sinner.'

Jennifer tapped her brother on the arm. 'Not now, Jonathan.'

'If not now then *when*? Over dinner perhaps? That wouldn't be polite. Guests have an obligation to be amusing.'

Jennifer nodded at the can of black spray paint. 'Feeling a bit poetic, were you?'

'It's not my best work.' He curled his lip, shrugged. 'Hardly worthy of a man who idolises Oscar Wilde, but it summed up my mood.'

'It will sum up the landlord's mood if I don't get rid of it before Saturday.' She shook her head. 'Do you want something to eat?'

'Sure.'

Jennifer slipped into the kitchen, the purple beads shivering in her wake.

Jonathan stared at Mary and Mary stared back at her brother, trying to fathom how he could be so different from Jennifer. He was pale with lank dyed black hair and a high white forehead. His long nose gave him a wolfish look, and there were traces of pink lipstick on his cracked lips, the same as on the used coffee cup on the table. The only feature all three had in common was their father's eyes.

'I'm a poetic genius,' he said suddenly. 'Ahead of my time like Oscar Wilde. I expect I shall die unheralded like most geniuses. My other great talent is marketing and promotion. Do you have a talent, Mary? Oh, of course, you play the piano.' He glanced at the poster of Michael Hutchence. 'He was a genius – Michael. So tragic. If I ever find someone with *his* singular musical ability I will be his marketing guru, put my own ambition on the back burner and serve his talent. When you serve the great they become your destiny. I read that somewhere.' He gave Mary a harsh, impenetrable look. 'Did our father leave us any money?'

'Dad would have pissed away any money he had,' said Jennifer returning with a plate of scrambled eggs and a mug of tea. 'More tea, Mary?'

'No thank you.'

No one spoke for several minutes then Jonathan pointed his fork at Mary. 'How did our father treat *you*?'

'He abused her,' said Jennifer softly.

'I see, so Jenny has tried her psycho-babble on you? Crocodiles in De Nile?'

'Talking it out makes it go away,' said Jennifer.

'It doesn't!' cried Jonathan with a sudden, savage change of mood. 'The pain never goes away. Nothing blots it out except –'

'Music.' Mary spoke so quietly both Jonathan and Jennifer leaned forward in unison.

'Excuse me?' said Jonathan.

'Music blots out the pain.' She gave Jonathan a long look. 'But you know this already.'

The expression of surprise on his face was almost comical. 'Who are you? Maria fucking Von Trapp?'

'No, I'm your sister.'

'That was a joke,' he said. 'Don't you recognise humour?'

'No.'

'We've decided to use this church for the service,' said Jennifer, abruptly changing the subject and indicating the paper with the address on it.

'You planned Daddy's funeral without me?' cried Jonathan, dropping his fork.

'Don't make a scene, please. You were asleep. I told you Mary was coming at ten.'

'Daddy's funeral,' he repeated, a skein of saliva oozing from the corner of his mouth.

Jennifer got up quickly, went to the door and unbolted it. 'Maybe you should go, Mary. Before Jonathan says something we'll all regret.'

'I'll see you when you come for dinner, Jonathan, and then you can decide if I have any musical ability,' Mary said, collecting her bag. 'Saturday night?'

'Whatever Jennifer decides. I loved him, you know,' he said, eyes brightening with tears in another lightning fast change of mood. 'In spite of everything I loved him.'

'Come on, Mary.' Jennifer led her out into the hallway, pulled the red door shut and leaned against it. 'Doesn't matter what I do, I can't shoot his crocodiles.'

'What kind of drugs is he on?'

'Is it so obvious?'

'His mood swings are dramatic.'

'I'm so used to them I hardly notice any more.' Jennifer's chin dimpled. 'Heroin. Same as Mum. He says he'll commit suicide if he doesn't have it. The emotional pain is so bad.' A little catch in her voice. 'It costs me nearly all my wages.'

'*You* pay for it?'

Tears slid over the perfect planes of her face. 'What else can I do? He can't hold down a job and I can't let him die. Our father fucked all three of us, Mary. I escaped into nature. You

124

escaped into music. Johnny escaped into drugs. My brother is a tortured soul.'

'*Our* brother.' The music curled around her like smoke. 'We're a family now.' *The three musketeers.*

A fleeting look of hope passed across Jennifer's face. 'Come on, I'll walk you to the corner and wait with you until you see a cab.'

They waited in silence until Mary hailed a cab.

'I'll organise Dad's funeral and I'll pay for everything,' said Mary, looking up at the woman who was, in her opinion, the most beautiful creature nature had even given life to. 'You can pay me back when those seedlings grow.'

'Thank you, Mary.' Jennifer blinked and looked down at the pavement. 'Don't judge Johnny too harshly. Today was a bad day but next time you see him he'll be different.' And with that she turned and walked briskly in the direction of home and their troubled brother.

LIGATURE

Curved line connecting notes to be sung or played as a phrase

At five o'clock she waited on the pavement for her second cab of the day. For the second time she gave an unknown address, this time Robert's, 10 Hope Street Vaucluse, and again she sat in the back seat watching her music irradiate the sky. The taxi took her across the Harbour Bridge and onto the Eastern Distributor, this time exiting at New South Road and heading towards the most expensive part of Sydney where many of the internationally rich and famous had their Australian residences.

What could she play for Robert? She couldn't even recall if he'd mentioned a piano but obviously he had one. What sort? And who had played it before? Pianos absorb the characters of their owners and don't always welcome strangers. She hoped the piano was friendly.

She turned her attention to the slipstreaming view: multi-storey, architecturally designed houses whose compact gardens of washed tiles and potted plants abutted the street front. Such a contrast to the sprawling lawns and faded opulence of Cremorne. After driving for about twenty minutes the driver turned left off New South Head Road and headed seawards down a narrow winding street, then two streets back from the harbour, he turned right into a wide cul-de-sac of gated mansions with turrets, chimney stacks, and peaked roofs peeping over high sandstone walls and stopped outside number ten.

After paying the fare Mary stood quietly on the pavement, listening for the music that would ease Robert's pain. *Something flowing and gentle*, a melody that sang of water over rocks. Only when the bubbling chords broke did she open the wrought-iron gates -S-H-A-L on one and A-M-A-R on the other. The sandstone path was canopied with spreading trees that looked more English than Australian. Jennifer would know what type they were.

Inside the gates the city vanished. As she drew closer Shalamar was an imposing pink and ochre mansion with twin columns descending from the upper floor balconies and a sweep of granite steps leading up to a heavy wooden front door with a brass knocker in the shape of a lion's head. Before Mary could knock, the door opened and Robert stood there, unshaven, the top buttons of his shirt undone.

'How did you know I was here?' she asked.

'There's a sensor on the gate. Come in,' he said, stepping aside in the marble-tiled hall. 'I haven't started on dinner. After calling you this morning, I fell asleep again. The sensor woke me.'

'You should have phoned. I can come back another time.' She half turned.

'No! It's fine. Please.'

'I'll just play for you if you don't mind. I've had two breakfasts today and I'm not hungry.'

'I'm not hungry either.'

'Do you have a piano?' Mary asked gently.

'Would I ask you to play if I didn't have a piano?'

'I'm sorry.'

'It was Jillian's. Come on...this way.'

Mary followed him into a beautifully proportioned room where a baby grand stood in an alcove that opened onto a conservatory. The room glowed with golden light.

'This is lovely,' said Mary.

'Yes, Jillian didn't get her hands on this one. It was my mother's favourite room.'

'Did your father like it, too?'

'No. Mum and Dad had opposite tastes. They led separate lives. Fortunately my father wasn't home much. He preferred the office or his club and the company of his current mistress. But he did die here.'

'I'm so sorry.'

'Don't be. He had the decency to die in his own bed.'

Mary felt a chill, sensing ghosts.

'I planned to fill this house with love and children.' He laughed – a bitter, hollow bark. 'Sorry to talk about myself. Did you manage to organise your father's funeral?'

'Yes, thank you.'

'Why didn't you tell me he died? You *can* talk to me, you know.' He squeezed his eyes shut. 'James could have talked to me, too.'

'I didn't want to burden you. Let me play something.' Mary moved to the piano where a breath of Channel and an echo of a Brahms melody rose from the board when she opened the lid. 'Who liked Brahms?'

His eyes snapped open. 'You're doing it again. Uncanny. Brahms was Jillian's favourite composer. Tell me something else, Mary. Why did James commit suicide?'

Because an angel lured him to his death. 'He was very confused. Did Jillian wear Channel No. 5?'

'And again! It was her favourite perfume.'

She began with a melody that washed briefly into the cracks between the keys but something held her back. Jillian didn't want her playing. Or the piano was protecting its previous owner. 'I'm sorry, Robert. I have no music today. Perhaps we need to talk instead. My sister swears it helps.' Mary sat opposite Robert.

A smile. 'Your sister thinks I should get counseling. Talk it out. But I'm sick of talking.'

The room seemed to balloon and hollow, dwarfing the two

people who watched each other uncomfortably, uncertain how to proceed.

'I thought I might work from home,' Robert announced suddenly. 'It would save money. I can bring my clients with me.' He hesitated. 'Would you mind working here?'

'It's a beautiful house but –'

He rushed on. 'I could turn one bedroom into an office for me and another for you.'

'Robert, my plan was to leave once you got back from England.'

'Oh.' He drooped, his head on his chest.

'It's time I focused on my music.' *Before anyone else gets killed.*

Somewhere in the huge empty house, a clock chimed the hour. Six even bells.

'Why don't you make a studio and paint?'

'How did you know I wanted to be an artist?' he snapped. 'You can't have guessed that, too.'

'James told me.'

'I didn't think he'd remembered,' he said softly.

'He was sad for you.'

'Was he? My father said I had no talent.'

'Prove him wrong.'

'It's a little late in the day, isn't it? And I have no passion left, Mary. I can't find a reason to get up in the morning.'

She went to him, sat beside him and held his hands. 'You have beautiful hands. It was one of the first things I noticed about you. Artist's hands.'

He crumpled into his pain. 'I wanted such a different life. Art, the noise of children in this big old house...but I'm going to die alone and leave nothing behind.' He pulled his hands away and covered his face. 'I'm sorry to burden you. Perhaps you should go now rather than seeing me like this.'

'Robert, forgive me.' Her voice broke.

'Whatever for?'

'It's *my* fault James is dead. *My* fault Jillian died. I've brought ruin to your firm. If there was any way I could make it right –' the rest of her sentence was lost in sobs.

'No, Mary. Don't blame yourself. James lost his nerve and I never had it. You've been heroic.'

'I've been stupid,' she said furiously. 'I thought I was in control.' She scratched her palms savagely, drawing blood. 'But *he* was.'

'Who?'

But she didn't reply. And what happened next should not have happened. He leant towards her and touched her lips with his. 'This sounds feeble and pathetic...but you seem to be my only friend,' he said, holding her. 'I had no-one else to turn to today.'

'Tell me how I can help you, Robert...'

'You can let me kiss you again.'

'If it will help.'

And so she allowed his kisses, like rain and hunger on her lips and face. She allowed him to lay her on the couch. Allowed him to love her.

Afterwards she dressed and called a taxi. She kissed Robert on his brow as he lay sleeping.

Before leaving, she whispered, 'Forgive me.'

MOTIF

Primary theme or subject that is developed

It was dark when she reached home. From the street, she could see a light inside her apartment as if someone was restlessly carrying a lantern from room to room.

'Where have you been?' he asked, when she unlocked the front door.

'With Jennifer and Jonathan.' She looked away quickly. 'And then with Robert.'

'Robert?' His voice held suspicion. 'Why?'

'I needed to tell him I was leaving work.'

'Oh.' With an approving grin, he drew a bouquet of red roses from behind his back and held them out for her. 'I brought you these.'

'Why?'

'No reason.'

She took them warily. 'Thank you. They're lovely. I'll find a vase.'

'I wouldn't really have killed your brother and sister,' he said, following her to the kitchen.

'You killed my best friend.'

'He meddled. In any case I only nudged him, left a little imprint on his window, a suggestion of flight. He chose to jump.'

She gave him a look that would freeze lava. 'He thought he could fly.'

'It is a well-documented fact that even under hypnosis people won't do things they don't believe in. He wanted to die, Mary.'

She filled the vase with water, said nothing as she arranged the roses.

'Your friend was bored,' he persisted. 'He'd lost his highs and lows. He was desperate to fly.'

'Four people have died to foster your ambition.'

'And yours.'

'Mine?'

'You want the world to hear your music. Don't deny it.'

'I'm not in denial about anything!' She swished past him. 'I don't know why everyone thinks I am.'

'Who else thinks you are? Robert?'

'Jennifer thinks I'm in denial about my father.'

'Did you tell her I saved you from him?'

'Hardly.' She placed the roses next to the picture of Jennifer and Jonathan. 'Yes it's true that I want the world to hear my music but I wouldn't kill for it, Gabriel.'

'You might be surprised what you would do to serve your ambition.'

'I don't like surprises. And I'd never commit a crime.' She moved the roses a fraction to the left.

He watched her. 'Did you like your sister?'

'She's beautiful, brave, kind, lovely and –'

'Broken.'

Tears blurred the room and the angel. 'Yes.'

'The three musketeers won't happen after all?' His voice was gentle.

'When did I tell you that?'

'When you were a child you told me all your hopes and dreams. You trusted me then. Do you remember when it was just you and me against the world?'

'Yes.'

'Why can't it be like that again?'

She swung past him on her way to the kitchen. 'Because you've killed since then.'

He followed her. 'Such a pity Jennifer and Jonathan had no angel to protect them like you did.'

She bowed her head, paused in front of the sink. 'I haven't forgotten what you did for me when I was a child. I'll always be grateful.' She filled the kettle with water. 'Would you like some tea? Do you eat and drink?'

'I don't need to but sometimes I do it for pleasure. Tea would be delightful, thank you. Mary, your music will heal your brother and sister and when I add my light it will heal the world.' He raised his wings slightly, feathers glittering. 'People will look up to heaven instead of down at the same tired paths they have trudged for a lifetime and they will dream again. Such grand dreams.'

'Milk and sugar?'

'Just a little milk, no sugar.'

She handed him a mug. 'You wake up from dreams, Gabriel.'

'I know but dreams are the Petri dishes of creation. By the way, your mother's rung several times today.' He nodded at the phone. 'I heard her messages on the answering machine while I've been waiting for you.'

'I left a message for her to call me. I have to break the news about Dad's death.'

'It's a blessing.'

'You *are* in denial, Gabriel. You're a murderer.' She went to the hall table, picked up the phone and dialed her mother's number.

'One day you will understand the end justifies the means. I will create heaven on earth, Mary.'

Kathleen's voice was slurred. 'Hello?'

'Mum, it's me. Please sit down. I have something to tell you.'

Suddenly alert. 'Mary, love, what's wrong?'

'Dad died last night. I'm sorry.'

Kathleen said nothing for a long minute. 'Who told you?'

'Jennifer Granger ... my sister.'

An intake of breath. 'Was he alone? Or was that barmaid with him?'

She looked across at Gabriel. 'He died alone.'

'He never came back, Mary ... never even sent me a birthday card.' Kathleen's voice was wild.

'Do you want me to come over? I can call a taxi.'

'No, I need to be alone tonight. To think. To remember. How did he –?'

'A heart attack. The funeral's on Thursday. I arranged it with Jennifer today.'

A beat. 'Do you still have that old Bible I gave you?'

'Yes.'

'Read a verse for your father and me before you go to bed.' A shivered breath. 'I love you, Mary. You're the best of me.'

'I love you too, Mum. Goodnight.'

Gabriel watched her, sienna eyes glittering. 'I did a good thing getting rid of your father. It brought your siblings into your life and it will set your mother free.' He sat with his wings spread along the back of the seat.

'Poor Mum never knew the truth about Dad. She loved a man who deceived her with her own daughter. Is there a worse betrayal?' She clenched her fists. 'She deserved loyalty and love. She gave it.'

'Her life isn't over yet.'

'Isn't it?' She looked at him through tears.

'She'll love again. Passion is in her nature. She'll be more discerning next time.'

'How do you know? You don't *know* my mother.'

'I pick up vibes.' He smiled at her. 'You get your passionate nature from her.'

'My passion is dead, Gabriel.'

'Is it?' He raised his hands, circled an imaginary spotlight.

'Imagine it, Mary, you on stage, the auditorium hushed, the audience a faceless sea of watchers in the dark. And when you make your first entrance, emerging from the wings into the spotlight, the sudden flare blinds you to the crowd as you move towards the piano, your fingers already tracing the melody. And all you hear apart from your music is the whisper of silk against your thighs as you walk. Red silk.' He pointed to the roses on the piano, each bloom with its own fiery nimbus. 'That colour. And when your fingers touch the keys, nothing else exists in the world. You, Mary Granger, are the mistress of another universe, a splendid, magical, safe world of your own creation. All who enter obey its laws.'

'No one dies in my world, Gabriel. Not any more.'

'I will clear your path to fame – a straight, true path that humanity can follow. Their enlightenment will be the most natural thing in the world.'

'Natural? Jennifer said there are no straight lines in nature.'

'She is forgetting light. Let me guide you, Mary. Put your faith in me.'

'James put his faith in you and you killed him. You killed Jillian.' Panic rose in strangled little sobs. 'Then my grandmother.'

'I told you I didn't touch her.'

She ignored him. 'I can't bear to hurt people. I can't bear it, but they die because of me. Because I know you.' She pointed an accusing finger at him. 'Because I put my faith in you!'

Gabriel folded the weeping figure into a pine and rose-scented embrace. 'Hush now, try not to think of those sad things. Think of your music and leave everything else to me.'

Her fingers drummed a hesitant tune on his chest. 'Dom, dah, dah, dom, dah, dah, dah...'

'Yes, exactly. I will clear a straight path for you.'

'But Jennifer said –'

'Allowing for a few natural curves and variations. A little death here gives life to a more beautiful aria there. Birth and death are partnered to perpetuate life. What could be more natural? Go and play the tune you're strumming on my chest.'

As she played Gabriel stood behind her, his fingertips resting on her shoulders absorbing the music like breath. When she finished playing she bowed her head and her tears fell into her palms. 'I miss James.'

'Ah, Mary' – he touched her cheek, tracing a tear's track – 'haven't you wept enough for one lifetime? Isn't it time for some joy? When you're famous you must take a lover in Florence. The Florentine moon throws quite a different light and looks larger than in any other part of the world.'

'It's the same moon, Gabriel.'

He ignored her. 'Once in the 1600s, I was standing on a balcony admiring the Duomo after making love to a woman who always left her window open for me and the moon was so close I could have caught it in a net.'

'I'd like to catch the moon in a net, take a lover in Florence, but I can't. Today I learned something –'

'What?'

She shivered. 'Jennifer said that our father shut down my sexuality, and hers, and I think she's right. When Robert made love to me this evening I felt nothing.'

'*What*? You let that pathetic human touch you?'

'I comforted him.'

'No! No! No, Mary! Accept only the best. You need a skilled lover who will delight in you and delight you. You are precious. Stop giving yourself away to those who don't deserve you.'

She caught his hand. 'How do you make your light feel like flesh?'

'I'm a master of creation. I can be as anything – flesh, light, water, air, rock, ideas … music. An artist in all things, Mary. Even love.'

'Robert wanted to be an artist.'

Gabriel shrugged, moved away. 'What's stopping him?'

136

'His father told him he had no skill. It broke his spirit.'

'Fathers. Robert Goodman must fight back. And so must you. You can have anything you want, Mary Granger, once the world hears our music.'

'But I can't. I told you...I felt nothing tonight. What if a part of me is dead forever. I don't want a life without love, Gabriel.'

'You will have a lover beyond compare. I promise you.'

She leapt up, went to her bookshelf and took down the bible. 'Mum wants me to read a verse for her and ... Dad tonight.'

'Song of Solomon.'

'Sorry?'

'Read the Song of Solomon.'

She opened the bible. 'Jennifer thinks I hide behind my music.'

'You are your music, Mary.' He moved closer. 'How do you know you would feel nothing in the act of love?'

'Because I felt nothing with Robert.'

'Robert!' he scoffed. 'Has Robert ever lived in Florence? Admired the moon? Flown onto balconies and truly given himself to another?'

'He gave himself to Jillian.'

'He drained her. A lover consummates the beloved before he takes his own pleasure.' He shrugged. 'It's a well-documented fact, and in any case, some things just come naturally. "How beautiful you are, my love, how beautiful! Your eyes are like doves". Song of Solomon. For him, love was like breathing. Read it later.' He took the bible from her and returned it to the shelf.

'Follow me.'

'Where?'

'You'll see. Just look into my eyes and trust me.'

'What are you going to do?'

'Restore what your father stole from you.' He touched her lips in a feather-light kiss and she felt a trembling response in the pit of her stomach, heard the soft chime of a distant bell.

'Let the bell lead us where it will,' he whispered, kissing her again, his eyes open and holding hers. 'You are your music, Mary, and I *am* part of your song. Tonight we will create heaven on earth.' He took her in his arms, his flesh warm and solid, perfumed with pine and roses.

'Oh, dear,' she muttered, knowing resistance was futile.

Tenderly he removed her dress and lowered her onto the carpet. 'I will love you, Mary, as you have never been loved before. Never will be again. Just for tonight' – he breathed in her ear – 'let's pretend no one else in the universe exists. Just you and me and the music.'

The scent of roses mingled with her symphony. She pressed her palms against his chest, maintaining the slimmest distance between sin and urge. 'Gabriel, this *must* be a sin.'

'Where is it written?' He was powerfully beautiful, erotically confident, seasoned with centuries of conquests. He pulled her hands from his chest and eased her into a dance ancient as Eden. Slowly, patiently, increment by increment, he increased their pleasure until she joyfully accommodated the release of his angelic seed into her womb.

And when they lay twined, his head cradled between her breasts, he said, 'Name the child after me. Gabriel will suit either gender.'

'Child?' she sat bolt upright.

He pulled her back down, stroked her belly with his fingertips. 'I can *give* life as well as *take* it, Mary. You will bring forth my child.'

'Or Robert's.'

He laughed. 'Robert could never do what I have just done.'

'Amen to that.'

'I have quickened the womb your father's abuse made barren.'

'Barren?'

'Your father broke you, Mary. No mortal seed could blossom into life.' He kissed her belly, still damp with love. 'You will have a child conceived of music and light.'

'A child.' She imagined a baby with golden curls, dimples and enquiring eyes. A perfect child who never cried or gave her a moment's worry. A child who would fit seamlessly into the routines of her life. 'I'll take her everywhere with me: to work, on my walks, to Jennifer and Jonathan's, to Mum's. She will be my best friend.'

'Mary, the child is a boy and when the vehicle ripens I will appoint a son of heaven to live on this earth as flesh. Did you not understand me earlier? I intend to create heaven on earth. I will populate the earth with angels, Mary. Servants to my vision.'

'What do you mean?'

'Heaven is a mess. The angels are rootless and drifting. Someone must call them to order and give them purpose.'

'Surely God –'

'Father's gone,' he snapped. 'There is only me and you and the music now. All future creation depends on us.' He turned, kissed the tip of her nose. 'Your eyes are the same colour as Miriam's soul.'

'I remember you telling me that when I was child. She's the lady with the blue and gold soul.'

'Yes. I wonder if she remembers me at all. Probably not. She has swum the waters of Lethe many times since then.'

'The what?'

'Lethe – the waters of forgetfulness – the great gift of rebirth. She has had many names since I knew her as Mary, taken countless lovers and born myriad children far less spectacular than our son. I daresay she has long forgotten me.'

'Poor angel, how you loved her.'

'Don't be ridiculous. Love is for mortals. Angels soar above human need.'

'Why are you so afraid of love?'

'It's unreliable.' He stood up, and with a sleight of hand swathed himself in robes of light. 'I must fly now. I'll be back tomorrow night.'

'Gabriel –'

'Yes, Mary?'

'Will I really have a baby?'

'In nine months time you will give birth to a son of heaven.' He stopped at the balcony door. 'My brother Rigel smells of jasmine. Don't forget.'

He left in a trail of firefly light resolving into glitter.

She was lying on her bed setting the extraordinary day and evening to music when the phone rang.

'I'm sorry to call you so late but' – he sounded hollow – 'but I need to talk. Do you mind?'

'No, Robert. I don't mind.'

She listened until the rising sun cast glittering shards of broken sky across the inlet. A magpie caroled the dawn. Soon the lone singer was joined by a chorus of birds.

'And,' he continued, now sounding brighter, 'I've decided to take your advice and turn one of the bedrooms into a studio.'

'Good for you, Robert.' She yawned.

'Sorry, I'd better let you get some sleep.' He hesitated. 'James' funeral is on Friday. Can I pick you up? I don't want to arrive alone.'

'Of course.'

'Thank you. Good Night, Mary.' He laughed. 'I mean, Good Morning.'

She hung up and breathed slowly. 'Not even God could have imagined a life such as mine.' She paused a moment to watch the brilliant dawn. 'But God is gone. Only me and

Gabriel and the music are left to orchestrate the world.' She touched her belly. 'And you, my boy child whom I don't yet know.'

ELEGY

An instrumental lament with praise for the dead

On the morning of James Oldfield Jnr's funeral, sunlight streaming in through the open balcony doors woke Robert at dawn. He flung off the sheets and leapt out of bed, quietly excited about the forthcoming day. He would see Mary again.

'I feel happy,' he said, testing the statement against reality. 'I'm not in pain.'

Of course he was sad about James but his partner had lived on the edge all his adult life, seemingly courting tragedy. His sympathy was with James Snr. who had lost so much: his wife, his health and now, his only child.

'I feel happy,' he repeated as he wandered out onto the balcony where he took a deep breath of rose-scented air and surveyed his garden: the acre of sloping lawn and established trees that Jillian had quartered with orderly beds of pink rosebushes. The roses were still in full bloom as if her spirit was bewitching them into permanent fecundity: a constant reminder. *I'll ask Jennifer to underplant them with lavender to break the monopoly.*

The arbor at the bottom of the garden was a mess of purple trumpet vines. The adjoining pond was overgrown with lily pads and the fountain was dry. *I'll reconnect the power and get the water running again.* There was a tool shed down there as well, half hidden by trees. *Jennifer can use it for storage.* It was too far from the house for a studio and anyway, Mary's idea about turning one of the bedrooms into an art studio was splendid. He could get up in the middle of the night and paint if he felt inspired.

He studied his hands, turned them over. 'Artist's hands, Mary said. What do you think, Jill? Do I have the talent or was Dad right?'

He realised with a shock that he hadn't dreamt of Jillian for the first time since her death.

'I'm ready to live again, Jill,' he said softly.

He went inside, showered and changed into a black suit. As he put on a tie he spoke to his reflection in the mirror. 'What's the worst that could happen? I could make an ass of myself.' He took a deep breath. 'OK, so what? Even if I fail as an artist I'll still have Shalamar and I'll live and die on my own terms. Not my father's. I refuse to give up on life like poor James.'

He went downstairs and called Mary to remind her to wait for him on the road.

'Hello?' a sleepy voice answered.

He laughed. 'Good Morning, Sleepy Head. Did you forget I'm picking you up in an hour?'

'Oh, is that the time?' She yawned. 'Thanks for reminding me, Robert.'

He felt a stab of jealousy. 'Late night?'

A pause. 'I have a friend I play the piano for most evenings. He stayed rather late last night.'

'I didn't know you had someone special in your life. Does your *friend* know that we slept together?'

Another pause. 'Yes. Robert, I really should get ready now. I'll be waiting out the front for you in an hour.' She hung up.

He stood there with the receiver in his hand for several minutes trying to get his head around the idea that shy little Mary had a boyfriend who knew they had slept together. Why hadn't she mentioned him before they made love?

Suddenly, it was Jillian's fault. If she hadn't died and left him prey to the vagaries of heartless young women with boyfriends they *never bothered to mention* he wouldn't be feeling so old and ridiculous. So much for waking up in a good mood. He slammed the receiver back down.

'Damn you, Jillian! And damn you, too, Mary.'

As he pulled out of the drive, a melee of savage memories returned: Jillian playing carols on the piano last Christmas urging him to sing along as if nothing was amiss. Jillian painting the house in carnival colours, pretending life would go on. Jillian in one of her quiet moods, turning her back on him in bed. He never asked her what was wrong and she never told him. She was increasingly dissatisfied in the last few years of their marriage as if something was missing. But what? She had a beautiful home, plenty of money, no pressure to work, a loving husband. No need to do anything at all except desecrate Shalamar with bizarre colours.

On the bridge, he wound down the window, letting the wind dry his tears.

'What did you *want,* Jillian?' he asked.

'Purpose,' sighed the wind, cooling his face with an uneven pressure that felt like fingers. 'And children.'

They had tried so hard, turning to expensive IVF implants when natural methods failed. After the last embryo died, Jillian said she would never try again. He assured her that she was all he needed, but when he made love to her, she shrank from his touch. He let it go. She would bounce back. Their nights would sparkle again. Maybe they could adopt but that idea faded. Jillian's quiet moods grew more frequent and finally, when death beckoned, she followed.

He thumped the steering wheel. 'What about me! You left me with nothing!'

'Why does it always have to be about you, Robert?' sighed the wind.

'Because our entire marriage was about you, my darling!' He slammed the poor steering wheel again. 'Your colours, your moods, your garden! What remains of me now that you've gone?'

'Whatever was there before I met you, you selfish boy!' Her ghost sparked indignantly and left, trailing white rags of foam across the darkest part of the harbour.

'I wanted to be an artist,' he said softly but there was no reply.

By the time he reached Cremorne, he had regained control. Mary mustn't see that he'd been crying. Men don't cry.

Mary was waiting. In a simple black dress and with her hair in a chignon, she looked different. Elegant. Confident.

'You look lovely,' he said, opening the door for her.

'Do I?'

'You sound surprised.'

'You've never commented on my appearance before.' She got into the car, clutched her bag on her knees.

'How was yesterday's funeral?' he asked.

'Mum and Jonathan cried. Jennifer and I didn't. We came back to my place afterwards so everyone could get to know each other.'

'But Jennifer said you were very close. Inseparable.'

'Oh we are,' she said quickly. 'But Mum doesn't know them very well.'

'Did anybody else go to the funeral? Partners? The friend you play the piano for?'

'No one in my family has partners. The person I play for isn't exactly a friend.'

'What exactly *is* he, Mary?'

A pause. 'It's complicated.'

Especially now that you've made love to me, he thought irritably. 'What does your friend do for a living?'

Sweat broke out on her palms. 'He doesn't work.'

'Is he rich or on welfare?'

'Why are you so interested, Robert?'

'Why didn't you tell me you had a boyfriend?'

'He's not my boyfriend.' She looked out the window. 'Can we change the subject, please?'

It was Robert who broke the silence. 'We slept together, Mary. We need to talk about it.'

'Why?' She looked back at the harbour, scratching her palms and humming softly.

He stared at the road; saw his future in its gray monotony.

'Because it meant something to me,' he burst out. 'Could we at least discuss it after the service? Over lunch?'

'Yes.'

'Thank you.' He wound his window down. The wind teased, taunted, and laughed in his face. *You old fool,* it seemed to be saying. *She's in love with someone else.*

At Saint Mary's Cathedral a substantial crowd had already gathered in Queen's Square.

'Who *are* all these people?' said Robert. 'They can't be his friends. He had none and Lucinda and James Snr. are his only family.'

'I was his friend,' said Mary, scanning the faces.

'Who are you looking for?' he asked tersely.

'My sister.'

'You'll never find her. Too many people.'

'Yes, I will. Jennifer would stand out in any crowd.'

'I hope that's a good thing.' He led her towards the door. 'Come on, we'll find her after the service.'

They took their places in the front row next to Lucinda, dazzling in a chic Carla Zampatti suit, blonde hair pulled back into a shining knot at the nape of her neck. At the end of the row sat James Snr. in his wheelchair, head drooped, parchment-skinned hands clasped tightly in his withered lap. Next to him was his nurse, looking bored and holding a box of tissues.

Throughout the long Catholic service, Lucinda wept beautifully into a black lace hanky, her attractive grief illicitly caught by popping cameras and journalists scribbling notes on palm-size pads. The media ignored the old man until he crumpled into belching sobs when his son's coffin was borne away to the strains of Pachabel's *Cannon*. Only then did they give him their ghoulish attention, exploiting his pain for the morning papers and the evening news. The bored nurse offered him a tissue.

When the service was over, the old man remained, staring at the empty bier.

'I should say something. But what?' Robert said.

'I'll speak to him.' Mary stood up and gave Robert her handbag. 'Mind this.'

James' coffin had been covered in white lilies. Robert remembered that *other* coffin had been covered in pink roses. Jillian had organised the roses in advance. She'd also organised the music –*Imagine There's No Heaven*. You could have heard a pin drop when the first line rang out in church. *Imagine there's no heaven, I wonder if you dare.*

'He was the love of my life,' Lucinda Oldfield was announcing as she stood in the aisle, cameras flashing around her, microphones under her chin. 'I don't know how to go on,' she said directly into the Channel 7 lens. But she did go on. She glided towards the main entrance through the parting crowd who made her exit look like a Hollywood entrance. The media boys waggled after her like dogs on heat.

'Vampire! Jillian couldn't stand her.' Robert said under his breath. But Mary was on her way back, thank God, cutting off his fury. 'Let's get out of here,' he said. 'I'll take you to lunch and we'll ... talk.'

147

'First Mr. Oldfield Snr. wants me to play one song for James. The priest has agreed. Then I must find my sister.'

'Can you play the organ?'

'No.' Her gaze, always unnerving, carried a charge. 'The music will teach me.'

'Mary, don't make a fool of yourself.'

She gave him a look he couldn't quite read. 'I trust the music.'

Mary ran her fingers over the layers of manuals as if feeling for the organ's pulse. Then she tipped her head to one side, listening.

'F is your favourite key,' she told the instrument.

'If you usually play the piano,' said the organist, bustling up behind her, 'use the swell pedal as you would the sustain and stick to the main manual, which is slightly smaller than a piano keyboard.' He switched on the blower motor underneath the console creating a whistle of wind that rushed through the pipes. The instrument had begun to breathe. 'Don't play for too long.'

Mary let her hands float over the manual. 'I'll play something in F.'

The fifth death occurred while Mary was pressing the swell pedal and touching the keys. Wind-bellied music issued from the pipes, and, in the silences between the notes, unearthly light shivered, illuminating the saints and angels planed in the stained glass windows: heaven's apertures. Those about to exit lingered in the great arched doorways, conversations dangling, grief suspended.

Mary saw a suggestion of white robes and the pulse of glowing wings reflected in the organ's polished pipes, and sighed. 'What are you doing here, Gabriel?' she asked under her breath.

'I couldn't miss our first public appearance. And in my

Father's house. How fitting! I am here to add my light, Mary. That was our agreement. I do, after all, own the rights to this music. You just keep playing and pretend I'm not here.'

He touched Mary's music with light, raising the soulful melody to intoxication. The crowd pressed back into the Cathedral, silent and transfixed by the music.

'What a team we are,' said Gabriel, sienna eyes glittering. 'They're immobilised.'

It was true. There wasn't a sound or a movement while she played, every eye trained on her.

'Intensify the rhythm now, Mary,' cried Gabriel. 'Make them look up to the light.'

Mary's hands flew over the manual, opening vistas of possibilities, fields of dreams.

'The old man,' said Gabriel softly. 'Let me reunite him with his family.'

'I said no more deaths.'

'Look at him, Mary.'

Mary glanced down. James Snr. was caved in with pain. 'Just this once. But never again.'

'Yes. I agree,' said Gabriel before he flew to James Snr. and hovered above him. The old man looked up and gave a single shiver of joy. The nurse, blinded by the light didn't realise her charge was dead until much later.

For Robert, Mary's music brought joy and hope: he would paint like Nolan, love again and die surrounded by his children. When the last note rang out, he leapt to his feet, leading the enthusiastic applause.

Mary stood and looked around for Gabriel but he had gone. Somewhere in that sea of radiant faces she searched for Jennifer and found her inside the backlit arch of the Cathedral, her hands gripped under her chin. She wore the same black dress she had worn to their father's funeral the day before.

Robert followed Mary's stare to see who had hijacked her attention and saw a woman of exceptional beauty who shone like a beacon in the black-garbed crowd.

VOLTI SUBITO

Turn the page at once

Jennifer and Jonathan had arrived late and only caught the tail-end of Mary's music but they heard enough to convince them that their half-sister had a rare gift.

'Her music touches the heart,' said Jonathan, tapping his chest with his forefinger. 'It almost makes you think –'

'That miracles are possible?' said Jennifer.

'Yes indeed. Who would have guessed she was such a genius. She seemed a bit odd to me. Did she seem odd to you, Jen?'

'I like her.'

'Here she comes. Now don't argue with me no matter what I say. All right.'

'For God's sake, Jonathan, what are you planning?'

'Our future, princess.'

'Don't *ever* call me princess,' she said in a low voice.

'Sorry, Jen, I forgot that's what Dad called you.'

'I thought you weren't coming,' said Mary, slightly out of breath after pushing her way through the admiring crowd to reach her siblings.

Jonathan kissed her hand. 'We wouldn't have missed it for the world, sister. You were very coy about your genius.'

'Genius?' Mary touched her throat. 'No, I'm just talented.'

'More than that, I think. You sly little fox. That music makes a person dream of empires. That's what I imagined anyway. What did you think of, Jen?'

'I saw myself as a mother with children' – her voice breaking – 'of my own.'

A look passed between Jonathan and Jennifer that Mary couldn't quite read.

'Let's talk some more over lunch,' Jonathan said.

'I'm sorry. Robert wants to take me to lunch. It was a rather sudden decision.'

'Not to worry. Another time,' Jennifer said.

It was then that she noticed a tall, attractive man moving towards them, his gaze concentrated on her as if she had just been birthed in a half-shell. He carried a handbag, the only discrepancy in an otherwise flawless picture of heterosexual attraction.

'You must be Jennifer,' he said, handing Mary her bag without looking at her. 'I'd love to say *I've heard so much about you* but Mary's never mentioned you. Why don't we all have lunch together?'

'I thought you wanted to talk,' Mary said, confused.

Robert ignored her. 'I'm so sorry about your father,' he said, still gazing at Jennifer.

Jonathan's expression underwent a lightning change from charm to grief. 'It was devastating. Burying him was like losing him all over again. Daddy and I had a complex relationship. Love-hate. I loved him. He hated me.'

Robert dragged his gaze from Jennifer to her brother and saw a foppish young man in black leather pants and a black satin cloak. Apart from his spectacular blue eyes, he was nothing like his sisters, and, unlike them, he wore make-up.

'Fathers and sons can have very challenging relationships, Jonathan. My father was difficult.'

'Was he really? We must talk about it sometime. Talking it out really helps.' He winked at Jennifer.

'Yes, sometimes,' said Robert, his attention drawn back to Jennifer. 'Do join us for lunch.'

'Splendid idea,' said Jonathan. 'Our little sister's told us so much about you.' *Like the acre of garden and the mansion in Vaucluse, the rich, dead Daddy, a well-to-do Mummy in England, a dead wife, no children.* 'Family's the most important thing on earth. Trumps all material wealth, wouldn't you say, Rob?'

'I agree.' Robert's attention was elsewhere.

'Mary tells us you have artistic aspirations,' he continued.

That broke the hold. He looked at Jonathan and engaged with him. 'I've turned one of my spare rooms into a studio. Mary convinced me I should try and today when I heard her music –' He turned to Mary. 'Why didn't you tell me how gifted you were?'

'I wasn't sure.'

'So modest,' said Jonathan, putting his arm around Mary's shoulder. 'Jen and I have always said that, haven't we, Jen?'

Jennifer looked at the floor rather than argue with her brother. 'Shall we go and have lunch?'

'Yes,' said Robert. 'My shout. I'll take you to my favourite café on the Quay.'

'I'm sorry about your partner, Robert,' Jennifer said quietly, walking beside him.

'My wife died ten months ago.'

'I meant James.'

Robert looked at her vaguely. 'Of course. Poor James. Follow me.'

Robert led them into Queen's Square, cleaving a passage through the crowd.

When Mary appeared at the top of the stairs, news cameras flashed in her face and the journalists who were still prowling for a story bulleted questions.

Mary scratched her palms in rising panic. 'Please leave me alone. My friend has just died.'

'My *sister's* exhausted.' Jonathan materialised at her side and slipped a supportive arm around her waist. 'No more questions now. No more pictures.'

But the cameras kept clicking and the questions kept coming.

'Make them stop,' whispered Mary, leaning against him.

'Don't you people realise how traumatic this is for Mary … Mary Granger,' he shouted. 'My sister saw James Oldfield jump to his death.'

Mary pulled away from him. 'He didn't jump! That's a lie, Jonathan.'

A sibilant buzz. The press scrawling notes. A volley of fresh questions were hurled at her.

Jonathan leaned closer, breathed in her ear. 'Was he pushed?'

'No, he tried to fly.'

'Don't say another word, sister,' said Jonathan, pressing his face so close she could see the stubble of his beard under his pancake. 'If you want to be famous, leave the press to me.' He swung back around. 'It took so much courage for my sister to play today. James was her best friend and we buried our father yesterday.' He swaddled her in his cape and followed Robert and Jennifer down the stairs. 'That's enough for now,' he confided. 'They'll be panting for more.'

But I don't want that. A hard knot tightened in Mary's belly like a clenched fist. First Gabriel seducing the crowd with his light, then the excessive adulation, and now Jonathan playing the press like fish on a line. There was a madness in the atmosphere unlike any she had ever known.

'Why did you tell them about Dad? It's none of their business. Nothing to do with today,' she asked in a whisper.

'It's your pitiful back-story. They'll love it. Fame is a dirty game, Mary,' he said, shepherding her through the crowd. 'And the price is your privacy and your soul.'

'My soul?'

'Mary?' It was Jennifer. 'Are you all right?'

154

'She's fine.' Jonathan answered smoothly. 'She's just a little shocked that fame isn't all glitter and roses.'

Mary shuddered.

Jonathan patted her shoulder. 'Just think of the music. Let me handle the money and' – he thumbed at the crowd – 'them. It's what I do.'

'Jonathan, leave her alone,' Jennifer said. 'Take us to this café, please Robert. Let's get out of here.'

'Why do they keep looking at me like that?' Mary asked as hungry eyes followed her.

'Like they could eat you?' Jonathan laughed. 'That's what they want.' He snapped his teeth like a shark. 'Eat you alive, Mary.'

'Stop it, Jonathan,' said Jennifer.

He ignored her. 'Fame is all about supply and demand, sister. Your music is a drug and I intend to supply it.'

Mary moved away and clung instead to Jennifer's arm. She allowed her sister to shepherd her away. 'My music was supposed to make them feel happy. I don't understand.' *Gabriel said it would enlighten them, make them look up. Why hadn't it worked? How much music did they need?*

Jonathan laughed. 'We don't want them *happy*. We want them hooked and wanting more.'

'What do you mean?'

'I mean we'll bleed 'em dry before the next big thing comes along. We'll make a fortune, Mary. Isn't that exciting?' Jonathan swung his cape over his shoulder, and headed off along Macquarie St. with Robert, Mary and Jennifer following. The bulk of the crowd in Queen's Square tracked Mary's departure with dazzled eyes but others were drifting off, already bored.

PRECIPITANDO

Rushing, headlong

'The reason we were late,' Jennifer was telling Mary, 'was that as we were leaving I had a call from a solicitor. Apparently Dad had made a will leaving everything to me. I've just inherited three hundred thousand dollars.'

Mary scratched her palms. 'But where would he get that much money?'

'Horses. An extraordinarily lucky win. He banked the money last week and committed suicide before he blew it all. He wanted to make sure I'd get his winnings.'

'Suicide?'

'Penance for his sins. The coroner said it was a heart attack, but it wasn't. He managed to make it look that way.'

So Gabriel hadn't killed him after all. They walked on in silence for a block, each lost in thought.

Jonathan swung around. 'Catch up, ladies. Robert is telling the most amusing little story about hounds and foxes.'

'We're good,' Jennifer replied, waving him on. 'Mary, it means we can move out of Newtown. I'll find a nice place for Jonathan.'

Circular Quay was at its busiest – the lunch-hour rush. Ferries nosed in and out of the wharves every fifteen minutes like track ponies. The restaurants lining the concourse jostled for trade,

156

poster size menus on artists' easels out front. The Opera House berthed on the right prong of the horseshoe-shaped harbour, white sails gleaming, and directly across on the left, the convict built piers squatted in drab formation.

'This place does the best Spaghetti Marinara in Sydney,' Robert said, pushing open the door. 'As well as stocking my favourite wine, Grant Burge Stillwell Shiraz. We could all use a drink today, I'm sure. To celebrate Mary's triumph.'

'And toast James,' Mary added.

'Poor old James,' Robert replied.

'He wasn't old,' Mary whispered to Jennifer.

The waiter welcomed Robert like an old friend and after offering his condolences, showed him to a table for four. The restaurant was filling up fast, conversations melding into white noise.

'Would you like me to order for you?' Robert shouted above the noise.

'Only if you do it in Italian,' Jonathan replied.

The waiter returned quickly carrying a bottle. Grant Burge Stillwell Shiraz. 'On the house today, Robert ... in memory of James.'

He filled four glasses while he and Robert exchanged some coded shortcut that translated into an order for lunch.

Robert raised his glass. 'Here's to Mary's success and new beginnings all round.'

'And to James,' said Mary.

'To James,' said Robert.

They all drank to that.

'I know this is out of place after what we just heard...but would you consider working for me just until I find a replacement.' Robert had turned to Mary, his face serious.

Jonathan answered. 'She'll need time to practice, Rob.'

'I'd love you to stay on a bit longer.' It was Jennifer asking.

'I want the challenge of that acre of garden in the city but it would help if you were there too. For a while.'

'I already gave Robert my notice but –'

'Please.' The look was beseeching.

Robert was watching them. 'Three days a week, Mary. How's that until you play Carnegie Hall?'

Carnegie Hall. The last notes rang out from the piano, a beat, two beats, then a thousand bodies rising as one, applauding, stamping their feet as she stood up to bow, the spotlight striking her face like a search beam. She felt beautiful. A bunch of red roses tossed on stage matched her gown. Then Gabriel was there beside her, stealing her applause and challenging her to value her music. Was it worth anything without him? Was she worth anything without him?

'Mary? Did you hear me?'

She turned her head slowly. 'Yes, Robert, I'll stay until you find someone else.' *I'll stay until you stop lusting after Jennifer. Or until I'm certain she has the upper hand.*

As the restaurant filled to capacity, the background noise congealed into a solid mass of conversations. Throughout lunch Jonathan barely paused for breath on the subject of Mary's fame and fortune. 'You gotta seduce your crowd like a first-class whore,' he said, waving his glass around. 'Now there are certain techniques …' While the others ate, he talked rapidly, brightly, barely touching his food, drinking steadily. Robert ordered a second, then a third bottle of Grant Burge. An hour later, Jonathan had scarcely drawn breath.

'My sister's music inspires people. Jennifer said it made her think of –'

'That's enough, Jonathan,' Jennifer said sharply.

'Sure, Jenny. How did Mary's music make *you* feel, Rob?' Slugging back a half-glass of Shiraz.

'It made me feel as if nothing could ever hurt me again. Is that how you felt, Jennifer?'

158

Jennifer looked down. 'I *never* feel like that.'

'I'll play just for you,' said Mary gently.

'Yes, please.'

'Soon.'

They looked at each other. Smiled. They would never deal with pain alone again.

Myriad needles of light played across the harbour and a single note of music blocked out the extraneous noise. A delicate salty breeze drifted in, carrying the scent of pine and roses. Mary scanned the ferry-dotted harbour, taking in the seagulls sentinel on the rock wall, the tourists strutting the concourse, displaying themselves like brightly plumed birds. *Where are you, Gabriel? We need to talk about why the music left them hungering for more.*

'You'll fund my efforts to promote Mary, won't you, Rob?'

'No,' Mary said, defiant.

'Yes.' Robert was looking at Jennifer. 'If that's what she really wants.'

'If that's what *who* really wants?' Jonathan sneered. 'You're looking at Jennifer, but we're discussing Mary.'

Jennifer felt for Mary's hand and squeezed. 'Let's respect Mary, please. If she says *no* she means no.'

'But I make the decisions,' said Jonathan. 'If I'm her marketer…'

The rest of his sentence was lost as a crash of tympani heralded a blaze of horns and Mary imagined a lone, hunted stag rearing – the wildest part of his nature frustrated and aflame, driving him past caution. A triple drum beat echoed pounding hooves as if he tried to outrun danger.

'Have you ever been married, Jennifer?' Robert asked.

'No. Can we change the subject, please?' Her voice low.

'Doesn't mean she won't,' said Jonathan, rather too loudly.

'Don't ever speak for me, Jonathan,' Jennifer snapped.

The stag leapt up and over the heads of the people on the

concourse, body silhouetted against the steel-gray docks. Its horns were broken, which meant it could never hold its place in the herd. Such neutered creatures were cast out, their wild natures expressed in isolation or never. The stag paused where it had landed, raised its shaggy head and sniffed the air. As if finding her scent, it turned and stared straight at Mary – its eyes terrified, the whites showing fear, its wild spirit broken. Then it dissolved, leaving a vapour trail like a fallen star. And yet the terrified eyes remained. Mary realised she was looking at her sister.

'I need some air. Come with me, Mary?'

'You don't need Mary to hold your hand, Jenny.' Jonathan winked at Robert.

'Please.'

'Of course. Excuse us, please.' She stood up.

Jonathan and Robert stood too. Jonathan swaying. 'How long will you be, Jen?'

'Only a moment.'

'What is it?' Mary asked, close to her sister on the busy mid-afternoon concourse where office workers swerved past, conducting business on their cell phones, and couples wound symbiotically around each other.

Jennifer stood framed under heaven's blue canopy, the sun fracturing and falling like rain into the harbour behind her.

'I can't bear the way Robert's looking at me.' She fished in her bag for a cigarette and lit up.

'You're a very beautiful woman. It's not surprising. But I promise you he won't take advantage of you.'

'How do you know?'

'He's a gentleman. On my first day I dropped my bag spilling everything on the floor and he knelt and helped me retrieve it. He was wearing a designer suit.'

'That was kind,' Jennifer agreed. 'And he's never taken advantage of you sexually?'

'No, he hasn't.'

'You'll be there for a while. And Jonathon. He protects me from predatory men.'

Jonathan was raising his empty glass. 'How about you order another bottle of this exceptional drop while we sort out the ground rules?'

'Ground rules?'

'Yes,' slurred Jonathan. 'Now the girls are out of hearing I can explain things to you.'

'All right,' said Robert patiently. 'But how about you eat something?' He signalled the waiter. 'Pasta OK?'

'Sure.' Jonathan propped his chin on his hands. 'The first rule is I come with Jennifer. The second rule is the same as the first. I come with Jennifer.'

'OK.'

'Go ahead, ask me.'

'Ask you what?'

'If Jennifer has a boyfriend. You're burning to know.'

'Well, does she?' Robert felt his stomach tighten and braced himself for disappointment.

'No.' Jonathan grinned. 'She's all yours, old man, if you play your cards right. No one gets to Jennifer except through me.'

PESANTE

Heavy

There is a place in Sydney's northern beaches, between Palm Beach and Avalon Beach, where tumbled rocks abut the tide. Halfway up the steep sandstone face, a cave swallows the windblown spume and homecoming bats. He had found it four centuries earlier and it provided a perfect hiding place when he was looking hideous and needed to raise his clinging flesh to light.

Now the cave was home.

He leaned against the rocky mouth, contemplating the stars, greeting each one by name as they popped to light. He knew them as intimately as a mother knows her children, for they had existed in his imagination long before they were birthed into form. For three weeks now he'd been holed up in the cave waiting for Mary to forgive him. The falling out had been about so little. It had happened on the night after her first magnificent performance.

'They looked drugged when I finished playing today,' she had said when he arrived on her balcony ready to celebrate their victory. 'Not enlightened.'

'Drugged?' he repeated lamely. 'Mary there's a thin line between inspiration and hallucination…it's a well-documented fact. Those people were inspired.'

'And furthermore,' she said, ignoring him, 'I think you

162

like to kill. I think you're addicted to the power of taking lives.'

His instincts warned him not to dignify that accusation with a response. However …

'This is more of your sister's psycho-babble. I'm sorry I ever brought Jennifer into your life. Sorry I made that horse win so your father could leave her some decent money.'

'So, it *was* you!'

'Since your grandmother left *you* money, it was only fair. But I'm sorry I did it now. She's come between us and I won't …' But Mary had slammed the balcony door, locked it and drawn her curtains. He could have passed through her walls as light – his energy was raised and joyful after their triumph at the Cathedral – but why bother? She wasn't speaking to him and Mary could be stubborn. Better to give her the *space* she needed. And time to see reason. She'd eventually realise he was right.

That was three weeks ago and he hadn't heard a note of her music since. Not even in her mind. She was deliberately blocking every melodic pulse.

He punched the rock wall, startling a few straggler bats that had not yet left the cave for the night's foraging. 'Women make no sense at all. They're the greatest mystery known to any man, mortal or divine.' He, a master designer and creative genius, could not untie the Gordian knot of the feminine mind, could not unravel those twisted loops and coils called feminine intuition. He resumed his contemplation of the familiar stars. Humanity might speculate about the possibility of surprising worlds out *there* but he knew better. There was nothing surprising *out there*. All that was surprising lay unimagined within. And the greatest puzzle of all, a woman's mind, remained a mystery.

'Mary, I see what you cannot. Know what you do not. And yet you question and prod my decisions. You are so like Miriam.

Always arguing with that same infuriating blend of stubbornness and strength.'

And like Miriam, Mary had the courage to see wings where others were blind.

SPIRITO

Spirited

He had first seen Miriam at a well, the sunlight weaving silver threads in her blue-black hair, her eyes so dark they held infinity in their depths. She showed neither fear nor amazement when he appeared to her in his full glory.

'I am the Archangel Gabriel,' he told her, half expecting her to faint.

'And I am Miriam. But my friends call me Mary. *You* may call me Mary.'

'Well, Mary, I have chosen you above all women. Let me explain why I'm here.'

She listened patiently as he explained her part in the plan that would raise humanity to the light. 'So, now that you are acquainted with the facts, are you willing to help me?'

In answer she dropped her ewer and then her robes, and, when she stood naked before him, her eyes reflecting every nuance of his light, he thought *he* might faint.

'Let it be done,' she said.

'Let it be –?'

'Done.'

He took her in full view of heaven and a passing camel train, his senses thrilling to heights of hitherto unequalled ecstasy, and, even though her womb had well and truly quickened, he took her again. And again the next day. And again. In fact, they met by the well every day for the next fortnight, his temporary flesh tingling, his soul consumed with thoughts of his beloved.

And he probably would have stayed earthbound if his brother Rigel had not come to fetch him home.

'You are a son of heaven.' Rigel reminded him. 'There are other worlds in need of Father's message. Why do you linger?'

'It's Mary –' he began.

'Is she in need of you, brother?'

Gabriel's eyes strayed to the indented patch of sand where he and Mary had earlier made love. 'I fear it is I who am in need of her.'

'My poor brother. Her worship has inflamed your heart. Father has warned you about your vanity.'

'No, it's not like that at all...this time.'

'How is it then brother? This time.'

Gabriel shook his head. 'You know how Father wants the very best for us?'

'For *all* living creatures.'

'Yes, I meant that. This woman loves me in a way that I have never known.'

Rigel smiled. 'But you don't believe in love, Gabriel.'

'I know but Miriam...*Mary*...loves me with such *tenderness*.' He looked at his brother bleakly. 'I fear I have become rather attached to her generous consideration.'

'This brand of human love sounds exceedingly attractive.'

'I would stay and learn more about its potential application. We may be able to use it to further Father's cause.'

Rigel frowned considering his brother's dilemma. 'Or do you wish to stay with this woman?'

'Of course not!' cried Gabriel. 'Nothing comes above my loyalty to Father.'

'Be calm, brother. I'm not accusing you. It was curiosity that prompted the question. I can find no fault in this generous human love and one day we must learn more about it. Perhaps together. But right now you are needed elsewhere and must come home.'

Gabriel bowed his head. 'Give me one more day with Mary. Let me say goodbye.'

The last time they made love he cradled her in his arms. 'Mary, you *do* understand that our child belongs to heaven, don't you?'

She sat up, her hair coiling over her breasts. 'What do you mean?'

'I mean, he will only stay as flesh until his message reaches the world. You mustn't get too attached.'

She laughed, teased the golden curls back from his damp forehead. 'He's my son. I will get attached. Poor angel, don't you know anything about love. About maternal love?'

He tried again to make her understand. 'This child is not yours to keep' – he paused – 'any more than I am.'

She darted a frightened glance at him. 'You're leaving? But I'd hoped you would stay and help me raise our son.' She fought back tears. 'I thought you loved me.'

'You always knew this was just a job for me.' Even as he said it he knew how clumsy it sounded. 'That was –'

'Cruel.' She stood up, donned her blue robes.

'Mary, be grateful that of all the women on earth I chose you to carry a son of heaven.' He reached for her but she shrank from his touch.

'The first thing I will teach my son is how to love so he will be kinder than his father.'

'He has a job to do, woman. As do I.'

'And as his mother it will be my job to guide him as I see fit.'

'Mary, please understand, once the message is delivered, heaven will call him home as it now calls me.'

She picked up her ewer and went to the well.

167

'Don't try to keep him from our Father's business, Mary.'

She turned her back on him and drew fresh water. 'When you see your Father tell Him the world is far too old to change.'

'The world will bend to my Father's will.'

She put the ewer down, went back to the angel and kissed him, her tears tasting like salt on his tongue. 'I love you, Gabriel. Remember that when the world grows dark.'

Something akin to a pulse fluttered in his breast. 'I was only sent to prepare the way. I cannot stay with you.'

'If you change your mind, I'll be waiting.'

'I'm not at liberty to change my mind. I am a son of heaven.' He could not meet her eyes. 'I must go now. My Father has other business for me.' And he flew away without looking back, leaving her pregnant, unwed and burdened with a son of heaven who would be ripped from her arms in due course.

Centuries later, the world hadn't changed and he could still taste her tears on his tongue.

'You did not wait for me, Miriam. I came back and you were gone. And the world has become dark without you.'

Unable to sate the hunger in his soul, he suppressed it with a baser appetite. On the floor of the cave, the remains of the bats' last meal – bits of fruit and a half-eaten rat. Squatting down, wings dragging in the guano of millennia occupation by the creatures, he broke the rat's bones, sucked a little marrow. Not too far below, the green and bronze-weeded waves gnawed incessantly at the bellied-up rocks, an echo of the pain gnawing at his soul. He tossed the last of the rat into the roiling sea and lay down in the dust and guano.

A sweet strain of melody drifted into the cave. He sat up, cocked his head and listened for a few bars.

'She's playing again.' He leapt up, dusted off his robes and flew out over the sea, a million familiar pinpricks of light puncturing the ebony sky.

'The world will change, Miriam. It must.' He winged towards Cremorne. 'I will make it bend to my will. Am I not my Father's son, inflamed with a greatness even I cannot comprehend?'

NOCTURNE

*A musical composition that has a romantic or
dreamy character with nocturnal associations*

Mary closed the lid of the piano, ran her hand across it, tracking the minute irregularities in the timber. 'Robert is lusting after Jennifer.'

'Why would you care? You're not in love with Robert.' Gabriel was lying on the couch, his right wing and right leg dangling onto the carpet, his sandals tossed casually on the floor next to a plate of cake-crumbs. He had arrived in a most agitated state, starving for food and desperate for music. After consuming the chocolate cake she'd made for Jennifer and Jonathan's next visit, he asked for music and she played him the piece she'd been working on when he arrived: a requiem in A Minor for James. The melody ended on an unresolved chord, incomplete like James' young life.

'You're not in love with that insipid human, are you?' He hoisted himself onto one elbow.

'No. It seems I can't inspire love.' She swept passed him, collecting the plate on her way to the kitchen. 'Or *lust.*'

'Is there more cake?' he called out after her.

She washed up the dish and returned, slumping down on the piano stool. 'If I was beautiful I would inspire love.'

'That kind of love doesn't last.'

'What do *you* know about love?'

'Forget Robert. He'd drain you of life if you gave him half a chance.'

'And *you* would never drain the life out of anybody.'

He adjusted his position. 'This couch is much more comfortable than a cold cave.'

'Cave? Is that where you go when you're not hanging around me?'

Gabriel studied his fingernails, five half-moons capping splendidly tapered fingers, but didn't answer.

'Don't you go to Florence any more? No windows being left open?'

'I'm too busy now. I have to save the world through your music – performance by performance.'

'Who are you to play God?'

'Someone has to.'

'Why?'

'People need a chain of command to give them direction.'

'Why can't nature take its course?'

'Control *is* nature's course.'

'No, it's not. Jennifer said nature follows a twisted line towards the light. Why can't we find our own way to the light, Gabriel? Don't you have faith in us?'

He pointed at the vase with the roses he had given her a week earlier. They were still in bloom, their petals a vivid, living red, their perfume mingling with his signature scent. 'They will never die nor age but remain in a state of perfection for eternity.'

'That's creepy. Everlasting roses...like plastic ones.'

He ignored that. 'And why? Because I added divine light to a bunch of ordinary roses. If I can do that for flowers think what I could do for humanity. No more illness and pain. No more death or the agony of birth. Just perpetual...'

'Stagnation.'

'Bliss. Heaven on an earth under my command.'

171

'*Your* command?'

'Someone has to tell them what to do.'

'And what will you tell them to do, Gabriel?'

'Stop fighting for a start. And then I will encourage a focus on the Arts and architecture like it was in the Renaissance. This planet of creative immortals will be the envy of other worlds, the jewel in the universe.'

'When you say there will be *no more agony of birth* do you mean giving birth will be painless?'

'No. I mean there will no more births. I will ban the entry of new souls.' He winked at her. 'They won't have heard the music, Mary. They'll be…ambitious.'

'What's wrong with ambition? I'm ambitious. You're ambitious.'

'There's only so much room at the top.' His eyes glittered as he studied his palm upon which the hint of destiny was etched. 'Mary, we can do it. Your music and my light will change the world.'

'Maybe the world's too old to change.' She brushed past him, en-route to the kitchen again.

'What did you say?'

'You heard me.'

'Just like Miriam,' he murmured as he followed her. 'You're too young to be cynical and faithless.'

'I'm not trying to save the world, Gabriel.' She hacked a slice of bread into eight pieces and arranged them on a plate.

'You seem a little agitated and why are you still feeding elves?'

'I need luck.'

'For what?'

'Love. In the Cathedral when all those people were staring at me as if they could happily eat me, I asked myself – would they want me without my music? Will anybody ever love me for myself?' She poured honey over the bread, picked up the dish and went out to the balcony.

He followed her. 'And what was your answer?'

172

Carefully placing the dish just so on the balustrade, 'I didn't have one at first. But when I saw how Robert couldn't take his eyes off Jennifer I knew no one would ever see past my plain face if I didn't have the music.' She pressed her fists to her forehead. 'Unless I was really lucky.'

Women, I will never understand them. 'Mary, everyone will adore you when you're famous.'

'For the music! I want to be loved for myself not my music. Or your light.' She held back a sob. 'Robert made love to *me* but I was completely forgotten the minute he saw Jennifer.'

He looked heavenward, hoping for a sign. None came. 'You don't want Robert.'

'And *you* were thinking of someone else.'

'I did say you remind me of Miriam.'

'And when my father ... when he forced himself on me he said ...'

'What?'

'He said I was plain compared to Mum.' She buried her face in her hands. 'Maybe my music's plain without your light. Maybe I will never be good enough to make it alone.'

'What if you aren't?' he whispered.

She jerked her head up and stared at him. 'I'd rather die than cheat.'

'But you're not cheating. I chose you because you're naturally brilliant.' He ran his finger over her cheek, tracing the track of a tear. 'No true artist is ever completely satisfied with her creation.'

'But where do I end and you begin when people hear my music?'

'Ah, the eternal dilemma of co-creation.' He raised his hand, indicating the sky. 'My creation is swamped with my Father's light. Where does that leave me? It's hard not knowing your own worth but the New World will be mine alone. With your help, of course.'

'Gabriel, I want something of my own. I need to know my music is good even without your light.'

'You'll never know.'

'Then I'll give it up.'

They stared at each other for a long moment, neither willing to give ground. Finally Gabriel spoke. 'You'll go mad.'

'I am mad.'

'Imagine a life without music, bound by routines you're too frightened to break. Every night wishing for a little luck only to discover what an angel once told you...elves bite. Your days blank, your nights tormented with dreams about stages and Steinways. Your music a sad haunting refrain singing of the glorious life you might have known. And when death comes for you at last, you'll embrace him like a lover.'

She buried her face in his chest. 'I don't have any choice, do I?'

'No-one has any choice, Mary.'

'You once said we all have choices.'

'I was wrong. The only choice is life ... no matter what it takes.' He stroked her hair. 'The life of an artist is fraught with doubt.' He held her tight. 'Try not to concern yourself with my part in your success. Just focus on your own role. Let us complete each other: your music, my light, *our* success.' He kissed her. 'My sins will never touch the music or the New World or our son.'

'But the sins of the fathers –'

'Let's not talk about fathers.' He scooped her up in his arms, carried her to the bedroom and lay her down on the bed. 'I've missed you these past three weeks, Mary. Please don't shut me out again.'

She gazed into his beautiful, mesmerising eyes. 'I've missed you too, Gabriel.'

'So, no more arguments? You'll play your music and let me heal the world?'

'The Renaissance did sound like a very productive time.'

'They were creating heaven on earth, Mary. And then it all went horribly wrong. The geniuses were snuffed out by bureaucracy. Ignorant men who thought they had a hotline to God changed the rules with every new leader. That's why there can only be one person in charge – me. It's just easier.'

'And people will be happy?' she asked cautiously. 'No more suffering?'

'It will be perfect bliss.'

She thought of the pain and suffering she had witnessed in her brief life: her father's cruelty, her mother's regret, James' messy life, her siblings' homelessness and misery, Robert's loneliness. 'Yes,' she agreed. 'Do what you can to help them, Gabriel.'

'Thank you, Mary. They'll never know what hit them when they see the light.' And then he kissed her, silencing any further questions, erasing any further doubt.

They made love until the moon was a silver bullet directly overhead. She was lying cradled in his arms – feeling sated and secure – when she remembered.

'I need to ask you something. My sister has a client, someone who promotes rock music. She wants me to play for him. If he likes our music, he might sign me and promote my career. Be my manager. Does that suit your plans?'

'Let it be done.' His eyes shone like lanterns in the dark.

DEVELOPMENT

Where the musical themes and melodies
are developed, written in sonata form

𝄞

They stood on the doorstep of the Italianate mansion in Bellevue
Hill owned by Jonté Fortune. The double front doors loomed
over them dark and imposing, a sombre contrast to the
otherwise white house.

'The house looks like a tomb.'

Jennifer nodded. 'It's meant to impress people. I think it just
scares them. What do you think of the garden?'

The beds were bursting with flowers in colours grading from
purple to hot pink. 'Beautiful. You've brought some colour to
the place.'

'Not without a fight, I can tell you. Jonté loves white and
insists on keeping all those naked Greek gods.'

There were at least a dozen life-size white marble statues
standing in contemplation of each other around the front lawn.

'They're a long way from Mount Olympus, right?' Jennifer
laughed.

'Was that a joke?'

'A lame one. Ready?'

'Another minute, please. I've been meaning to ask you...
what did my music make you think of?'

She looked past Mary at one of the incongruous gods. 'It
made me believe I'd be a mother one day. But since I can't

bear a man to touch me after what our *loving* father did to me, I don't expect children are on the agenda.' Her fingers flexed over an imaginary cigarette. 'I just have to content myself with getting Jonathan sorted out and you playing your music to the world.' She laughed. 'Assuming I can get you over this damned doorstep.'

'Don't waste your gifts.'

'What?'

'You have a gift for love. Please use it.'

'What do you think I'm trying to do here? Now, take a deep breath and think of the future.' Jennifer rang the doorbell. Moments later, the door swung open revealing a blinding white yet lightless interior: walls, marble floor and cavernous ceiling, all blaringly white. Soulless. Only silence emanated from the blank walls as if no one lived there. Jonté Fortune looked almost colourful in his brown moleskins and cream shirt.

He smiled, white teeth, cold eyes. 'Come in, Jennifer, and ...' he clicked his fingers.

'Mary,' said Jennifer.

Two toddlers at his heels started squabbling volubly. 'Go to Mummy, kids. Daddy's working. Emma!' he bellowed, voice echoing off the glacial walls. 'Jennifer's here with her sister. Lock the front door again, will you, Jen?'

The children's arguing escalated into high-pitched defiance.

'Enough!' Jonté raised a finger and they fell silent, chins trembling. 'We don't want Jennifer and ...'

'Mary,' growled Jennifer.

'...Mary to think you're a pair of spoiled brats, now do we?'

They shook their heads in unison. The children, a boy and girl, were identically dressed in blue jeans, white T-shirts emblazoned with I♥NY and mini red baseball caps worn backwards. 'Daddy's working. Now ... Mary ... I can give you fifteen minutes.' He hurried off down the hall, the children trotting after him.

'You'll see how good my sister is in *five* minutes, Jonté.'

'They all say that.' His mobile rang and he stopped dead, checked the caller ID. 'Hey Stan,' he held the phone to his ear, strode off with Jennifer, Mary and the children following. Within seconds, the children were bickering again.

'Hang on a moment, Stan …' Jonté stopped walking, bent over his kids. 'Janis, that's your brother's iPod. What's Daddy told you about stealing? Where's your iPod?' The child blinked at him. She couldn't have been any older than three. The boy looked to be about four. Mary wondered what earthly good an iPod would be to a toddler.

He stood up and bellowed again, 'Emma! Take the kids! I'm working!' He pressed the phone to his ear. 'Sorry, Stan, just sorting out a domestic issue. Emma!'

An attractive blonde woman in track pants and white T-shirt also emblazoned with I♥NY sauntered into the hall. 'Where's the fire, Jonté? Hi Jen, love your latest plantings. Some colour at last! I feel like I'm the Snow Queen in here.' She bent down and scooped up the two moppets, one under each arm. 'Now what crime have you committed?'

'Hang on a minute, Stan.' He covered the phone. 'Janis stole Hanson's iPod.'

'Do you want her flogged or put in stocks?' Emma winked at Jennifer.

'It's not a joke, Emma,' snapped Jonté.

Mary watched the glamorous mum struggling to suppress her laughter. Clearly she thought it *was* a joke.

'You heard Daddy, kids. It's a downhill slide unless I beat the devil out of you now. Shall we have some ice-cream and watch Aladdin? That's a good punishment. Very best of luck, Mary. Jen's been singing your praises. Wish I could listen but I have to entertain the monsters.' The children squealed with delight as their mother carried them off into one of the many rooms celled in the glacial labyrinth. Jennifer watched the children's departure, a sad downward curve to her beautiful mouth.

'Emma spoils those kids,' Jonté muttered.

'Children *should* be spoiled,' said Jennifer.

'You won't say that when you've got your own.' Resuming his phone call. 'Yeah Stan, I'm still here.'

'You're right,' said Mary softly. 'Children should be spoiled with love.'

Suddenly Jonté's mobile blasted with the sounds of a wailing guitar and a thumping bass. He held it out from his ear, looked back at Jennifer and rolled his eyes. 'No wonder half the people I manage are deaf by the age of thirty.' Someone was shouting above the music. 'Say that again, Stan!' He pressed the phone to his right ear, jammed his finger into his left, squinting in an effort to hear. 'Back in rehab? Shit! OK, we'll replace him when you get back … talk on the yacht. Gotta go, mate. Working.'

Jonté marched to the end of the hallway, stopped in front of a pair of heavily padded doors.

'Recording studio,' he said, ushering them into another white room with booths, drum kits, mikes, sound desk behind glass and a spectacular grand piano. He slumped onto a white leather couch, put his feet up on a glass coffee table and nodded at the piano. 'You have fifteen minutes to impress me … um …'

'Mary,' Jennifer reminded him between gritted teeth.

'It's all right, Mr. Fortune, no one notices me until I play my music.' Mary sat at the piano, raised the lid.

'James noticed you,' said Jennifer quietly. 'And he never heard your music.'

The sisters looked at each other for a long moment and then Mary smiled. 'Thank you for reminding me.'

'Fifteen minutes, Mary,' said Jonté. 'The piano's not really my bag. Rock bands, singer-songwriters, *young* people's music is what I understand. I make stars out of dross and everything I touch turns to gold.' He waggled his fingers. 'Midas touch. So…

as I said to Jennifer...I can't quite see where I'd position you in the marketplace but for Jen's sake, I'm prepared to listen.'

'You'll thank me, Jonté,' said Jennifer, eyes twinkling.

'We'll see.'

Mary placed her hands on the keyboard. The instrument felt tired, *flogged* like Emma had suggested for the children. But the piano *was* being regularly thumped. Mary murmured assurances to the exhausted instrument, calming it as a talented jockey might calm a highly strung, overworked racehorse.

'Fifteen minutes.' Jonté reminded her. *The girl didn't seem to be listening, damn it. She was whispering to the piano.* 'What are you? A piano whisperer?' He laughed. Sourly.

Mary snapped her attention to him. 'Was that a joke, Mr. Fortune?'

He tapped his watch. 'Can we get on?'

She began to play, her music gathering the dangling emotional threads in the room and weaving them into a melodic tapestry. Her own confusion about her worth was a golden thread, her sister's steady belief in her a scarlet tight-wire defying gravity, and seeping from the empty soul of Jonté Fortune was a thin green strain underscored by a darker seam of fear: his terror of the merciless young fans who screamed for their idols one minute and crucified them the next. So many stars had fallen off their plinths on his watch and ended up junked out of their brains, domiciled in semi-permanent rehab until they launched comebacks decades too late.

Then the music changed key and a bright sequence of notes pierced Jonté's cynical armour. Into the chink a subtle note of appreciation seeped and he realised that he actually liked what he was hearing, something he hadn't done since he was a teenager. When his phone beeped with a new message, he ignored it. For the first time in years he felt excited. And he knew that this music was so much finer than the noise and dated desperation he usually peddled. It touched the heart rather than the loins.

And just as she had at the Cathedral, Jennifer saw children in the music. Her children. Then came the last note – an unfinished E minor chord left deliberately incomplete – and the vision faded.

Jonté sat quite still while his mobile beeped on. 'I'll sign you,' he said, his voice not sounding like his own.

Jennifer whooped. 'Thank you, Jonté!'

He held up his hand. 'But you have to practice day and night, um ...'

'*Mary*! For God's sake, Jonté. Try to remember my sister's name. Do you want to be the only person not knowing her name when she's world-famous?'

'All right, Jen, calm down. Now ... *Mary*, playing in here is one thing, playing for the world takes nerves of steel. I've seen a lot of people break under the pressure.'

'I won't,' said Mary quietly.

'Good. I want you ready to record an album in six months. I want original tracks as brilliant as the stuff you played now. You *did* compose that tune, didn't you? I'm not signing a co-writer. Too much trouble.'

Mary pressed her hands to her belly where Gabriel's child was little more than a whisper. 'I get a little inspiration from an outside source.'

Jonté darted a look at Jennifer. 'I thought you said she composed her own music.'

'She means God, Jonté.'

'God's OK. He won't ask for royalties. I'll get your contract now. No need to waste time reading it. Just sign.'

'I'll read it first, Mr. Fortune. I am a paralegal.'

'Look, Mary, I don't want you finding some loophole and backing out when a better offer comes along from some two-bit promoter.'

'I'll keep my word, Mr. Fortune, but I prefer to know what I'm signing.'

'I'm only asking you to play your music to the world. I don't want your soul.'

A slight smile. 'They all say that.'

He looked at the girl who sat at the piano like a little Buddha, her face expressionless, her unblinking eyes fixed unnervingly on his face.

'I'm not like other promoters, Mary. I'm the best.' He left the room and returned almost immediately with a three page document and a gold pen. 'I promise you that within a year, you'll be a household name or my name's not Jonté Fortune.'

VERISMO

An opera written in a contemporary setting in
which the characters are modeled on everyday life

'No, what's pissing me off is that you went behind my back! My own sisters betrayed me.' Jonathan swished his cape as he paced back and forth, boot-heels click-clacking on the kitchen floor tiles.

'Can we talk about this at home? In private?' Jennifer had caught the warmth of the sun working in the garden that morning. Her face was flushed.

'At home? In private? Like civilised people?' Jonathan imitated his sister's tone. 'Am I embarrassing you with my ill-breeding, Jenny? I say, Robert, do make us some cucumber sandwiches, there's a good chap. Lady fucking Bracknell would like them with her tea.'

'Stop it, Jonathan.' Jennifer's face turned pinker with frustration.

'I had no idea Oscar Wilde wrote so colourfully,' said Robert, placing the teapot on the kitchen table. 'Do sit down, Jonathan. You're wearing a track in the floor with your pacing.'

'Sorry, Rob.' Jonathan sat at the table and toyed with his empty cup. 'This contract Mary's signed has caught me by surprise. Neither of my sisters told me what they were planning and then an announcement over tea, well, that hurts.'

'I'm sorry, Jonathan,' said Mary, 'I did blurt it out. It's my fault.' She caught Jennifer's eye and gave a helpless shrug.

'But Mary, you knew I'd made plans for you and yes, Jennifer, we'll talk about it right now so you can stop glaring at me. You don't mind do you, Rob?'

'No, of course not. And if my opinion counts, I'd say Jennifer's intentions were good.' He turned away and pulled a tray of scones out of the oven.

'Well, we all know Jennifer can do no wrong in your eyes, Robert,' said Jonathan.

Robert ignored that. 'Sadly, it means I'll have to replace Mary even sooner but who am *I* to stand in the way of her career.' He placed the scones on the table. 'No one should stand in the way of her career.'

'I don't want to hold Mary back,' snarled Jonathan. 'Quite the opposite. I have one gift – marketing – and I want to use it to help my sister.'

Robert placed bowls of whipped cream and strawberry jam next to the scones. 'Have a scone, Jonathan. Have two. Put some weight on your bones.'

'Are you saying I'm too thin?'

'Anybody struggling with heroin is thin.' Robert said it casually.

Jennifer and Mary gaped at him.

Livid blotches appeared under Jonathan's make-up. 'Who told you? Jennifer or Mary?'

'I worked it out for myself. Tea with your scone?'

'*How* did you work it out?' he asked suspiciously, casting a glance at his sisters.

'I wasn't born yesterday. Please understand I'm making no judgments.' He dumped a scone on Jonathan's plate. 'Eat.'

'I just want to point out that despite occasional lapses I am winning the war against heroin, and my years of addiction have not diminished my intellectual capacity one scrap.' Jonathan tore the scone open and slathered it with jam and cream. 'When did you work out that I'm a *recovering* addict, Robert?'

'The day we met.' He sat down and poured the tea. 'When you were high as a kite. But I'm very glad to hear you're winning the battle. That takes courage.'

'I've not used since then,' Jonathan said. 'Betrayed by both my sisters. You don't seem able to keep your promises, do you Jen?'

'What are you talking about?' Jennifer's face burned.

'We were going to move out of that dump. Upgrade, you said. Find something nice for Jonathan, you said. But you want to use the money for Mary's career. The career I had planned all the way to Carnegie Hall.' His eyes pinning Jennifer.

'You're keeping that money aside for me?' Mary asked softly.

'In case you need to travel.'

'No. Use it to move house. I have savings.'

Robert cleared his throat. 'Do you want me to leave the room so you can talk privately?'

'We've agreed we can speak freely in front of you, Rob. Besides, it's your house,' Jonathan replied. 'Jen got an inheritance from Dad – three hundred thousand dollars – a piss in the park compared to your millions but enough to give us a new start in a decent place. But she's changed her mind.' Jonathan took a savage bite out of his scone.

'So you want to live somewhere pleasant, Jonathan?' Robert spoke as if he held back a secret.

'Obviously.'

'Well…an idea has been brewing. I have a proposition for the Granger siblings.'

'All three of us?' Jonathan asked. 'Oh you *are* wicked! I suspect Mary has already acquiesced and I won't say no.' He threw a sly glance at Jennifer. 'Which only leaves you. *Ménage à quatre?*'

'Stop it, Jonathan.' Jennifer's cheeks burned.

'Wrong kind of proposition, Jonathan. Now hear me out before you say anything else. There are six bedrooms in this house, four of them empty, and I'm fed up with my own company. I'd like the *three* of you to move in here.'

The three Granger musketeers stared at him.

'You'd have total freedom and the run of this house. And Mary, the baby grand is waiting for you.'

But the piano doesn't like me, thought Mary.

Jonathan dropped his scone. 'Move into Shalamar?'

'Yes. What do you think, Jennifer? No strings attached. No hidden agenda beyond me wanting company.'

'We have some...er...problems we wouldn't like to inflict on you,' Jennifer said, with a quick glance at her brother.

'Me?' Jonathan glared at her.

'I've told you I know about that,' Robert replied. 'The rule will be no drugs in this house.'

'I wouldn't dream of it.' He flicked an angry look at Jennifer. 'I suggest you accept Rob's kind offer too. Do this for me, sister, since you just ruined my career.'

Jennifer blushed. 'My own room?'

'Of course.' Robert turned away. 'Mary?'

'I don't think it will work. I practice the piano at night and I'd disturb everyone.'

'You wouldn't disturb me,' said Jennifer quickly.

'Or me,' Robert added.

'And I put up with everything decided by my sisters,' Jonathan said.

'I'm sorry but I need to live alone. And Robert, I also need to hand in my resignation.' She looked from face to face. 'I'm sorry, everyone.'

'Don't be.' Jennifer smiled. 'This is your chance, Mary. Take it.'

'And to hell with me.' Jonathan threw down his knife.

Nobody said anything for several minutes. Mary tapped her

186

fingertips on the table, drumming one of the melodies that would soon erupt into the world's consciousness. The ticking of the grandfather clock in the hall underscored the rhythm.

Jennifer broke the silence. 'Robert, did you say you'd turned one of your bedrooms into a studio?'

'Yes, for my painting.'

'Could we see some of your work, please?'

'Oh no, I'm not ready yet.'

'Please, Robert, show us one of your paintings.' Mary added her encouragement.

'Oh God,' muttered Jonathan.

'I only have one canvas at this stage,' said Robert.

'Go and get it,' said Jennifer.

'All right, but no laughing.'

When Robert was out of earshot, Jonathan turned on Jennifer. 'What do you think that arsehole Fortune can do for Mary that I can't?'

'For God's sake, Jonathan, you've never even had a job! You'd gamble with Mary's future like –' she stopped.

'Dad? Like Dad gambled with ours? Is that what you were going to say?'

'No, I –'

He made a fist, held it up and shook it. 'Marketing is my gift from God, like yours is gardening, and Mary's is music, and Robert's' – he twisted his mouth with distaste – 'may or may not be painting. Jenny, you've got your chance to shine here at Shalamar, Mary's music is about to go viral and any minute Robert will come downstairs with a painting we must pretend to like…'

'It might be good,' Mary interrupted. 'The painting – it might be good.'

'And pigs might fly. The thing is, Jenny, I wanted the chance to promote my own sister. Now she's signed up to a soulless, tin-eared twat. Listen to the crap he usually promotes for God's sake – white noise, one-minute wonders. All I ask is a shot at life.'

'Sorry, I took so long.' Robert burst into the kitchen carrying a massive canvas. 'Look…I only started painting a month ago… and I'd rather you were honest.' He balanced the canvas on a chair while his eyes darted from one face to another.

Jonathan rose and approached the painting slowly.

Jennifer frowned, tipped her head to one side. 'It's –'

'Colourful,' said Mary quickly.

'Yes,' said Jennifer. 'Not many people would think to paint a cow red and a' – she frowned – 'is that pink thing a pig with' – she shot a look at Jonathan – 'wings?'

Robert sighed. 'No, it's *you* actually working in the garden. I painted you with wings because I see you as an angel. And that red thing's a wheelbarrow. *Your* wheelbarrow. You're my muse, Jennifer.'

'Oh yes,' said Jennifer brightly, 'now I can see. It's *great*.'

'You hate it,' said Robert, chest caving.

'No, I –' Jennifer swallowed. 'I don't know much about art, Robert.'

Jonathan stood close to the painting, his hands clasped under his chin as he studied it.

'I like the colours,' said Mary. 'Very –'

'Bold,' said Jennifer. 'Very …'

'Brave,' said Mary. 'A lot of people wouldn't use that many colours –'

'In the same painting,' said Jennifer. 'I'd honestly have to say this painting is…'

'A work of genius!' announced Jonathan. 'Extraordinary! You will be misunderstood at first ridiculed…maimed…your soul lacerated by the cruel pens of critics who never bare their souls. Only their teeth. But I' – he spun around, faced Robert, his eyes shining with tears – 'will shield you from their slings and arrows. I can fit you into my schedule now that I've lost my primary client. It's better this way, Rob. I can devote all my energy and expertise to promoting your genius now that we'll be living under the same roof. No one' – he glared at Jennifer – 'can steal you away from me.' He looked back at the painting. 'What have you named this masterpiece?'

'I haven't named it. I thought I'd paint over this canvas. Do something better.'

'Better?' Jonathan's eyes flew open in horror. 'You can't deny the world this treasure. Oh, Robert, Robert, thank God our paths have crossed in time.' He turned back to the painting, studied it for a long minute. 'I have it! It will be called *And Pigs Might Fly*.'

'But there aren't any pigs in it,' said Robert helplessly.

Jennifer covered her mouth to keep from giggling.

Mary looked from Robert to Jonathan to the painting and back again. 'If there are no pigs in it shouldn't it be called something else?'

Jonathan flipped his cape back over his shoulders. 'An artist must keep his public guessing. They'll all be looking for pigs and pigs will be seen as clearly as the emperor's Calvin Kline undies unless some precocious child spots the absence of porkers. Note to self *no kids at the opening*.' He squatted in front of the painting. 'Such fine brushwork, such bold colours. You're a natural, Robert and I' – his eyes brilliant with tears – 'am home at last.'

MADRIGAL

*A contrapuntal song written for at least three
voices, usually without accompaniment*

At first life felt slow after four years of following a fast-lane
routine. Her days and nights had little definition and stretched
uninterrupted into weeks. With nothing to do but practise her
music, Mary suffered a kind of vertigo, her mind dizzy with
arias and symphonies.

Gabriel rarely left her flat. He lay on her couch imbibing every
ambrosia note and asked numerous questions: what inspired her;
did she have a Muse; did the music come to her fully arranged
or note by note; and lastly, why did she use music to interpret
her inner world as opposed to words or paint?

'And how does the light come to you?' she asked him one
evening while they sat on the balcony admiring the view.

'I absorb it and reflect it...like the moon reflects the sun. I
used to reflect my Father's light. I was His messenger, reminding
mortals in every realm that they owed their souls to God.'

'Whose light do you reflect now that your Father's gone
away?'

'It's complicated.'

She had another question. 'You say you're *just* the messenger
but if you imagined the universe, you're a co-creator. Legally
speaking you're entitled to credits.'

'I haven't been entirely honest with you.' He shifted

uncomfortably. 'Father imagined the universe...but I made it work. I constructed the material world and made it all stick together with the laws of attraction. Then Father breathed His light into it and gave it life but He couldn't have done it without me.' He tipped his head back and took a deep breath. 'He needed me then, Mary.'

'Try to explain it to me. I really want to understand. Where do you find the light you add to my music?'

'I'm getting it from *you* if you must know.'

'Me? How?'

'I absorb the light of your soul when you're playing for me and reflect it back into the music when you perform, intensifying your natural glow like a mirror reflecting sunlight. Can we drop it now?'

They fell into silence. Mary sipped her wine. Gabriel stared sullenly at the stars peeping through the canopy. The rhythmic lap-lap of wavelets in the cove underscored the many night sounds.

'I'm not cheating,' he said suddenly. 'If that's what you're thinking.'

'I wasn't thinking that at all. I was wondering who you really are if you're not the light and not the music.'

'I don't know.' He sighed. 'I've become so bewitched with physical sensation I'm little better than human.'

She tipped her glass, capturing moonlight in her wine. 'Who created physical sensation? You or God?'

'Nature. It was a natural coalition of matter and energy. Life is sustained through the consumption of other life, so nature made eating pleasurable. She wanted her kingdom to survive. New souls are injected into physical form through sex, so Mother Nature made that pleasurable too. However, as I've discovered, physical pleasure is highly addictive, so I will eradicate it in the New World. I don't mean eating and drinking. I just mean sex. I will neutralise that urge.'

191

'You'll never make love to me again?' she asked sadly.

He smiled at her wickedly. 'I'll make an exception for us.'

'I'm hoping Jennifer will find a lover who will heal her. Can you make an exception for her too?'

'Oh, very well. Jennifer and her lover.'

'My mother deserves some happiness,' she added.

'For goodness sake! Everyone you know? I'm sterilising the rest of humanity. I don't want any more baby souls to train. I'm weary.'

They said nothing more for a while until Mary asked, 'What colour is my soul's light?'

'Blue shot through with pure gold. Like my Father's.' He shivered despite the warmth of the night. 'And it has the same innocence and naïvety that is the signature tone of His light.'

'Is God really naïve?'

'Profoundly. How else could He remain so idealistic?'

'While you do all the killing in His name.'

'Everything kills to –'

'I know … protect that which gives it life. You've protected your Father from blame for centuries. But who protects you?'

'I don't need protection,' he said gruffly. 'Listen Mary, my Father did what He had to do to preserve heaven. He kept the flame alive.'

'And turned a blind eye to suffering and injustice.'

'He lit the pathway home.'

'And now He's gone and to hell with humanity.'

'Stop it, Mary. My Father held the light for millennia. He's earned His freedom.'

'So, you don't hate your Father, after all. I thought you did.'

'Of course I don't hate my Father. Whatever gave you that idea?'

'Oh, just a few things you've said.'

'Ridiculous the way humanity hears what it wants to hear.

I may have said I wish He'd respected me enough to delegate.'

'Maybe He has…by leaving.'

'Maybe.' He bowed his head. 'No more questions tonight.'

They said nothing more for a while. 'Who do we pray to now, Gabriel?'

'I don't know.' A short beat. 'I must find Rigel and talk to him about it.'

'And if you never find your brother?'

'I said no more questions. Please.' A long beat. 'I *must* find Rigel. I need him more than ever. He'll help rid the doubt. It's a well-documented fact that the end justifies the means. My brother will sanctify my actions and bring me some peace.'

'Gabriel, you have to forgive yourself. No one else can do it for you.'

'My brother can!'

'It's not the same as forgiving yourself. It won't stick.'

'How do *you* know?' His eyes burnt like sienna flames. 'You have no sins to carry. You don't know what it feels like to crave God's light and know you may never bathe in it again.' He wrung his hands. 'Never feel that rebirth of innocence, never know the sanctifying love that only a soul without sin can bestow.' He paced up and down in the confined space. 'I can't forgive myself, Mary. I have no inner light to drive away the shadows. It went out centuries ago…because I *killed* for Him. Light is all that separates me from my Father now – the only thing that stops us being equal.'

'You *do* hate your Father.'

He leapt onto the balcony and perched ready to fly. 'Why am I bothering to explain myself to a girl who hears nothing but music and hides away in an imaginary world?'

'I used to hate mine,' she said softly. 'He was cruel and thoughtless, too.'

'Don't you dare compare our fathers, Mary Granger, and don't lecture me. I'm an angel. You're just a human. The only special thing about you is your music and that's mine. We have a contract.'

'A mere mortal I may be but unless you find your brother, I'm all you've got,' she said calmly. 'You said so years ago.'

He flared and sparked. 'Don't cage me in your little world, Mary Granger. I will leave when my Father summons me. He will realise universes are more than just light and ideas.' His focus shifted to a distant star. 'He *will* need me and I will go... after I've saved the world.'

'You'll leave me, too?' Her voice breaking.

'Those who have wings must fly, Mary Granger. Did you really think you could keep an angel bound to you forever?'

Tears stung. 'I know you don't love me...'

'I don't love anybody.'

'Not even your unborn child?'

He swayed as he remembered that other Mary. *I thought you'd stay and help me raise our son. If he had stayed, would humanity have crucified him?* 'I have wings,' he whispered. 'Why does everyone try to clip them?'

'It's all right. I won't try to cage you. And don't worry, I'll find your brother in spring when the jasmine is in bloom. He'll help you and then you can leave us all behind.' *Even me, the mother of your child and the source of your light.*

After he had taken flight she sat for a long time watching the disintegrating firefly trail of his borrowed light.

'Cages are evil things, Gabriel,' she whispered.

They come in all shapes and sizes and the bars are made of hate and envy and love. 'But sometimes you have to find your freedom within a cage. I did. Your Father didn't. He flew away the instant His jailer left the door open.'

Maybe no one was praying that night.

Or maybe the urge to fly was just too strong.

AD LIBITUM

At choice, freely

Mary rotated the teapot three times before pouring. 'Mum, sit down and have a cup of tea. You've been cooking all morning.'

'Nearly done. That's six containers of stew for freezing. All you have to do is add salad or vegetables.'

'I can cook for myself, Mum.'

'I know, but I don't want you having to fuss over meals while you're practising for Mr. Fortune.' Kathleen nodded at Mary's girth. 'Do you get any exercise at all?'

Mary pulled her dressing gown over the slight bulge. She hadn't told her mother about the baby because she wasn't absolutely sure it was real and in any case, how could she explain the paternity? *It was an angel, Mum.* Of course it might be Robert's despite Gabriel's claim. But her mother would insist Robert was told and the last thing she wanted was pressure for a shotgun wedding with her ex-boss.

'Are you listening, Mary? I asked you if you were getting any exercise.'

'I go for a walk every Saturday morning.'

'You need more exercise than that or you'll get positively fat.'

Yes, because you keep preparing such calorie-laden meals.

'Do you ever hear from Robert?'

How soon do babies start kicking? She felt her belly. Nothing moved.

'Mary, for heaven's sake, I only come here once a week. Can you stop thinking about music and have a conversation?'

'Sorry. No, I haven't heard from Robert. He's not interested in me now Jennifer lives in Shalamar.'

Kathleen huffed. 'Well, you *were* asked to move in, too. I still don't understand why you left a rich, handsome man all to your sister.'

'He prefers Jennifer.'

'There's something not quite right about that girl. And as for the boy –' she shook her head. 'Make-up and cloaks. He likes the boys, doesn't he?'

'He's very troubled.'

'Troubled about what brand of lipstick to wear. He's not much of a brother if you ask me. How disappointing for you after all the years you've wanted to meet them.' Kathleen poured the stew into six plastic containers. 'And as for your cold-hearted sister...'

'Jennifer's not cold-hearted.'

'There's *something* wrong with her.' Kathleen sat at the table. 'Sure that girl'd freeze a man's balls at ten paces.'

Mary's hands shook, her cup trembled and a few drops splashed the table. She jumped up, grabbed a cloth and scrubbed frantically.

'Mary, calm down. It's only a drop of tea.'

'Jennifer's suffered.'

'All right. Don't take on so.'

'I played for her, Mum, and it didn't help. My music's meant to inspire joy and hope but it had no effect on my own sister.' She began to sob. 'What if James and Jillian died needlessly.'

'For heaven's sake, Mary! We've talked enough about this nonsense.'

'I miss James. He liked me for myself.'

'Ah, cry it out.' Kathleen held her sobbing daughter. 'You've had no time to grieve for your friend. Your sister will sort herself out in time. She's strong. There's a saying in the bible *those who have ears will hear.* Your gift will touch many hearts. You just play your music and leave salvation to God.'

But He's gone.

'And when Mr. Fortune makes you famous I'll travel with you – be a shoulder you can cry on or a safe haven when you need to be alone.'

Mary pulled out of her mother's embrace. 'You'll be there, Mum? No matter what?'

'Through thick and thin, darling.'

So where were you when I was a child? No, my mother didn't know. I have to believe that.

She glanced at Gabriel who was perched in a tree outside the kitchen window like some great eagle looking down into Shellcove. She'd asked him to give her some private time with her mother, go back to his cave but he said he never wanted to see that cold cavern again. He had promised not to listen but suddenly he turned and smiled as he'd been following the conversation.

'What is it?' asked Kathleen, looking around.

'What do you see in the tree outside the window?'

'Leaves and branches. What should I see? Is there a nest?'

Mary took a deep breath. 'No, an angel. The one who's watched over me since I was child. He's watching me now.' *Again Gabriel gave her a knowing smile as if he was following the conversation.*

'Sure, he's your guiding angel. No one can see him but you.'

Unless he wants them to.

'Do you think the end justifies the means, Mum? Is there a case for suffering, even the occasional murder, to bring justice to many?'

'Sure. The Lord was willing to die for our sins. It was part of God's plan.'

'Was it?' *Or was God so blinded by His own light He couldn't see the danger?*

197

Kathleen crossed herself. 'Can't you just play your music and stop asking questions, darling? We've neither the wisdom nor wit to understand God's ways. But sure He wants you safe. He sent an angel to watch over you.'

'I think the angel found me by accident, Mum.'

'No, Mary, angels are sent by God to protect us from harm.'

'Did God send an angel to watch over Jesus and protect *him* from harm?'

'He sent the angel Gabriel.'

That explains it.

Gabriel turned his head just then and glared at Mary, sienna eyes narrowed and burning.

Kathleen handed Mary a tissue. 'Here, dry your eyes and stop worrying about our Lord. I daresay he's well enough. And stop worrying about your sister. Your music will make a difference where it's meant to. It's brilliant.'

'Is it, Mum? Is it really good enough to help troubled souls?'

'The curse of being an artist is never knowing if you're good enough. It's torture trying to bridge the gap between imagination and expression.'

'How do *you* know?' This unexpected wisdom stunned Mary.

Kathleen looked out the window, straight through the angel perched in view. 'Mama's music was as beautiful as yours, but she never thought it was good enough to be played outside our little cottage. The world missed out on something truly great because Magdalene Muir doubted her genius.' Impulsively she clasped her daughter's hand. 'Don't make the same mistake.'

ACCENTO

Accented, emphasized

The Saturday morning walks were a carefully orchestrated routine. At nine o'clock Mary left her flat and set off along Milson Rd, then turned right into a lane lined with tall, skinny Victorian terraces. At the end of the lane, she turned right again and walked for thirty minutes along a tree-lined boulevard with houses more like Shalamar: mansions behind sandstone walls. When she reached an alleyway, she turned right once more, then right again into Milson Road, completing the rectangle and achieving a satisfying geometry.

This particular Saturday the sun was shining but the air hinted of autumn chill. About halfway along the boulevard, she caught an alluring scent – the spring-like perfume of jasmine. Distracted by a lure more powerful than her fear of change, she walked in the other direction for several unfamiliar blocks until she found the source: a delicatessen.

She hadn't any money on her but she went in anyway, pretending interest in the shelves stacked with pickled and preserved vegetables, jars of condiments, packets of tea and canisters of cooking ingredients so unusual they might have been for witches' spells. The blocks of colour on every shelf ranged with perfect deliberation from fire engine red through the colour spectrum to forest green. She could find no fault in this design nor felt any impulse to straighten a single item.

Whoever was responsible for stacking the shelves had a mind as detail-oriented as her own.

Inside, the scent of jasmine was utterly overpowering yet the customers who were shopping or waiting for coffee beans to be ground seemed oblivious. Perhaps they were used to it. She looked for something that could produce such an enchanting perfume – scented candles, aromatherapy oil, soap – but there was nothing. And then she saw him. Behind the counter stood the most beautiful person she had ever seen. He bore a striking resemblance to Gabriel but there were no wings visible and why was an angel working in a delicatessen? She drew nearer to get a better look. He was serving an elderly woman, his sienna-coloured eyes focused on her with tender curiosity as if he was trying to understand her needs. *Or her species.*

He was tall and slender with golden curls and skin so translucent the veins in his temples showed as pale violet etchings. Above those beautiful eyes, his eyebrows slanted upwards like the brushstrokes of an artist disinclined to finalise his masterpiece. Suddenly he sniffed the air, looked around and found Mary, his eyes widening into shock. He swayed slightly and the dark-haired man standing next to him shot out a supporting hand.

'I'm fine,' he assured him with a gentle touch. Then he looked back at Mary and when their eyes locked, the scent of jasmine overwhelmed her and made her sneeze.

'If you have a cold, you should leave.' It was the old lady. 'He's sick enough already.'

He didn't look sick.

But then he coughed violently and a wad of tissues, proffered by the dark man, were speckled with blood.

'Forgive me,' he told the customers. 'I'll be fine. Please carry on shopping.' Again he touched the dark man's arm. 'Thank you, Alfio.'

Alfio's smile – a presenting of even white teeth – seemed a little strained. 'I'll close early.'

'No, I'm fine now.'

'At least sit down.'

'I'm fine,' he insisted. Again he sought Mary. 'Do you mind waiting until the shop's clear so we can talk?'

'I'll wait,' she said, her voice steady but her knees wobbly.

When Mary was the only customer left, Alfio put a CLOSED sign on the front door, locked it, and asked, 'What's this about, Rigel?'

'You *are* Rigel!' Mary swayed against the nearest shelf leading Alfio to place a supporting hand under *her* elbow.

'So you know my partner?'

'Partner? Gabriel didn't tell me his brother was –'

'Gay? I bet he didn't. Did Gabriel send you to spy on us?' Alfio sounded angry.

'No, he didn't,' said Rigel, his eyes fixed on Mary. 'How *is* my brother?'

'He misses you.'

'He could have called or paid us a visit,' Alfio said, stripping off his work apron and slapping it down on the counter. 'Since he clearly knows where we are.'

'He doesn't know,' protested Mary.

'So you just stumbled in here by accident?' Alfio raised his eyebrows.

'Yes.'

'Hmmm. Did Gabriel happen to mention that Rigel's *loving* family has disowned him for being gay?'

Mary stared at Rigel. 'Is *that* the real reason you left heaven?'

'No,' Rigel mouthed.

'Heaven?' Alfio laughed. 'Florence isn't heaven, my dear. It's a hypocritical old town with a long, dark, bloody history. But it is *close* to heaven. My grandfather lives just outside Florence in a little slice of heaven called *Bellesol*.' He spoke the name with reverence.

'His grandfather's vineyard,' explained Rigel, his magnificent eyes, so like Gabriel's, watching her tenderly. 'Be gentle with this lady, Alfio. She's deserving of mercy, having been so merciful herself.'

'Protecting Gabriel,' sneered Alfio. 'So, why are you here if not to spy for the family?'

'I smelled jasmine and followed the scent here.'

Alfio shook his head. 'That doesn't make any sense.'

Mary's focus was on the angel. 'Rigel, your brother's been looking everywhere for you.'

Rigel slumped down onto a stool. 'So, he's been home. He knows Father's gone.'

'Yes, he knows.'

'Rigel's been looking for his brother for the last six years,' said Alfio. 'No one in his family has called or written in all that time and now you turn up out of the blue claiming Gabriel misses him. And you live nearby? You walked here? By chance? Trailing the scent of jasmine? Please, Mary, don't treat us like fools. Gabriel sent you. What I want to know is why he didn't have the balls to come in person?'

'He has wings.'

'Please,' said Alfio. 'You think he's an angel?'

Rigel gave Mary a subtle shake of his head, warning her not to answer.

'A woman in love sees wings where there are horns,' said Alfio.

'How *are* you, Mary?' said Rigel.

'How did you know my name?'

'I remember you,' he said softly.

'But when did we meet?'

'Surely you remember,' said Alfio. 'I'm hungry. Shall we continue the conversation over lunch upstairs? Are you hungry, Mary?'

'I don't want to intrude.'

'You're not leaving until we've talked,' said Rigel. 'Stay for lunch, please. Alfio is a superb cook.'

'I am indeed. My grandfather taught me.' Alfio locked up the till. 'Could you manage something to eat, darling?'

Rigel shook his head. 'I used to love eating.'

'You loved every aspect of life,' Alfio replied.

They exchanged a tender glance, and Mary looked at Alfio properly for the first time. His eyes were topaz-coloured and kind, despite his gruffness. He was actually very attractive and had he been standing next to anyone but Rigel she would certainly have noticed him.

'Come along,' said Alfio, slipping his hand under Rigel's arm. 'Let me help you upstairs.'

As they climbed the stairs, Rigel looked back at Mary. 'Now I understand why I couldn't find my brother in Florence when I came to take him home. He'd found you.'

'Take him home?' said Alfio. 'But I thought you said his father was upset with him.'

'He was for a while but that was all forgiven long ago.'

'He was only following orders,' Mary added. 'Is there no tolerance in your family?'

'I like her!' Alfio laughed. 'You can't mess with Italian fathers, Mary, especially not when you go against the family.'

'*Italian* fathers?' Mary drummed a tune midair. 'But surely you know –'

'The Don has a long reach,' interjected Alfio, touching the side of his nose. 'The Godfather may be gone but one day Gabriel will be sent for.'

'Yes,' said Mary. 'He will be sent for and he will go.'

'Not even a fallen sparrow escapes our Father's notice,' Rigel said, pausing at the top of the stairs to catch his breath. 'Father cared for Gabriel more than he realised. But my brother can be so stubborn at times. Father hoped he'd listen to me. That's why I was sent to bring him home.'

'Where he'll be shot,' muttered Alfio.

'Hush, my love. But Father's gone so everything's changed at home. Tell me, Mary, has my brother been back to Florence in the last few years? He loved it once.'

'He spent a little time there a few years ago but he hasn't been back since.'

'Wouldn't dare,' murmured Alfio.

'I love the colours you've used,' said Mary, changing the subject.

'Alfio chose them all,' said Rigel.

The apartment was decorated in strong, rich Italian colours, the walls painted ruby red. Glazed pots sprouted luxuriant ferns and on one wall a fantastic tapestry hung, its ebony background covered in brightly-coloured birds clinging to ropes of stylized blue vines.

'A little piece of Tuscany,' Alfio said, leading the way to the kitchen where he pulled out a chair for Rigel and another for Mary.

Rigel coughed again.

'I have congestive heart disease, Mary,' he said. 'My lungs are filling with fluid.'

'We take it day by day,' Alfio added in a clipped, precise voice. 'Chat amongst yourselves while I prepare lunch.'

'This flesh was only intended to last long enough to find my brother.'

'Interesting way of putting it,' Alfio said cynically.

The kitchen was a compact room, neat as a pin with open shelving displaying crockery and cooking utensils in orderly rows of blocked colour. Alfio bustled about, humming.

'I'm sorry you're so ill,' Mary said. 'Is that why you stopped looking for Gabriel?'

'No. I fell in love.' He glanced at Alfio. 'And the experience has been worth every ounce of pain: physical and spiritual.'

Alfio turned around, hand on heart. 'For me, too, Caro

mio.' He swung away quickly, busying himself with his preparations.

Rigel watched his partner tenderly. 'He's a good man, Mary. Easy to love.'

Up close, the angel's eyes were not sienna like Gabriel's after all, but more the tawny colour of wild animals like lions or owls.

'What kind of spiritual pain have you had?' Mary asked.

He looked back at her. 'Cataclysmic. The changes are so profound' – he lowered his voice – 'they will cost me heaven, I'm afraid.' He spoke up again. 'I believe in love now, Mary. I no longer follow the light.'

'It's hard when you've been raised a Catholic,' Alfio interjected. 'The gay thing, you know. They don't see it as real love. But it is.'

'My brother found love once.' His eyes locked with Mary's. 'Has he found it again?'

'He only trusts light not love.'

'Still,' Rigel sighed, 'my brother is driven and possessed of the kind of genius that sets a soul apart. He is lonely.'

'I know.'

Rigel touched her hand. 'I'm glad you understand.'

'Oh, the flawed genius deserves our pity.' Alfio set the table with napkins, spoons and forks. 'But his dying brother is ostracised for being gay.'

'Be easy, Alfio. We have a very special guest.'

'With a very special bias. So, Mary,' Alfio asked with forced brightness, 'does Gabriel live with you?'

She made a minor adjustment to her spoon, lined it up with the fork. 'No, he comes and goes as he pleases.'

'How convenient.'

'My brother has always been like that. You mustn't be offended, Mary.'

'Oh no. We can't expect Peter Pan to grow up.'

205

Rigel ignored his partner's comment and smiled at Mary's arrangement of the spoon and fork. 'It's neater that way.'

She blushed. 'I get nervous if things are not in perfect order.'

'And yet you tolerate Gabriel's coming and going.' Alfio was filling a large pot with water.

'I can't force Gabriel to do anything. He hates being controlled.' She scratched her palms.

Rigel touched her hands. 'No need to scratch. I'm here now.'

His touch was instantly calming. Her palms stopped itching and sweet music began to flow, bubbly as water over pebbles. 'When did you lose your wings?'

'Wings again.' Alfio laughed. 'Every woman asks him the same thing. I sometimes wonder that myself.'

'I'm not like my brother. I prefer to blend in when I come to a new place.'

'You didn't want to look like an angel.'

'He can't help looking like an angel,' Alfio said. 'All northern Italians look like angels. Sadly, I'm just your typical dark-haired Italian.'

'I think you're handsome.'

'*Sono d'accordo*,' said Rigel. 'Do you speak Italian, Mary?'

'No.'

'I said, *I agree*. We speak Italian when we're alone.' He leaned closer. 'Start learning the language. You'll need it later.'

'I will?'

He smiled. 'Certainly. Alfio tell Mary about Bellesol.'

'Bellesol is in Tuscany. My grandfather's vineyard.' Again he placed his hand on his heart. 'I spent my childhood holidays there…flew to Italy every summer from the age of six. My grandfather makes the best wine in Italy.' He plucked a handful of fresh basil leaves off a plant on the window sill. 'You must come for dinner one night and share a bottle of my grandfather's Shiraz with us.' He coughed discreetly. 'Bring Gabriel.'

'That might be difficult.'

Rigel touched Mary's hand. 'I need to see my brother. Perhaps I could come to you?'

'Damn it, Rigel, you're sick! He can get his arse over here!' cried Alfio.

'He can't, my love, he's ... argh ...' Rigel pressed his hand to his chest. 'I'm sorry.'

Alfio was at his side in an instant with a glass of water and two white tablets. 'Five minutes, darling, and these will kick in.'

Rigel swallowed the tablets and patted Alfio's arm. 'Thank you.'

Alfio returned to chopping ripe red tomatoes. 'All right, darling?' he asked with forced calm after a minute or so.

'Yes, easing off now.' Rigel took a deep breath. 'Mary, I never knew what humanity had to endure. You're all so brave.'

'As if you're not human,' said Alfio, shaking his head.

Again Rigel smiled at Mary and shook his head. 'Let's change the subject.'

'How did you two meet?' she asked.

'I was in Sydney looking for Gabriel. I'd traced his scent to Australia after I left Florence.'

'Gabriel leaves quite a trail,' Alfio said. 'Broken hearts, broken promises, broken lives.'

'Anyway, I was standing on the Opera House concourse wondering where I would shelter for the night when Alfio kindly offered me a room here.'

Alfio huffed. 'I was trying to seduce him.'

'Don't listen to him, Mary. He's very kind. That was six years ago.'

'The happiest years of my life and now ...' Alfio swiped his hand across his eyes. 'I need some more onions. I'll just pop downstairs and get some.'

'So he can cry. He won't shed tears in front of me,' Rigel said. 'Mary, what is Gabriel planning?'

'To save the world and then leave.' She tapped a tune on the table.

'I see.' He looked at her hands. 'What are you doing?'

She folded her hands in her lap. 'I sometimes play the music I'm hearing in my head.'

Rigel closed his eyes, listening. 'Beautiful.' His eyes flew open. 'Does my brother hear your music?'

'Yes, that's what brought him to me. He plans to fill my music with light and use it to enlighten the world.' *Before he leaves.*

Rigel's eyes darkened to ochre. 'That would be a huge mistake. The world must remain as it is: muddled, messy and believing in love.'

'I agree.' Mary wrung her hands. 'People have died. People who got in Gabriel's way have died.'

'He's so stubborn.' Again he took her hands in his, instilling calm. 'I'll speak to him and try to make him understand he mustn't meddle. How many has he killed?'

'He says three but I think it's five. One death was merciful.'

'My family will take care of them.' Rigel glanced at Mary's stomach. '*His* child?'

'Yes. You seem sure. How do you know?'

'There's a pink glow around your womb. My brother is incorrigible but this time he must honour his heart and' – he glanced down at her belly again – 'not shirk his responsibilities.'

Alfio returned with a bag of onions. 'Holding hands the minute I turn my back. I don't know. Italian men are such flirts, Mary.'

Rigel laughed. 'You leave me alone with a beautiful woman what can you expect?'

They were joking of course. Mary knew that, but he had called her beautiful and the handsome Alfio had not disagreed. The jovial atmosphere continued over lunch. Mary told them about her music and Alfio spoke of winemaking at Bellesol.

208

Rigel smiled and listened, watching them both fondly as he picked at his small meal. The love between the two men was palpable and touched Mary's heart, despite the looming tragedy. Before she left, they planned the brothers' reunion.

'So – your place tomorrow evening at seven, Mary?' Alfio checked. 'I'll walk you home so I know exactly where to bring Rigel.'

Rigel squeezed Mary's hand. 'His heart is pure. You can trust him.'

'Gabriel?'

'No, *him*.' He nodded at Alfio who was re-stacking the colour-coded dishes.

It was dark when Alfio and Mary reached her gate.

'He's using you.'

'I know.'

'You're just a safe harbour for him while he figures out where he's going next.'

'I know.'

'But it doesn't matter?'

She shook her head.

'He has quite a hold on you, doesn't he?'

Mary swallowed. 'You think I'm crazy?'

'No. Maybe madly in love. Does he look like Rigel?'

'Yes, except for the wings.'

'Right. We worship at the same altar, Mary, but my angel's dying and yours will abandon you one of these days.' He kissed her cheek. 'For what it's worth, I like you and if you ever need a friend I'm just around the corner.'

'Thank you.'

He turned to leave.

'Alfio, who arranged the shelves in your shop?'

'I did. Why?'

'I like them.'

'I need order. It makes me feel safe.'

'You, too!' *It was the first time she'd ever met anyone like her.* 'For me, everything has its own special place and I get anxious if things are untidy.'

'I get anxious when things aren't colour-co-ordinated. It drives Rigel nuts at times.'

'I drive my mother nuts.'

He laughed and for the first time in her life she laughed, too. A fall of broken stars accompanied them.

'Look! A meteor shower.' Alfio pointed.

They watched until the last star burned away, their laughter intermittent ripples.

'Tell me,' said Alfio, 'why are two highly ordered people risking emotional chaos by falling in love with Da Vinci angels? Our lives will be a mess when they leave us.'

The laughter stopped. They looked at each for a long moment.

'But at least our shelves will be neat,' said Mary.

Alfio laughed out loud. 'Neat shelves. Life will go on.' He waved over his shoulder as he walked away, an occasional hoot of mirth punctuating his footfall.

'He made me laugh,' she said, marveling. 'I understood a joke.'

Gabriel was waiting for her, his light fracturing into a sunburst, his eyes dancing with sienna flame. 'Where have you been all day?'

'Out.' A bubble of mirth rose up and burst.

'What's so funny?' he asked suspiciously.

'Nothing,' she said, dissolving into giggles.

Gabriel stared at her. 'Have you been drinking?'

She shook her head. 'Your brother's coming here tomorrow night to talk to you.'

Gabriel swayed. Took a step backwards. 'You found Rigel?'

She nodded. 'He works in a delicatessen only four blocks from here. He has a lover – Alfio.'

210

'A *human* lover?' He shook his head, disbelieving.

'For the last six years.'

Gabriel's light swelled and receded as he processed this information. 'So that's why he stopped looking for me.'

'Yes. I'm sorry, Gabriel. He's very keen to speak to you, though. But I must warn you he no longer follows the light.' She didn't mention his belief in love or his illness.

'So, he won't help me enlighten the world?'

'Probably not.'

He stumbled to the balcony door. 'I need to think. I'll be –' he shook his head. 'I don't know where I'll be.'

'In your cave?'

He had sworn he'd never spend another night in that cold, guano-encrusted hole but he had nowhere else to go. 'Yes, I'll be in my cave. What time is he coming?'

'Seven.'

GRANDIOSO

Played grandly

Standing in the mouth of the cave, he watched sea and sky cleave in graded blue harmony, enjoying a brief connection before the sky bruised and cast a wine-dark stain on the sea. Seconds later the sun launched a spectacular volley of vermillion spears over the horizon just before it sank. The rising tide shattered breakers against the boot of the cliff and the seventh wave, always the largest in a set, exploded against the rocks, sending a jet of spume over him. He leapt back, shaking the water from his robes and hair, and moved deeper into the cave. The bats were stirring, squealing and stretching leathery wings, waking up for the night's foraging and soon a dark silent stream would head west to raid suburban bowers. The sky rapidly deepened from purple to indigo and a bright display of stars, planets, asteroids, comets – the flotsam and jetsam of past galaxies – popped to light.

He felt both excited and terrified about this meeting with his brother. A thousand years, even by angel measure, is a long separation and much can alter. Universes. Opinions. Hearts. Mary said Rigel had fallen in love. He could scarcely believe that his own brother, who had nursed him through the pain of Miriam's rejection, could now succumb to the same disease. For make no mistake – love was an illness. There was no recovery. Only remission.

A mere fortnight had altered Miriam's heart.

He had waited for her at the well, eager to tell her he'd changed his mind and was prepared to lose his wings, don permanent flesh and live as a human being with her. He would help her raise their son of heaven even though this decision would cost him his Father's trust. But what else could he do? He'd seen what human beings did to those who broke the rules – they were hung, ostracised, tortured, even crucified. Unwed mothers were stoned.

Mary would be stoned...unless she *married*.

'No!' he had cried aloud, imagining his beloved broken and bloodied, or worse, in the arms of a husband.

'No,' he whispered. 'I won't share you with anyone. Certainly not a human.'

And so, he decided to drop his wings for the woman he loved.

All day he waited by the well and finally at sunset she arrived, approaching cautiously, every so often glancing behind as if she expected to be followed. When she reached the well he leapt out of hiding.

'Miriam, I'm back.'

But she looked right through him as if he was invisible and then drew water from the well, her sights turned inwards, her movements mechanical.

'Miriam? It's me, Gabriel.'

She ignored him.

Her dismissal hit him harder than any other reprimand or rejection, even from his Father. In that moment, the light and hope in his soul bled away and he had never quite recovered his faith or equilibrium since.

And now his brother was in love.

He leaned against the rocky wall. 'Do not be fooled by love, Rigel. It is fickle and cruel and turns like a serpent. You will see. And after he has shattered your heart we will conquer love with light and no one will suffer its faithless pangs again.'

Miriam once told him he was addicted to control because he had no faith in love.

He slammed his palm against the rock. 'How can anyone have faith in something that alters on a whim? You said your heart was mine forever. You said you'd wait and yet you married Joseph.'

He held his hand up to the sky, capturing a little pallid moonlight on his palm. 'Light travels in a straight, unfaltering line. Now that is something you can put your faith in.'

The sea heaved and pitched, rocking the crescent moon like a bark. He remembered the time of the appointment. He had lingered long enough. Now that the stars were mapping their familiar patterns on the sky he dived out over the ocean, braced the rising thermal currents and flew south over the necklace of northern beaches towards Cremorne.

A star fell.

Treading water in the currents of air he watched it dissolve into vapour. How quickly things can alter. One minute burning gases and boiling rock, the next, cooling cloud and a handful of dust. He shuddered at the reversal, wondered if his Father had abdicated heaven in a similarly swift heel-turn instant, leaving his playground kingdom to the impulsive seraphim. His brother would know what had happened, and hopefully, he would also make a reversal. He *would* abandon fickle love and champion light.

If not, then Gabriel was the last sword-bearing angel in the holy battle for enlightenment.

RALLENTANDO

A direction to a performer to gradually play slower

Rigel placed one foot heavily in front of the other as he climbed the stairs, pausing every so often to catch his breath and then grimacing because this small life-sustaining act caused him pain. At one point he stumbled and would have fallen but for Alfio's support, and, even though the evening was balmy, he shivered under his heavy coat. By the time they reached Mary's apartment, each new breath rattled and hurt.

Mary gasped when she answered the door, for the angel had deteriorated dramatically in the past twenty-four hours.

'Come in,' she said, stepping back. 'Sit down, please.'

Alfio ushered Rigel to the couch where he crumpled.

'What's happened to you?' Mary asked.

'This flesh is failing because' – a dry, hacking cough – 'I won't need it soon. After I have spoken to my brother I will leave.' He looked at Alfio. 'But I won't go far.'

Alfio clenched his fists but made no comment. 'Do you need anything? A painkiller? Some water?'

'A cup of tea?' Mary offered.

He looked at them tenderly. 'Nothing, thank you. You're both so kind.'

'Alfio? Tea?'

Alfio looked tired. There were dark rings under his eyes and his mouth was set in a grim, sad line. 'Thank you, yes. Milk, no sugar.'

The scent of jasmine was infused with the sickly sweet odour of imminent death. Rigel coughed and pressed a wad of tissues to his mouth.

Alfio shifted his weight, glanced irritably at the front door. 'You'd think he'd be here on time after making his sick brother climb three flights of stairs.'

'He'll be here.' Mary hurried into the kitchen.

'Do sit down, my love. I've always gone to my brother. He doesn't usually come to me but he'll make an exception tonight.'

'Does he know how ill you are?'

It's just failing flesh not failing light. 'I'm sure Mary's told him.'

'Hasn't seen you in six years and he can't be on time.'

A thousand years actually. 'It's only seven fifteen.'

'It's rude and disrespectful to be late.' Alfio shot another furious glance at the door.

Mary returned with two cups. 'Alfio, why don't you and I have our tea on the balcony and let Gabriel and Rigel catch up in private?'

Rigel shot her a grateful look. 'Good idea.'

'I'd rather wait so Rigel doesn't have to get up to answer the door.'

'He'll let himself in. He…er…has his own key.'

'So he can come and go as he pleases.' Alfio rolled his eyes. 'He must be one hell of a lover.'

'The balcony is through the kitchen door. I'll meet you out there.'

'Be with you in a minute.' Alfio crouched in front of Rigel. 'Don't let Gabriel walk all over you the way he walks all over Mary,' he whispered.

'I won't.' His eyes danced with gold flame. 'Alfio…thank you … for everything. I'll never be far away from you.'

216

'Stop it. You're making me nervous. Maybe I should stay here with you.'

'No. Keep Mary company.'

Alfio looked at him for a long minute, his eyes shining. 'There will never be anyone else for me.'

'Don't close your heart to love.' He reached for Alfio's hand. 'I want you to be her Joseph.'

'What do you mean?'

'Look after Mary and her child.' His tone urgent. 'She's pregnant by my brother.'

'When did she tell you?'

'Yesterday.' His breath came in gasps. 'My brother won't look after them. His history with women is bad. Will you?'

'I can't.'

'Don't make me beg. Do it, please. For me.'

'Yes. For you.'

'Promise me.' His grip tightening.

Alfio nodded. 'I promise.'

Now Rigel relaxed his grip, leaned back and looked at Alfio for a long silent moment. 'Your features are recorded on my soul. I will know you the day I wake. Even the waters of Lethe won't let me forget.'

'Rigel, you're frightening me. Don't leave me...'

'I'll never leave you.' He smiled. 'Go to Mary now. I must speak with my brother alone.'

'I'll be on the balcony.' Alfio stood. 'If he makes some unseemly crack about your sexuality, you call me. OK?'

Rigel watched the man he loved walk away, recording every nuance of his manner forever on his soul. The balcony door clicked and he leaned back and waited.

They clung to their cups like crucifixes. Refracted light from across the inlet casting leaf shadows on their faces and hands.

'Shall we talk about Bellesol?' Mary asked, hoping the subject would engage him.

Wing shadows pulsed over them as bats made their silent passage to suburban boweries.

'Mary, are you pregnant?' he asked suddenly. 'Rigel tells me you're pregnant by Gabriel.'

No point in denying it. It would be obvious soon enough. 'Yes, I am. I haven't told my mother yet.'

'Why not?'

'She'll start organising my wedding.'

He looked at her sidelong. 'Has Gabriel asked you to marry him?'

'No.'

'I see. What does your mother think of Gabriel?'

'She doesn't know about him. She will think the child is someone else's.' *Robert's.*

Again he glanced at her. The girl was really very surprising, seemingly shy and quiet but clearly very popular with men. 'How many boyfriends *do* you have, Mary?'

'Oh, none. I mean...just Gabriel...and I had a one-night stand with my ex-boss.'

'Rigel made me promise to watch over you and the child.'

'I can look after myself. You mustn't worry about us.'

He was looking up at the sky. He was even more handsome in profile: aquiline nose, high forehead and strong chin.

'Why do you put up with Gabriel?' he asked.

'He knows me, and he's in love with' – she hesitated – 'my music.'

A beat. 'Rigel thinks he'll abandon you and your child.'

'He will.'

He swivelled to face her. 'That's absurd, Mary! You're worthy of love. True, loyal love!'

'I can't bear any other man to touch me,' she whispered.

'I see.' A pause. 'Why him?'

218

'Because he hears my music.'

'Everyone will hear your music when you record it.'

'But he heard it first. He made me believe in myself. Do you understand how important that is?' Tears sparkling in her eyes. 'You have to imagine what it was like to have no friends, no confidence, no hope...and then someone beautiful comes into your life and tells you you're special. Tells you that your music is so heavenly people will love you for it.'

'How do you feel when he touches you, Mary?'

She thought for a minute. 'Holy. Clean. Ecstatic. I was a plain misfit until the most beautiful, extraordinary man on earth claimed me.'

'You're not plain. You have beautiful eyes and a beautiful soul.'

She widened those beautiful eyes. 'Thank you.'

'I understand how it feels to be loved by an angel.'

'An angel?' Her palms itching. 'So you *do* know?'

'Rigel's an angel to me and I know you think Gabriel's an angel though if you ask me, I'd say he's a devilish rogue. But who am I to judge you? You and I are human after all.'

A flash of light shimmered over the inlet, silver-edging the canopy. Gabriel alighted on the balustrade, sienna eyes appraising Alfio, then Mary. 'Why are you holding his hand?' He sniffed the air. 'Jasmine. Is he inside?'

Mary nodded imperceptibly.

Alfio continued to stare at the inlet, oblivious to the angel perched in front of him.

'Open the door for me, Mary. We can't have the mortal thinking the place is haunted. And let go of his hand.'

Mary eased her hand free of Alfio's. 'I'll make more tea.'

Alfio half-stood. 'I should check on Rigel.'

'I'll do it. You relax.'

She opened the balcony door and went inside, Gabriel slipping in after her.

A flash of light, an explosion of pine and roses and, 'My brother!' His voice charged with emotion.

Or was it Rigel who spoke?

After making fresh tea she went back out to Alfio.

'Has Gabriel arrived?' Alfio asked as soon as Mary returned.

'Yes, they're chatting now. Please tell me more about your grandfather's vineyard.'

'Bellesol.' His eyes shone as he spoke of the place he called *a little slice of heaven*. 'The house was built in the 1700s. It has a cellar and a secret garden. It stands on the ridge of a hill overlooking the valley. Idyllic sunsets. My grandfather hoped I'd bring my children there.' He laughed softly. 'I'll never have children of course … but if by some miracle I did, that's where I'd raise them. Nonno, my grandfather, would love that.'

'Is there a Mrs. Nonno?'

'My grandmother died when I was a kid. Nonno has lived alone for many years.'

The music showed her a house on a hill accessed by a long, cypress-lined drive. A beautiful place. But lonely.

He pulled a chain linked to a small key from under his shirt. 'This is the key to the front door. Nonno has one and I have one. I'd hoped to take Rigel there.' Alfio sighed. 'Why did Rigel ask *me* to look after you and your child? We hardly know each other.'

'Because he trusts you.'

The key momentarily glowed. 'He can. There will always be a place for you and your child at Bellesol.'

'Will you move to Italy after –?'

'I can't stay here. Too many memories.' He shivered despite the warmth of the evening.

'Did you say Bellesol is near Florence?'

'Only a twenty minute drive.'

He loves Florence. If Rigel can persuade him to stay earthbound he'd be happier if I lived near Florence.

220

'My grandfather really *does* make the best wine in Italy,' he continued. 'His secret is that he harvests the grapes when he first sees the moon in the daytime sky.' He traced his thumbnail with his finger. 'A sliver of moon and then the grapes have to be picked that day.'

'I can see it,' she said, her music building pictures of sun-ripened grapes purpling in clusters on nuggety vines. She plucked a grape, held it up to the sun. The dark seeds chambered within would incubate great wines and new vines. Back on the balcony, a sudden breath of wind shivered the canopy and wires of lightning streaked down from the clear sky.

Alfio leapt up, his eyes glittering. 'Was that a meteor? Did you see it?'

But Mary was tuned inwards to her womb which fluttered with life for the first time.

'Wait here, Alfio,' she said calmly. 'I'll just check how things are going.'

'I'm coming with you.'

'Trust me. I won't be long.'

He sank back down onto the chair as she locked the balcony door behind her.

ANIMA

Soul, spirit in the music

𝄞

Gabriel stood in the centre of the room, the air around him glowing, crackling. He did not look at her but raised his hand slowly, indicating the couch. 'You need to see to my brother.'

Rigel lay with his eyes closed as if in sleep, his face soft with peace.

'Is he –?' *But she knew the answer.*

'Dead?' Gabriel laughed. 'No. He has cheated death. And me.'

'How?'

'My brother bathes in the waters of Lethe while I remain here tortured with memories. He will be born again. To you, Mary.'

So that's why he asked Alfio to look after him.

'I'd better get Alfio.'

How can I deliver the news?

'The mortal can wait. My brother refused to support me.' His eyes flashed. 'He *ordered* me not to meddle with humanity. I, who created all that can be measured, have no stake in the future.' He stared bleakly out the window. 'I am lost, Mary.'

'Did he mention me at all?'

'Yes, he told me to stay and help you raise the child who will be both my son and my destroyer.'

'I don't understand.'

'Rigel said he will thwart my plans. He would drain your music of light.' His lips faltered. 'The Renaissance is over, he said. Forget the past, he said.'

'Stay with me, Gabriel.'

'You don't need me. Your music stands alone. My brother says it must.' He nodded at the balcony. 'He wants you to go to Italy with the mortal. He wants to stay with the man he trusts more than his own brother. Oh, yes, my brother explained it all very carefully to me. The world doesn't need light. Only love. *Love*.' He laughed bitterly. 'Nobody needs me, Mary.'

'I need you, Gabriel.' Scratching. Scratching.

'You don't. You're spectacular.' He gave her a tender look. 'Why else would I have chosen you?'

'Then stay with me.' She beat her fists against his chest. 'Love me!'

'I can't. I'm sorry.' And with that he left her. His fading soul moved through the balcony door, passed by Alfio unseen, then rose and melted into the night, a ripple across the moon.

Mary sank to her knees, rocked back and forth until she heard a pounding on the balcony door as strong as the pounding of her heart. She got up slowly, moved across the room and unlocked the door. 'I'm so sorry, Alfio.'

'What's happened?'

'It's Rigel. I'm sorry.'

He rushed past her. Then froze.

'Rigel?' He took a tentative, disbelieving step toward the couch. 'Are you sleeping, my love?'

Mary leaned against the piano, her hand soothing the fluttering soul in her womb.

'Rigel?' He knelt and stroked the limp arms and chest. Kissed the beautiful face.

'Rigel.' The truth seeped into his soul until he collapsed under its weight. He sobbed silently.

Mary could only watch, wait and nurse her own grief.

Moments passed. Then Alfio cried out in raw, guttural agony before lifting his beloved in his arms and walking to the front door.

Mary hurried to open it. 'I'm so sorry.'

With neither a word nor a backward glance, Alfio carried his lover into the night.

DRONE

Dull, monotonous tone. A bass note held under a melody.

All day the women came and went from the well, their robes black sails on the horizon, the shimmering heat making flotilla mirages of their departure.

After Miriam had ignored him at the well, he had returned to heaven, hoping to be given a new assignment. To forget Miriam. But his Father had refused, saying, 'You tempted a woman to fall in love with you knowing you would leave. It was a simple message, Gabriel. I gave you a straightforward assignment. How many times have I warned you against complications? I want you to take time out and think about your behaviour.'

But all he could think about was Miriam.

'You took advantage of her, my son,' said his Father a week later when they spoke again, 'and now you are feeling the consequences.'

'She needed me Father. I was only thinking of her.'

'You fed off her adulation, my son. Once again your vanity has conquered you.'

Gabriel's knees had buckled and he knelt. 'Forgive me, Father. Please give me another chance – an assignment far from earth. The Pleiades perhaps?'

'The Pleiadians have seen the light. No, Gabriel, maybe it's time I relieved you of your post and assigned another messenger.

Your brother, perhaps? Rigel will resist the temptations of the flesh.'

'Do you think you would be strong enough to resist the temptations of the flesh, Rigel, if Father made *you* the messenger?' Gabriel asked his brother when they were alone.

'I think so. I find the concept of temptation unreal, brother.'

'I hope your innocence remains unspoiled. Humans can be very alluring.' Gabriel looked longingly at earth. 'I have to see her again, Rigel.'

'My brother, why would you risk everything for love? You don't even believe in it.'

'She's all alone and she thinks I don't care for her. I *do* care, Rigel. The least I can do is tell her.'

'I will not pretend I understand this torment of the flesh you suffer from but I can see how conflicted you are, my brother. Go to her. I'll cover for you if Father asks. But don't stay away too long.'

The very next day Gabriel snuck back to earth to find Miriam.

And so the archangel Gabriel waited for Miriam by the well. Every day he looked for her amongst the sloe-eyed beauties whose gaze passed over him, unseeing. But Miriam did not come. Then it occurred to him that he may have forgotten her face. Miriam insisted her features were common enough and she'd be lost in a crowd. But her soul was unique: blue as the sky inflamed with light. There was no forgetting that.

After two weeks, his anxiety increased. Had her family realised she was pregnant and locked her away, awaiting stoning for her sin? And then there was the constant nagging worry that his Father would find out he had truanted and be angry with him. No angel could bear God's wrath. It was never delivered violently. It was gentle and imbued with disappointment that lingered like slow-working poison in the soul.

Gabriel sighed as the sun sank below the dunes and the desert air cooled rapidly. Long shadows bled across the sand. Two weeks and no sign of her. The sudden appearance of a woman on the road alerted his senses. She was hastening towards the well alone and carried no ewer. Flowing around her indigo robes was a familiar bluish glow. Closer still and he recognised her distinctive walk, the sway of her hips, her proud carriage and above all, her colours: blue shot through with gold.

'Miriam!' He leapt up and spoke with passion. 'I love you with all my heart and soul. Mary!' He used the intimate version of her name reserved for her friends.

She looked past him towards a man of middle years who approached from the opposite direction.

'All right, Miriam,' he said when he reached her. 'I've come. At sunset as your note instructed. But why must we meet in secret? Why can't we meet in the light of day? At a *respectable* hour.'

The man called her Miriam so he wasn't a close friend.

'What I have to say is not respectable, Joseph.'

He looked around nervously. 'You know my good reputation, Miriam. I offered you marriage and you refused.'

'Joseph,' she said, raising her chin. 'I am with child.'

'Mary, don't tell him!' cried Gabriel. 'He'll cast the first stone. He's just said he's *respectable*!' But she did not or *would not* hear him.

'And the father?' Joseph asked, his eyes patient, his expression kind.

'He's abandoned me,' she said unflinchingly.

'No, Mary! I haven't abandoned you!' *Still* she did not hear him.

'Was he young and handsome? Will you now accept me?' There was a note of sorrow.

'Will you still have *me*?'

'NO!' cried Gabriel. 'I'm here!'

Joseph looked down. 'Do you still love the father?'

Gabriel held his breath.

'I will always love him.'

Gabriel sank to his knees in the sand. 'And I will always love you.'

If she heard she gave no sign.

'Have you any feelings for me at all?' Joseph pursued.

She drew her blue cloak around her and shivered. 'I respect you.'

The sky had turned from purple to ebony and the first stars appeared like fairy torches. 'I would give anything for your love, Miriam, but if respect is all you can give, then I thank God for this small mercy.'

'Thank you, Joseph. I will try to make you happy.' She kissed his hand.

'Kneel and pray with me.'

Miriam knelt but did not pray. While Joseph made his pledge before God to protect her and the unborn child, she stared vacantly at the sky, looking straight through the angel who knelt in front of her.

'When shall we tell our parents the news?' Joseph asked her.

'Tomorrow is soon enough. Go now.'

When he left, Miriam beat her fist against her heart. 'Gabriel! Gabriel!'

'I'm right beside you, my love. Look at me!' he called frantically.

But her soul, once open to him, was now sealed. He left the desert that night believing he'd lost her forever.

Now, two thousand years later, he listened intently as his brother whispered these words with his dying breath. 'Mary is Miriam. Don't you recognise her soul?'

It was as if lightning had struck and split a koan, the truth revealed in the small, encrypted signatures that even time could not erase: her light, the familiar phrases, the way she looked at him, questioned him, challenged him, her strength and courage, and, finally, her glow. Why hadn't he recognised her glow?

Mary Granger is Miriam Bar Boaz?

'Don't you recognise your beloved, Gabriel?'

The truth sank deeper, creating a pressure that cracked his long-sealed heart.

'What shall I do now?' Gabriel flexed his wings. 'Where shall I go?'

'Love Miriam' – Rigel laid down his head – 'in Florence' – and died.

From the mouth of the cave, he could see that the sky was ripening. Around him a slipstream of bats made their nightly exodus, moonlight-drugged and fruit-tugged. He sniffed the air, inhaling the evening bouquet of salt water and tree exhalation: the sweat of earth and sea. Near the horizon, moonlight ghosted the hull of a fishing boat and from somewhere on the beach the faint sounds of a guitar and laughter drifted up mingled with the slush-hush of waves.

'Love Miriam in Florence.' He stood up, shook the dust from his robes. 'Florence.'

Florence where geniuses sought to paint him.

Florence where women fought to taint him.

Florence where he was just another Da Vinci angel.

Florence where lovers kept windows open for him.

'But she's not in Florence.' He shrugged. 'Still, I could go there while I decide what to do next.'

VIRTUOSO

A person with notable technical skill in the performance of music

The night was filled with fragrance: eucalyptus, lavender, a hint of jasmine and the tang of citrus from a lemon-scented gum in the canopy. But no pine and roses.

The evening sounds – the cry of a plover, the hoot of an owl, the rustle of leaves marking the passage of possums through the trees, the thrum of traffic on the not-so-distant main road – accompanied *Mood Indigo* played by the saxophonist next door...who was improving. But no whirr of wings.

'He's never coming back.' Mary touched the place on her balustrade where she used to put the elf dish. She traced the circular stain in a whimsical invocation of luck. 'I need never again fear for those I love. I'm finally free of Gabriel.'

Finally free of the demonic, murderous, cunning companion who had controlled her since childhood.

'So why do I feel so empty?'

Stars twinkled through the canopy and a half-moon cast a tessellation of leaf shadow on the walls. A beautiful night in a safe major key. The world that once shimmered with the prospect of magical descants now obeyed a baton of measured beats: days turned into weeks, weeks into months, months becoming years that fossilised into eons. What was the point of it all? The child growing within her squirmed in his watery cage as if to say, *love makes sense of it all and softens the passage of time.*

'Where are you, Gabriel?' she asked the stars. 'Has a beautiful woman left a window open for you? Are you planning a New World with her?'

Jonté Fortune was well into his preparations for a blazing New World for her. *Another Mozart*, he'd promised. And tonight she would record the music that would make her famous.

'Our dream is coming true, Gabriel. Do you remember when you said my dream was your dream, too?'

The doorbell rang. 'Come in, Jen, door's open!' She called from the balcony.

Jennifer burst in, face flushed, car keys jiggling in her hand. 'Nervous?' she asked, joining her sister. 'Wow, this is some view. It always stuns me.'

'It's all right, I guess.'

Jennifer laughed. 'You're too used to it. Let's go. You're going to make history tonight.'

Before locking the balcony door, Mary whispered, 'Good Night wherever you are.'

'Who are you talking to?'

'Just a ghost.'

'Of Christmases past?'

'Of a past lover.'

Mary clung to Jennifer as they made their way down the three flights of stairs.

'The baby's father?' asked Jennifer.

'That subject's taboo.'

'OK. OK. But why such a big secret?'

'It's hard to explain,' Mary said, climbing slowly into the car.

Jennifer pulled out onto Milson Road. 'It's Robert's, isn't it?'

'He told you? He had no right.'

'He said it only happened once. Not sure why he felt the

need to confess. I'm not judging.' A pause. 'Is he the father?'

'This is *my* baby, Jen.'

Jennifer said nothing for a minute. 'He'll find out eventually.'

'It might be his but most likely it's –' she stopped speaking.

'You never said you had a boyfriend.'

'He's gone. Please don't ask his name. I have no other secrets from you. Let me keep this one.'

'I don't like it. But I won't ask again.'

'I love you.'

'I love you, too.' A moment's silence and then, said with tears, 'I'm going to be an aunty.'

The view from the Harbour Bridge never failed to dazzle, the skyscrapers reflected in the water alongside ladders of green and red lights from the ferries chugging in and out of the Quay. All in concert with the stars.

'He left me six months ago.'

'Bastard.' Jennifer made no further comment until they reached the Eastern Suburbs. 'He'll come crawling back when you're famous.'

The house had changed since Mary last saw it. The glacial white interior was softened with the pastel shades of Jennifer's landscaping. And there were signs of occupation, tiny fingerprints on the walls, and dolls and Lego scattered on the floor. Jonté seemed more relaxed. His jeans were stained with ice-cream and his shirt needed a wash.

'Mary!' He gave her a hug and patted her belly. 'Not long now.' He kissed Jennifer's cheek. 'Your mother's already here.'

Jennifer's eyes widened. '*My* mother?'

Jonté hurried down the hall. 'She told me she had to be here for her two girls. Good-looking woman. I can see where you get your looks from Jen. You, too, Mary.'

Kathleen emerged from the studio and ran to Mary. 'How

232

do you feel? I wish Mamma was here. Jennifer, you look a bit pale. Is everything all right?'

'I feel a bit nervous, Kathleen.' Jennifer explained.

'So do I, me darlin'. You come and sit by me.'

Jonté herded them into the recording studio and locked the door. 'Now ladies, there must be no talking. No whispering. Understood?'

'Yes,' said Jennifer and Kathleen in unison as they sat side by side on the white leather couch, holding hands.

Jonté took Mary into the sound booth. 'Don't be nervous.'

'I'm not nervous, Mr. Fortune.'

He looked away from those faintly disturbing eyes. 'Right then, we'll get started. Pop the headphones on.'

Mary put on the headphones and ran her hands over the piano. It gave her a soft buzzing response, maybe a purr.

'Whenever you're ready.' Jonté's voice in the headphones sounded so close. So intimate.

The music curled from the board like smoke, her hands drifting through it. Swirling images held for a wavering beat before dissolving into notes. The melody told the story of Gabriel who had become as permanent and solid as the unseen layers of rocks that gave the spinning earth its ballast. Even before he came to her window, she had sensed wings and a shimmer of light that watched over and protected her. *Or spied on her.* Now, as her hands flew over the keys, she imagined he was breathing light into the spaces between her notes. His light. Her light.

As she drew towards the end of the piece she fought the grief that sometimes caught her unawares. She missed him. She would never have another lover. Nor would Alfio. For who can accept a mortal after being held in the arms of an angel?

Jonté's voice in the phones broke the spell. 'Do you have a name for that piece, Mary?'

233

'I call it *Song for Gabriel*.'

'Someone you know?'

'Someone I *knew*.'

'Next piece. Whenever you're ready.'

She played the melody she had heard when they had made love for the first time, when the great moments in creation had fused with her soul as tiny fragments, his mouth on hers sealing a covenant between earth and heaven, known and unknown, born and unborn. She played the brush of feathers on flesh, of light on air. The colour of his eyes was reflected in every variation and the last note was the burning sienna of his fierce stare.

'What's this one called?' Jonté asked.

'*The First Time*.'

The next piece was for Florence where artists painted him and women opened their windows for him. For five hundred years his love affair with Florence had persisted yet, of all the women he had known, Miriam was the only one whose name he remembered. Her tears fell onto the board, seeped into the crevices between the keys. She imagined Florence awash with rain as her music serenaded the drenched streets, the glistening statues of angels and washed-out fountains. If she ever took up Alfio's offer and accepted a room in Bellesol she would be twenty minutes by car from the city Gabriel loved.

'And this piece?'

'*Florence*.'

The last track was the most difficult – a requiem for those Gabriel may or may not have murdered to pave the way to her success: Jillian, Magdalene Muir, James Oldfield Jnr, James Snr and her father. *Everything kills to protect that which gives it life. Or light. That's Nature's way.* If they were trees and she a vine that had strangled them to reach the sun, would they forgive her? If they knew she did it to light the world?

'Brilliant work. You can relax now, Mary. I'm coming in.'

She pulled off the headphones, folded her hands in her lap and waited. When the door cracked open, a trapezoid of light fell across the floor and flared on the white leg of the piano.

'What do you want to call that last piece?'

'*Thank you.*'

Jonté scribbled on a notepad. 'And the CD?'

'*For Gabriel.*'

'Great.' Jonté was grinning. 'Go and celebrate with your family. They've been holding hands for the last hour.' He laughed. 'And their breath, too. I'm going to post *Song for Gabriel* on You-Tube and iTunes tonight and watch it go viral.' He nodded at her stomach. 'When's the bub due?'

'Next month.'

'OK. I'll give you six months to get bub settled and weaned and then you'll be on the road – Europe, UK and New York. How does Carnegie Hall sound?'

'It's always been my dream,' she murmured sadly.

He didn't notice. 'In two years you'll be playing to a packed house in Carnegie Hall.' He put his hand on his heart. 'My pledge to you.'

VOLANTE

Melody flying fast

'I'm so proud I could burst.' Kathleen's cheeks were flushed after her third glass of champagne.

'Me too.' Jennifer sipped more slowly while looking out over Shellcove. 'This view is even better at night.'

'It's lovely, to be sure. Mary, love, you're very quiet. I suppose it's finally sinking in. Mr. Fortune said people will be wanting your autograph everywhere you go when *Song for Gabriel* goes...what was his word now...*toxic?*'

'Viral, Mum.'

'I knew it sounded like a poison. Aren't you even a little bit excited?'

'I suppose so.' Her voice flat, expressionless.

'Isn't it what you've always wanted?' Kathleen asked.

'Yes, but when you get what you want, it leaves nothing to look forward to.' Mary clung to her cup. She was the only one drinking tea.

'What about your baby? Isn't that something to look forward to?' Kathleen caught Jennifer's eye. 'Even if the father's done a runner. Whoever he is.'

'Mum, I don't want to talk about the father. Ever. He's gone and he's never coming back.'

'Fame and fortune might lure him,' Kathleen replied, tightlipped. 'But I'll never like him.'

236

'Nothing on earth would bring him back. Life goes on. What doesn't kill you makes you stronger...it's a well-documented fact.' Her voice broke.

'Was it James?' Kathleen asked gently.

'It wasn't James.' A rag of cloud drifted across the moon, casting a frayed shadow. Mary sighed deeply as she hauled herself up. 'The spare room is ready and there are clean sheets in the cupboard for the couch. You decide who sleeps where. I'm going to bed. I'm tired.'

'Of course, darlin'. It's been a big day.'

'We'll sort ourselves out,' said Jennifer. 'You get some sleep. We'll be here in the morning.'

Mary leaned against the doorframe. 'Mum, Jen, thank you both for everything. Family is so important.'

Kathleen went to her daughter. 'A life without love is hard, *I know*, but it has its moments, darling, and yours will be many.' She ran her finger over her daughter's cheek. 'Who knows, when he hears your music, he may be back.'

Mary kissed her mother. 'He's never coming back, Mum.'

The night was so still, the harbour looked like a spill of oil with shimmering droplets of mercurial moonlight. *I imagined he was with me today, glorying in every note I played and pouring his belief into my music.*

In Florence the same moon posed for tourists, swelling like a slattern seeking coin. Gabriel sat in an open window, his naked buttocks bracing the same stone his cheeks had warmed in Renaissance times. As they invariably did when he had no distraction, his thoughts returned to Mary. To Miriam. Earlier that day he had tuned in to her soul and heard her playing her music, his heart leaping at the depth of feeling in her melody.

'Do you ever think of me, my love?' he whispered. 'No, of course not. You don't need me. You have your family and soon you'll have the world.' He clenched his jaw. 'We made that music together as we made the child. You would be barren but for me. You were frightened until I spread my wings over you. Do you remember me at all, Mary?' *But who ever remembers me? I'm only seed and inspiration. The unsung co-creator of the universe.* 'You forgot me, Miriam.' *His Father had forgotten him and moved on. Rigel had forgotten him and would soon be born again with a new name and a new life.*

'Everyone forgets me,' he said out loud.

'Angelo Gabriel?'

His lover had woken. She had the beauty of an Italian woman: dark curls, eyes dark as chocolate, red lips pouting for another kiss. 'Come back to bed.' She stretched out her arms and raised her hips seductively.

Sex is all well and good but like candy one can sicken on too much sweetness. But a warm bed and a warm body offered comfort for him while he decided what to do with himself for the rest of eternity.

He stood up, forced a smile, and wandered slowly back to her bed, willing himself to tumescence.

DOLCE

Tenderly, sweetly

Jonathan tucked the black canvas bag under his cape, turned off his bedroom light, and crept downstairs. Jennifer was staying with Mary and wouldn't be home until morning. Robert was closeted in his studio, painting, and didn't want to be disturbed. Over dinner he'd announced that his Muse was with him and he would paint until dawn.

So, Jonathan was alone. More or less.

Carefully, he closed the kitchen door behind him and hurried from the house, keeping to the shadows, avoiding the pale spear of light thrown from Robert's studio, avoiding Jennifer's new garden beds which would record his passage in the freshly turned soil. Jennifer had broken all the straight lines, curved every border and introduced more colours. The effect was a semi-wild, fey landscape like the Constable painting hanging above the fireplace in the living room.

Jonathan was proud of his sister's talent for gardening. He'd never admit it, of course, but in those long, harsh years when they lived in that dump in Newtown, those verdant little seedlings gave him hope. If they could erupt from the dirt, sprouting tiny green wings, then one day he might fly too.

He paused and looked back at the house, checked that Robert hadn't spotted him. The curtains of the studio were open. Robert stood in front of the easel, paintbrush in one hand, palette in the other, contemplating his work. Robert may be stuffy and prematurely aged but there was no denying his artistic genius.

'You lucky fart,' Jonathan said under his breath. 'God overlooked me.'

Yes, he boasted about his marketing skills, but what else could he do when he had no true talent except the Salieri ability to recognise it in others.

And envy it.

'You may be a genius, Robert Goodman, but without me you'll remain unnoticed.'

Robert didn't fit the usual mold of artistic genius: flamboyant, prone to tantrums, self-indulgent. He was pedestrian in his approach to both his life and his work and perhaps it was this ordinariness that blinded Mary and Jennifer to his talent. But the detection of genius was Jonathan's oeuvre. Jennifer said nothing. She was kind, laughed at his lame jokes, listened to his lectures about art and just about tolerated the adulation he lavished on her. Jonathan knew that Jennifer liked Robert. The man was exactly like his surname. How clichéd and boring and sad. And how *old* – one of those people who had never been young. Jonathan imagined him middle-aged at twenty.

He continued on his way to the arbor at the bottom of the garden, to the gardening shed, his nerves tingling with excitement. Inside the shed something scurried into hiding. He lit a candle and sent whatever it was – probably a mouse – deeper into the nooks. He left the shed door open so he could see the stars. Robert wouldn't spot the tiny spill of candlelight. The trees would block it. He undid his cape, threw it across the bench and laid his precious paraphernalia on the black silk – syringe, belt, spoon, lemon, lighter, a bottle of water and the magical, mystical junk. Excitement already ran in his veins.

He was careful not to move any of Jennifer's gardening tools. She would spot even the smallest disturbance. Her tools were lined up, everything in its right place, as if Mary had organised them. There were a dozen shovels hitched to the wall in descending order of size, a red wheelbarrow tucked neatly into a corner, five pairs of gardening gloves suspended on hooks, several straight rows of potted seedlings on the work bench, and cuttings in buckets lined up underneath next to a dozen newly grafted roses and two pots of bougainvillea awaiting planting.

'You make up for all my missing gifts,' he lovingly told his paraphernalia. Then he threw a spiteful glance outside and addressed the guardians of nature. 'Faeries, why was I overlooked? Wasn't I worth a gift? Or two?'

Jennifer had read to him when he was little, told him stories about Faery Godmothers who visited the cradles of babies and gave them magical blessings and special talents that would enrich them when they grew up. One child might be given the gift of beauty. Another intellect. Or strength. Endurance. Artistic talent.

'What's my gift?' he had asked her, eyes wide with curiosity.

Jennifer had frowned. 'We'll have to wait and see. It will be something special.'

It wasn't. He had no gift at all. By the time he was fifteen, he knew he'd been overlooked. The faeries hadn't bothered with the dark, silent child who lay in his crib glowering at the world. Or perhaps they had used up all their gifts. Cruel faeries. Maybe that was why he felt compassion for his father where his sisters felt only hatred and repugnance. James Granger knew what it felt like to be nothing. His lack of talent warped him. It twisted him into thieving from his children. Into raping them. Perhaps the selfish James recognised a similar paucity in his son – which was why he cradled him so tenderly after the pain of invasion. After the whispered assurances: *I never meant to hurt you. I loved you.*

Jonathan wanted to believe him. Love involved pain. Pain and love. Love and pain. The two went together. And all his subsequent lovers, the men who paid him for five minutes of sex against a wall, delivered the brand of pain he associated with love. They never knew his name, never whispered words of love, never told him he was special. It was better that way. The strong, compassionate man of his dreams could remain, forever imagined, behind his closed eyes. The man who adored him and whispered that he was special. The man he would never meet.

But his mistress, heroin, made him feel special. In her thrall he felt great and powerful and capable of conquering the world. So despite his promise not to use drugs at Shalamar, sometimes he needed a fix of her sweet lies. And technically, he wasn't using in the house. Just the shed.

He began the culinary process of preparing the drug, mixing it with lemon juice to make it compatible with water, heating it on the spoon, sucking it into the needle. When this was neatly done, he rolled up his sleeve to expose his skinny pale arm and to tighten the belt above his elbow. He quivered with excitement as he waited for the vein to swell. Then, came the stab, that pinprick of delicious pain laced with anticipated pleasure. Soon Lady Heroin's sweet lies would intoxicate him with a joy even more exciting than imagined acts of love with the man of his dreams.

Finished and fulfilled, he loosened the belt, cleared the bench and lay down, turning his face to the stars. Immediately he was floating on the surface of a pink lake, aware only of the stars. As he watched, they swelled to the size of ping-pong balls. His mistress bid him count them. He did, but the unreliable things kept bouncing about.

'Never mind the stars, Jonathan,' she whispered. 'Redesign the universe.'

'I can't. It's too big.'

'Shrink it.'

So for the next few hours, he shrank the universe, brought the stars within reach as jewels to be plucked.

'Now decide the fate of humanity.'

'Humanity?' he asked nervously.

'Kill them if you wish.'

The sky was beginning to stain with pale light. Soon Jennifer would be home and Robert would be buying the Sunday croissants. Needing to be back in his bedroom before his absence was discovered, he didn't have time to decide the fate of humanity. *Were people worth saving anyway?* They were always at war, the rich grew richer and more cavalier about the environment while the poor huddled in faceless legions and died unnoticed. A good old-fashioned biblical drowning was in order, but he decided to be merciful. Simply let them be. Jenny said mercy was strength.

'I will show them mercy,' he whispered.

'Ah, so you are weak,' his mistress replied and turned her back on him.

'But Jenny said –'

'I don't care what Jenny said.' The fix was wearing off and his mistress was acquiring fangs and scales. How serpentine were those jeweled eyes. 'Be a man, Jonathan Granger. Kill something.'

'But Jenny –'

'Shut up! You are nobody.'

He curled into a ball. 'Jennifer loves me,' he murmured.

'Jennifer loves everybody. She even loves that old fool Robert.'

'No. She's just being kind to him.'

Always be kind, Jenny told him when they had lived on the streets. No matter how they treat you, be kind and merciful. In all those long, sad years he never heard Jennifer say an unkind word to anyone.

'No. She loves him. Soon they won't want you around.'

He blocked his ears. 'No. No, Jennifer will always look after me. She promised.'

'Soon she won't want you. She's happy now. Haven't you seen her laugh?'

It was true. Never before had he heard his sister laugh. Now she laughed often: at Robert's jokes, at his own impersonations or quotes from Oscar Wilde. Outside, tending the garden, she laughed for no reason at all. When he asked her why, she replied that Shalamar made her feel safe, that she loved the house, she adored the old Camphor Laurel trees. She said the house with its lichen-stained walls had history and she wanted to be part of its story.

'He'll marry her, Jonathan, and then you'll have to leave. Where will you go?'

He turned his head slowly, and looked at the ceiling. A mouse was peering down from a beam, its black eyes gleaming in the burgeoning dawn, whiskers twitching, ears stiffly alert.

'What are you looking at?' His words stretched out like a slow-running tape. The mouse continued to stare. The hit was fading fast. He felt the terrifying vertigo of the *exchange* – the moment when heaven and hell flipped. The surface of the pink lake was breaking up and when he plummeted to the hard plane at the bottom, he ached with saturating cold. The candle had long burned out. Soft drizzling rain misted the fountain, pond and arbor. The reality of a cold gray dawn was working its way into his bones. He curled up tighter, closed his eyes against the painful truth.

When the sun broke through the mist, a pair of strong arms pulled him off the bench and light-filled sky-blue eyes watched him.

'Daddy?' he asked.

A curtain of blonde hair fell over his face. 'It's me, Jonathan.'

'Jenny?'

'Who else?'

He succumbed to the enveloping warmth of his sister's arms.

'I've been bad,' he whispered. 'Will you tell Robert?'

'No.' Her voice surprisingly calm.

'But he'll know when he sees me.'

'He won't see you. He's out at the shop. He thinks you're in bed.'

'Have you got my stuff?' His voice held panic.

'Yes. I packed it in your black bag. I've got it.'

'How did you know where I was?'

'I figured it out. Your bed hasn't been slept in.'

'Did you just get home?'

'Half an hour ago.' She helped him up to his room, helped him undress, and get into bed. 'I'll tell Robert you're sick today.' Again the curtain of blonde hair, warm and smelling of apple shampoo. 'It's a long road, Jonathan, but we'll get there in the end.' She kissed his forehead. 'Do you need anything?'

'I need to know you'll always look after me.'

'You've got me for life, Johnny. I'm not leaving you.'

'And if something happens to you?'

'I'll take you with me. Sleep now.' She turned away and closed the door behind her.

'Even unto death,' he whispered, closing his eyes and falling into a dreamless sleep.

Sunlight streamed through the kitchen window. In the morning light, her eyes were the colour of an English lake, beautiful enough to drown in.

'How's Mary?' He put the croissants in the oven. 'She must be very excited about her success. That song for what's-his-name has gone viral.'

'Yes, she's always wanted to be famous. Even as a kid.' This small lie, at Mary's insistence, to keep the illusion of family intact would not stain her soul.

'Robert maybe you should call Mary and catch up on her news. You two haven't spoken in a while.'

'Let's ask her to dinner before she flies off to London or New York.' He sat opposite her. 'Jennifer, we need to talk.'

Her stomach clenched. 'You're going to ask us to leave?'

'God, no. Why do you think that?' He paused. 'Are you happy here?'

'Yes. Why?'

'I want you to stay, that's all. But I suppose sooner or later you'll meet someone and leave.'

'I doubt it,' Jennifer looked away quickly. 'Robert, let's talk tomorrow morning. Right now I want to start clearing the arbour. The Morning Glory is about to invade and I have two bougainvilleas to plant in its place.'

'May I help you?'

He might see the shed and guess about Jonathan. 'I prefer to work alone.'

'Please.'

He was always so polite, asking her permission in his own home. It was rather sweet. Had she collected all the incriminating evidence? Yes. She was used to covering for her brother. Maintaining his lies. 'All right.'

The sun glanced off her eyes again, highlighting the green undertone. And then he remembered where he'd seen that lake. It was in the Cotswolds. He and Jillian were on holiday. After walking all day, just as the sun was setting they stumbled into a valley where the lake was the colour of turquoise and gold, as if the sun had drowned in it. Jillian swore it belonged to the faery folk. Back then, he thought that nonsense. Now, he wasn't so sure.

'Wear something old and comfortable,' Jennifer was saying. 'I'll get changed and meet you out there in fifteen minutes.'

She laughed. 'I'll give you a shovel and tell you what to do with it.'

'Just what I deserve, right?' He laughed too.

At the arbour, she asked him to wait while she dashed into the shed and did a quick scan. Nothing. She grabbed two shovels.

'Here,' she said, handing him the smaller one. 'And after we dig out the Morning Glory we have to burn it or it'll grow back.'

'Burn it? That's cruel.'

'Nature is cruel, Robert. Can we use the barbeque? Will you ever cook steaks on it?'

'We're vegetarians.'

'Jonathan and I are but you –'

'I'm a vegetarian now.' He'd changed after she'd moved in. 'I could no more eat an animal now than fly through the air.'

'As long as you're sure, because Morning Glory sap is poisonous.'

'I'm sure.'

She nodded at the fishpond. 'I'd like to get that fountain going again too. The water needs to flow. And I'd like to put goldfish in the pond. What do you think?'

'Anything you want.'

She studied the vine, tracking it to the fence line, looking for the point of invasion. 'There! That's how it got in.' She pointed to a thick cord of stem that had crept under the stone wall. 'I'll seal that off next week. Cement it over.' She kicked at a loose flagstone with the tip of her work boot. 'I need to grout these as well.'

'Is there anything you can't do?' Robert asked.

She ignored his question and swatted at an insect. 'Start digging there.' She pointed. 'I'll get the wheelbarrow and we can load it up ready for the barbeque.'

He struck his blade into the earth, leaned on it as hard as he could, and gouged out a single root ball.

'I did it!' he cried triumphantly, tossing it into the wheel barrow. 'Man conquers nature!'

'One small step for man, a giant leap for mankind.' She drove her own blade into the earth, split the ganglion roots with practiced ease and hurled the remains.

'You make it look so easy.'

'I'm used to it.'

'Where did you learn about gardening?'

'I borrowed books from the library. I had no education...so I read.'

'I wish you trusted me,' he said softly.

She stopped digging. 'I do. You're one of the very few people I do trust, Robert.'

'I wish you trusted me with your heart.'

She froze. He saw.

'I'm not saying this very well. I mean...one day people have to risk love.'

'Some pain is too much to bear ... even given love.'

'Try me.'

'Please. Don't talk about it. Let's just work.'

He plunged his shovel into the earth again and they fell into a rhythm, both of them applying their blades to the suckered vine root. By midmorning there was a pile of wilting green and purple stems in the wheelbarrow, but they seemed to have made little impression on the vine.

'Did you know my house was named after a famous garden?' Robert wiped his forehead.

'No.'

'The garden was designed by Shah Jahan – the same man who built the Taj Mahal. Both the Taj Mahal and Shalamar were in memory of his wife who died in childbirth.'

'That's a magnificent legacy.' Jennifer blinked several times. 'I'll just go and burn this lot. Excuse me.'

Robert watched her push the wheelbarrow up the slope, her

bearing dignified and self-protecting. As if she was holding herself together. He wondered, not for the first time, if someone had interfered with her. Maybe an uncle or her father?

'Oy, get back to work! I'm not paying you to stand around,' she called on her way back.

'You don't pay me at all! I'll put in a complaint.'

They continued their banter, working in harmony: one digging, one tipping roots out of the wheelbarrow. They worked hard, but the plant was without ending. Then a tendril looped itself around Robert's ankle and clung.

'Jennifer, that vine just latched on to my ankle.'

She laughed. 'Don't be silly!'

But then a vine caught *her* ankle and gripped. Struggling to extricate herself, she lost her balance and tumbled into Robert's arms.

'I'm so sorry,' she said, blushing.

'Don't mention it.'

She unwound the vine only to be tripped by another tendril and fell again into Robert's arms. 'This is ridiculous! The vine is grabbing my ankles!'

'That's what I said. Bewitched!' He gazed at her. 'Bewitching.'

She wore no make-up, and in the late morning light her skin was faintly blushed. Sunlight burnished the thick plait that fell halfway down her back. Robert imagined releasing the golden coils perfumed with apple blossom.

'I'm not normally this clumsy,' she said.

'That's perfectly all right.' His face was close to hers. 'Jennifer –'

'Maybe we should leave this for a while.' She tugged at the vine looped round her ankle and tumbled onto the flagstone tiles surrounding the pond.

'I don't know what's wrong with me today,' she repeated, brushing leaves and broken flowers off her overalls.

Robert sat beside her. 'I would never hurt you.'

249

'I know that.'

'Please tell me if I'll ever have a chance with you.' His heart was hammering in his chest. 'If it's a No, I'll never mention it again. Promise.'

She stared into the pond. 'No man has a chance with me after what *he* did.'

'Who?'

'My father,' she whispered. 'He broke me in every conceivable way.'

Their bodies touched and the air was fragrant with crushed purple trumpet flowers. A dragonfly skittered over the pond. When he put his arm around her shoulders, she stiffened but did not resist. For some time they stared into the overgrown pond, saying nothing.

'People break, give up and stop growing,' she said after a while. 'But nature grows in spite of everything. I've seen pictures of stunted pines growing in mountain crevices. Where do they find the courage?' She raised her chin. 'Jonathan isn't sick today.'

'I know.'

She spun around. Met his eyes. 'You know?'

'Of course I do. After you left, he was wildly excited. I knew what he was planning. I told him my Muse was upon me and I would lock myself away in my studio and paint.' He shrugged. 'I didn't know what else to do after I'd been so definite about the house being a drug free zone.'

'He's never done it in the house.' Jennifer held his gaze. 'He uses the shed.'

'Ah, of course. Should I try to stop him ... next time?'

'I don't think there's much point.'

'So we just have to be patient with him.'

'Some wounds never heal,' she whispered.

'His wounds *will* heal. Your wounds will heal. Mine have healed.' He dared to stroke her hair. 'One day I woke up and realised that for the first time I hadn't dreamt of Jillian. Life can go on.'

'I can never have children.' The light drained from her eyes. 'When I was seventeen, a doctor told me that the scarring was too severe for a foetus to attach to my womb. I'm barren.'

Life offers moments that, if unclaimed, never come round again. He touched his mouth to hers. Again she stiffened at his touch but did not pull away. He increased the pressure slightly, felt her tremble and, despite his own ache, pulled back. 'If you marry me –'

'I can't!' She reeled back. 'I just told you why.'

'Hear me out, please. If you marry me, I will never come to your bed unless you invite me. And I do not expect children.'

'But that's not fair to you.'

'I love you, Jennifer. It's enough for me to have you with me. And I can help with Jonathan. Marry me, please. You do like me, don't you?'

'I love you, Robert,' she replied. 'You are utterly good. And very kind.'

'Well, then...'

'No, wait. There's something else I must tell you. My father may have broken me but he didn't break Mary. She didn't want me to tell you –'

'Tell me what?'

'She's pregnant, Robert, and the baby might be yours.'

The newfound joy drained away. 'What should I do?'

'What any decent man would do. Offer to marry her.'

'But I'm in love with you.'

She raised her chin higher, her eyes cold and clear. 'That's irrelevant. Every child deserves a decent father.'

EXPRESSIONISM

To play expressively

Rain, rain and more rain. The pavements were awash, rivulets corrugated garden beds, the inlet was a lumpy gray mass undifferentiated from the sky, and windows wept. Mary tossed and turned. No matter what position she settled in, she wasn't comfortable. Jonté had rung earlier to let her know that *Song for Gabriel* had gone viral on U-Tube and the CD was outselling even the most popular teenage idols, boy bands and glamour girls.

'You start touring next year,' he said. 'Remind me…when are you popping the bub?'

'Any minute.'

She tried lying on her back, but the weight of the baby pressed against her spine, so she got up, waddled out to the kitchen and made a cup of tea. There was a knock at the front door. Nine o'clock. She wasn't expecting anyone – and who would brave the rain? She flung on her dressing gown and answered the door.

'Robert!'

Her ex-employer stood there, water dripping off his nose and chin, a huge bunch of soggy pink roses in his hand.

'For you,' he said, glancing at her bulging tummy. 'They looked great when Jennifer cut them but the rain – May I come in?'

'Is everything all right at home? Jennifer?' She paused. 'Jonathan?'

'Jen's fine.' He didn't mention Jonathan.

'Come in. I'll get you a towel.' She left him in her living room dripping onto her carpet still clutching the damp bouquet.

'Your music is on every radio station,' he called out. 'Everyone's playing it.'

'Here,' she said, returning with the towel. 'Dry off and then explain what brought you all the way to Cremorne in the pouring rain.'

He gave her the roses. 'They might perk up with some water.'

'More water?' She smiled. 'Cup of tea? Kettle's just boiled.'

'Thank you.' He followed her to the kitchen. 'Why didn't you tell me, Mary? Why did I have to hear it from Jen?'

'I asked her not to tell you.'

'Why?'

She sunk into a chair. 'Sorry, I have to sit down. I get so tired. It's not that I don't trust you. It's just that this baby is mine.'

He sat, too. 'It might also be mine.'

'It's not,' she said, looking past him, out the window.

'Damn it, Mary. You don't know that for sure. This is the only child I'm ever likely to have. We can get a DNA test to establish my rights if need be.'

She turned slowly to face him, her eyes shining with tears. 'Please don't, Robert. Be an uncle if you wish but not the father. Please.'

'The child deserves a loving father, Mary,' he said gently. 'Especially after the way your father treated you.'

'Jen told you that, too?'

'Today. I will give this child every advantage in life.' He rubbed his forehead. 'Jennifer wants me to ask you something.'

She looked at him tiredly. 'What, Robert?'

'Will you marry me? For the sake of the child. It can be an agreed arrangement. No need to –'

'Sleep with the man who's in love with my sister? No, Robert. But thank Jen for me. I know what it must have cost her to force you out in the rain ... with roses.'

'Cost her? What do you mean?'

'She loves you. The woman you should be offering marriage to is Jennifer.'

'I did. She sent me to you.'

'And I'm sending you back. Ask her again.' She laughed. 'I'll keep the roses though.'

His relief was palpable. 'Whatever happened to your musician boyfriend?'

'He left me.'

'I'm sorry. You and your child will always be welcome to live in Shalamar.'

After he left, she went to the piano.

'How are you, old friend?' She ran her hands lovingly over the keys. 'No matter how many Steinways I play in my career, you hold first place in my heart.'

The rain was heavier now. It drummed against the windows and drenched the leaves and grief-bowed the branches in the canopy. She played *Song for Gabriel*, the tune that had captured her heart long before it caught everyone else's. At its ending, she swung around half-expecting to see the archangel standing behind her, wings raised, robes glistening, smile teasing, finger wagging. *Did you think I wouldn't find you?* But she was alone. He was never coming back.

She lay awake, longing for the oblivion of sleep, when there was another knock at her front door.

'What now?' she asked, as she made her heavy way to the door.

'Alfio!'

'I walked from the deli.' He looked thin and pale and unshaven. His hair and clothes were saturated. 'How are you?'

'We can talk later. First, you need a hot shower and dry

clothes. There must be something of mine that will fit.'

After showering Alfio inspected Mary's clothes and chose her track suit. It was several sizes too small but better than nothing.

'Could I have something to eat?' He gave an apologetic shrug. 'Suddenly I have an appetite. I've been living on canned beans and toast since –'

'Sit.' Mary ushered him into the kitchen and pulled out the chair that Robert had recently vacated. A frozen stew was soon warming in the microwave. 'Hot veggies or salad with your hearty beef stew?'

'Don't go to any trouble.'

'Which?'

'Salad, please.'

They said nothing while Mary prepared his meal, nothing while he ate every morsel.

Finally, he pushed the plate away and stared vaguely out the window. 'There's no grave. I didn't know his date of birth. Or his surname. I scattered his ashes into the sea off the rocks at Palm Beach. I took him there at dawn so that we'd be alone.' His chest rose and fell in ragged breaths. 'There was a moment, Mary, when the sun burst over the horizon and I almost felt that God had come to take him home.' For a moment he was silent. 'Why didn't Gabriel stay and help me bury his brother?' His eyes snapped into focus, tortured, hurt. 'I just need to know.'

'He isn't emotionally strong like us, Alfio. He left me, too.'

'Left you to raise his child alone while he saves the bloody world. Or has he given up that notion?'

'He's given it up.'

'He gives up on everything, doesn't he?'

The baby wriggled and bucked. Mary tried to soothe it with gentle strokes. 'Be calm, little one –' her voice breaking. 'Gabriel tried to please his Father, but he failed. He still hopes his Father will forgive him and send for him.'

'I thought their father was dead.'

'No, He left home.'

'Like father like son? We all have to grow up sometime and be true to ourselves, Mary. I should have come sooner. I'm sorry.'

'I'm not your responsibility, no matter what Rigel said. Oh, do settle, little one, please.'

'May I try?' Alfio stretched a hand. Tentatively.

Mary held it against her stomach.

'I felt a kick.' His eyes shone. 'It's Alfie here, little one. You're safe.'

The baby settled instantly but Mary felt a different pain low in her abdomen.

'Ouch! Oh, dear.'

'What's the matter? Not labour starting, is it?'

'I don't know.' Her eyes widened with fear. 'I don't think so. The pain's gone now but it was pretty bad this time. I've been having them for hours but spaced out so...so it's not labour. Surely.'

He leaned back and sighed. 'I've been hearing your beautiful music on the radio. Gabriel must be hearing it, too. You'd think –' he took a deep breath. 'Even if he does come back I don't think he deserves you.'

Mary shook her head and opened her mouth to speak.

'No. Please hear me out. Rigel asked me to watch over you and the baby and I promised him I would. That's why I'm here. Mary, I want you to come to Bellesol with me.'

'Italy? Now?'

He laughed. 'Not tonight. After the baby's born. As soon as you can both travel.'

To be near Florence...the city he loved.

'Argh!' This time the pain was overwhelming and lasted much longer. Mary bent over. Clung to a chair. 'Alfio...maybe I should go to hospital.'

Alfio leapt up. 'I'll call a taxi.'

'My bag...Arrgh...is next to the front door. Oh, Christ this bloody hurts. Call a fucking taxi now!'

In the cab, she clung to Alfio.

'All right, hold on. You have to breathe,' he said, remembering something he'd heard somewhere. 'Mary, there's something I have to tell you.'

The driver discreetly watched them in the rear vision mirror.

'We need to get married.'

'What? Why?'

The driver grinned.

'My grandfather will insist.'

'Doesn't your...arrgh...grandfather know you're gay?'

The driver's jaw dropped.

'Yes, but he'll insist the child has our name. It'll be easier for residency. You can have lovers.'

'I don't want lovers!' she hissed. 'Only your brother.'

'I don't have a brother.'

'*Rigel's* brother. You know what I mean for God's sake. Why are you arguing with me?'

Now the driver was having trouble keeping his eyes on the road.

'I don't want another lover either,' he said after a moment.

'ARRGH!' She dug her nails hard into his arm. 'You think I want to go through this again?'

'My arm!' Blood gathered in the row of stab marks.

'Alfio! This is....unbearable.'

'Breathe. Come on, I'll breathe with you...in one, two, three...now out slowly.'

'Here we are.' The driver looked relieved as he pulled into the emergency bay where a nurse waited with a wheelchair.

'Call Mum and Jennifer. Look under Granger,' Mary said as the nurse pushed her away.

'OK. Will you marry me or not?'

'Yes. ARGHHH! For fuck's sake! Alfio, don't leave me!'

'I'm right behind you. Breathe! In and out! Deep breaths.' Then he remembered the driver. 'How much do I owe you?'

'It's on me, mate. I haven't been so entertained in years.' He slapped Alfio's shoulder. 'Good luck. You're going to need it.'

Kathleen, Jennifer, Robert and Jonathan cast curious glances at the handsome man in the ill-fitting tack suit who sat opposite them.

'Is Alfio Ferranti an Italian name?' Kathleen asked politely.

Alfio dragged his gaze from the swinging doors of the operating theatre. 'Yes, I was born in Italy ... in Tuscany ... near Florence. You're Kathleen?'

'That's right. Mary's mother.'

'She's mentioned you.' Then to Jonathan, 'She never mentioned *you*.'

'I'm Jonathan, Mary's brother. Our little sister failed to mention she had a handsome friend tucked away in the closet.'

'I'm not in the closet. Haven't been for years.' His eyes were back on the doors.

'Fascinating,' murmured Jonathan. 'Does Mary know?'

'So how did you and Mary meet?' Kathleen asked, overriding Jonathan.

'She came into my delicatessen one day.'

The conversation dried up for some minutes.

'What instrument do you play?' Robert asked.

'I'm sorry?'

'I said what instrument do you play? Mary told me you were a musician.'

'The guitar. But I would hardly describe myself as a musician.'

'How *would* you describe yourself, Alfio?' Robert narrowed his eyes.

'Confused,' Jonathan muttered.

'That's enough,' Jennifer warned. 'We're very glad you and Mary have sorted things out. Welcome to the family.'

'Thank you...Jennifer, is it?'

She nodded.

'So what made you come back, Alfio?' Robert couldn't hide the sarcasm.

'The baby,' he said. 'Why is this taking so long?'

'The baby? Not Mary?'

'Both.' Alfio finally looked Robert in the eye. 'Do you have some problem with me?'

'Yes, as a matter of fact.'

'No,' Jennifer said. 'We don't have a problem with you. Whatever happened between you and Mary is your business and whatever you decide is fine by us. As long as she's happy.'

'Why aren't you in there with her?' Robert's voice hardened. 'Oh but of course...being with her is not your style.'

Alfio was about to respond when a nurse appeared. 'Mr. Ferranti?'

He leapt up. 'Yes? That's me. Is Mary all right?'

'She's fine. Your wife's just delivered a beautiful baby boy and she's asking for you.'

Alfio, beaming, trotted after her.

'Wife?' Robert, Jennifer, Jonathan and Kathleen spoke in perfect unison.

'Did I hear him correctly? Did he say he was out of the closet?' Jonathan asked.

'Don't you go getting ideas, Jonathan Granger,' Kathleen said sharply. 'The man's Italian. He couldn't possibly be bent.'

'Or gay.' Jonathan got to his feet and swung his cape over his shoulder. 'I'm going to get some coffee. Anyone else?'

Robert rose too. 'I could use some. It's been quite a day.'

Once they had gone, Kathleen turned to Jennifer. 'When did my daughter get married?'

'I have no idea.'

'Why didn't she invite her own mother to her wedding?'

'Maybe she dragged him to a registry office before he could take off again.'

'She's been so miserable without him. I *told* her the music would bring him back. I want to hate him after what he's put her through but –'

'He's so nice,' finished Jennifer.

'He's charming. I can't stay angry with him. Oh, well, they're a family now. That's the main thing.'

'Kathleen, I have some news for you too. Robert and I are getting married.'

'Oh my goodness…another surprise! Good for you, darling girl.' She dabbed her eyes. 'You'll invite me to *your* wedding, won't you?'

Jennifer laughed. 'I was rather hoping you'd help me plan it.'

Mary handed the blue-rugged bundle to Alfio. 'He's beautiful,' she whispered.

Alfio took the baby, tears welling. 'I checked you in as Mary Ferranti. It seemed easier. That way he gets my name on his birth certificate. You did agree, after all.'

'Look at your son.'

'My son.' He blinked back tears. 'Hello you,' he whispered. 'Welcome home.'

At the sound of Alfio's voice the baby opened his eyes, gazed up and smiled.

'He smiled at me.'

'That's wind, Mr. Ferranti.' It was the nurse, now at their side. 'Babies don't smile for several weeks.'

Alfio caught Mary's eye, mouthed the words. 'He smiled at me.'

'I know.' Mary mouthed back.

'Do you have a name for your son?'

'His name is Rigel,' Mary replied.

'Rigel?' Alfio whispered.

Mary smiled. The baby gurgled and grinned.

'Yes,' Alfio said. 'We're naming our son Rigel Ferranti.'

A PIACERE

At pleasure. The performer is not
bound to follow the rhythm exactly.

𝄞

Home. *A space defined by four walls, a gathering of family and friends, a place where milestones are celebrated and rooms trigger memories.*

Bellesol, a beautiful house in an idyllic landscape, was not home, despite the enthusiastic goodwill of Alfio's grandfather, Nonno, and the stream of neighbours who arrived with gifts for *la famoso compositore, Mary Granger,* her husband, Alfio, not after all *finocchio,* and their *bellissimo angelo bambino, Rigel.*

Home was Cremorne Point where her piano waited in the alcove gathering dust. Mary could not decide. Should she sever the links with the past, sell her place and her old piano and tour the world as Jonté wanted? As her CD sold and her fame grew? As Carnegie Hall became more than a promise. Or stay where she'd been happy with Gabriel.

'Why don't you play the piano here?' Alfio would ask.

I want my own piano. My dear friend.

'I need time to settle,' Mary always replied.

Alfio nodded and left it at that. The Yamaha baby grand remained untouched.

Rigel whimpered in his sleep.

'All right, little one?' She leaned over the crib and marvelled at her son's flawless beauty. 'Gabriel, we have a beautiful son,' she murmured. 'Not that you care. You weren't even curious enough to linger until our child was born.'

She soothed the baby back to sleep, then went to stand at the window. The night was still and soundless. A three quarter moon laminated the hills and turned the espaliered vines into silvery webs. Gabriel was right – the moon looked larger in Tuscany. Close enough to catch in a net. The faint glow of Florence hovered over the furthest hills.

'Are you in Florence, Gabriel? Are you posing for an artist or looking for an open window?' *Or has your Father summoned you to a distant galaxy?*

She yawned and turned away. She was always the first to go to bed. Night feeds and missing Jennifer and her mother exhausted her. After her departure, Alfio and Nonno raked over the day in Italian, but tonight footsteps in the hall, the low burr of a conversation and the final click of bedroom doors meant they weren't far behind her. If Nonno wondered about their arrangement, separate beds, separate rooms, he never asked. It was enough that he had family around him. And he was the cog in the wheel for Alfio and Mary and Rigel, the heart of the family, his kindness communicated in warm smiles and the bunches of wild flowers Mary found next to her placemat at mealtimes.

'He's a perfect grandfather. The one we all wish we'd had,' Mary had told Jennifer. They talked often by phone.

'And how's married life? He's not trying to take off again?' Jennifer had asked.

'He's staying put. We're blissfully happy,' she lied. 'And you?'

'A child.'

'What?' Mary almost dropped the phone. *Gabriel had said Jennifer was barren. Had Jen too been visited by an angel? Impossible.*

'We're going to adopt a little girl,' Jennifer said, joy and wonder in her words. 'From an orphanage in Thailand. She's three.'

Mary was stunned into silence.

'We had to marry quickly to be eligible so it was a trip to the registry office and Kathleen was upset she missed out on another big white wedding. I told her we'd have a big white Christmas in Bellesol instead...sorry...should have asked you first. Would it be OK? With Nonno?'

'It's brilliant. Maybe I can talk you into staying forever!'

Jennifer laughed. 'I'll organise it this end. Kathleen's missing you fiercely.'

'Maybe Mum could stay on.'

'Maybe. She's learning Italian. It's a surprise. You didn't hear it from me.' She had chatted on about Robert's painting and how Jonathan was determined to get him an exhibition despite a conspicuous lack of interest from galleries. 'So how's Italy? Rigel?'

Mary told her sister everything. Except the truth – that her heart was broken and her soul felt hollow and she longed day and night for Gabriel.

The moon had risen higher, glancing off the windowsill, delineating a second horizon.

Once I left dishes of honeyed bread for the elves on my windowsill and an angel had come.

Gabriel has left me hungering.

Dissatisfied.

Lonely.

Next door, Alfio was talking loudly on the phone. That was odd. And so late. His voice was intimate, warm and...he was speaking in English!

'Thank you, J!' he said. 'Thank you!'

She lay awake staring at the sky framed in the window. Did her husband have a lover? So soon after Rigel's death? She quashed a stab of anger.

'Who the fuck is J?' she asked. *J*? Australian?

It had better not be Jonathan.

The next morning a posy of fresh daisies lay by her breakfast plate.

'I picked them,' Alfio said shyly. 'I thought you might like them.'

She filled a glass with water for the flowers. 'Peace offering?'

'Sorry?'

'Nothing.' Mary sat down and smiled at Nonno. 'Good Morning, Nonno.'

'Did we have an argument?' Alfio asked, puzzled. 'Or did you have a restless night?'

'I slept like a top,' she lied. 'What about you?'

Picking up the tension, Nonno focused on Rigel in his basket.

'We can talk later. No need to worry –' he nodded discreetly at Nonno.

'No. I'm being silly. Petty and stupid. Alfio, I want you to be happy.'

He looked at her for a long minute. 'And I want *you* to be happy.'

They left it at that. The conditions unspoken.

After breakfast they went their separate ways, Alfio and Nonno to the cellars to check the fermenting Bellesol shiraz and Mary to the hills with Rigel snuggled into a possum pouch. She climbed to the top where the valley spread below like patchwork fields stitched with rows of cypress, pine and poplar. There, she imagined Gabriel in Florence, posing for a new artist, preening and enchanting and achingly beautiful. *Do you ever think of me?*

After feeding Rigel, she lay on the grass and gazed at the sky. Gabriel was right about the Tuscan sky: it *did* hold light in suspension and the blue *was* shot through with gold. She caught one of her baby's small hands, reaching upwards, and pressed it to her cheek. 'You're an angel but they must never know,' she said before sleep overwhelmed her.

When she woke the air had chilled and the sky was bruising russet and bronze. Rigel had managed to wriggle free of her grip and slept with both hands curled tightly under his chin as if he had caught and held a piece of sky. Shivering, she gathered up her child and headed back down. Outside the house, the sound of an engine punctuated an otherwise pristine silence and on the dirt road a puff of dust curled in the wake of a truck. Rather late for a delivery of bottles but she didn't give it much thought.

Alfio and Nonno were waiting for her on the front porch, excitement sparkling in their eyes.

'What?' she looked from one to the other.

'You see,' said Nonno. 'Come. Come.' His eyes were smiling.

'Rigel needs changing,' she murmured.

'It can wait,' Alfio said, taking the baby. 'First you must see this.'

She followed them along the hall to the room painted a rich ruby. Nonno opened the door and stood back for her to enter.

'We thought...Nonno and I...this might make Bellesol feel more like home.'

Under the far window was her old piano.

She clasped her hands. Fought back the urge to cry. 'When did you arrange this?'

'Last month. Jen arranged the transfer her end and I sorted out the delivery this end. We spoke last night.'

Jen? J. She laughed at her stupidity. 'You spoke to Jen! I thought –' she stopped.

'What?' Alfio frowned.

'I thought you had a lover. I heard you on the phone last night. I'm sorry.'

He smiled softly. 'And did it bother you?'

A pause. 'Yes.'

'Hmmm. Good.'

Nonno touched her hand. 'You play now.'

She approached her old friend, raised the lid and touched the keys.

'Thank you both.' She turned to them, eyes shining with tears. '*Now* this is home.'

A hush, a beat and then came music that sang of the ever-changing light of Bellesol, its reflection in her son's eyes, the hot summer nights when the moon rode full and high, and the Christmas that was coming when her family would be together. Snow would be falling on the hills outside while inside a fire roared and Nonno opened a bottle of Italy's finest wine.

She played on until the moon blistered the Duomo with a silvery corrugation of tiles and dew. Nonno and Alfio sat on, listening intently and quietly while Rigel added his own small vocal harmonies.

And in Florence, he heard. He rose from a lover's bed and crept to the open window, straining to catch the fine threads of melody which came on the wind and wound around his heart. Tighter and tighter. The harmonies held him spellbound as he been all those years ago.

He unfolded his wings.

He flew out into the night.

MAGNUM OPUS

A great work of art, especially an artist's finest work

She twisted her waist-length hair into a knot and secured it with a diamanté clasp at the nape of her neck. A dash of red lipstick to match her gown and she was ready.

The stage manager knocked. 'Fifteen minute call, Miss Ferranti.'

There was no music playing in her head. Not yet, but it would come when it was ready. Another knock on the door.

'Come in.'

Alfio burst in, face flushed. 'The auditorium is packed. I'm so nervous. How about you? Stupid question…of course you're nervous. But you'll be brilliant. You always are. Don't worry. The entire family is in the front row. Stand. Turn.' He articulated a circle in the air with his finger. 'Just need to adjust this clasp… that's better.' He placed his hands on her shoulders. 'He might have sent flowers.'

He gave me roses once. Red. I've still got them in a box under my bed. They haven't faded and the petals glow with inner light.

'Forget him. He's not worthy of you. Never was.' A reassuring squeeze of her shoulders. 'Don't be nervous. This is what you've always wanted.' And then he was gone.

'I'm not nervous.'

Another knock on the door. 'Five minute call, Miss Ferranti.'

'This is it,' she whispered. 'Everything I've ever wanted.' *Family, fame, love, recognition and a burgeoning fortune.*
So why this heartache?

The music made its first shy appearance as the auditorium darkened, the notes riding in on hushed and excited whispers. Her fingers traced the melody as she stood in the wings. Tentative at first, it built in response to the anticipation of the two thousand souls who waited beyond the stage.

Mary waited too, tendrils of memory binding her to the past, trapping her in that first moment when she knew her music could bridge heaven and earth. When Gabriel had kissed her and she had felt the world pitch towards a light more compelling than the sun. He had said they would orchestrate salvation and fill souls with light. They would forge enlightenment. They would triumph. Together.

From a faraway time and place, she heard her name announced.

'Ladies and gentlemen, Carnegie Hall is proud to welcome Mary Ferranti.'

And she stepped forward into the spotlight and walked towards the piano, her music pulsing like breath, exhaling the past memory of Gabriel's kiss, inhaling the present. The audience held its collective breath while she sat down and took a moment to listen and tune her emotions to the instrument. Then she touched the keys, her hands flying over the board sleighting cycles of melody that were more exciting, more moving, more fabulous than anything she had played before. As the last notes rang out, two thousand bodies rose as one, applauding, shouting Encore! Encore!

'*Song for Gabriel!*' someone cried out.

A swell of applause.

She sat again, taking a moment to compose herself. Then she played the piece that had secured her fame. Four bars in, she glanced at the audience, acknowledging their love, their admiration, their support and their secret joys...and shame. She smiled as if to say *I know, I've been there, too.* Listen. Listen. Follow my music wherever it leads. *And if you need a refuge, as I once did, it is here for you. As it still is for me.*

When the last note rang out, a bouquet of red roses landed at her feet – the colour of her gown and scented with pine.

'Gabriel?' She twisted to stare into the glare of light.

A whisper of wind. The brush of feather against her cheek. *Did you really think I would not come back?*

'Gabriel!'

But her cry was drowned in the drumming of feet and the thunder of applause.

FINALE

Movement or passage that concludes a musical composition

'From the private balcony, the apartment has a view of the Duomo. It was used as an artist's studio in the Renaissance,' the estate agent continued. 'Even the great Da Vinci hired it from time to time. His favourite models sat for him here.'

'I'll take it,' Mary said.

This was where they met. Alone. Because of course he must never come to Bellesol. Never hurt anyone. Never meddle with the way she and Alfio raised the children: those angels who lived as flesh and learned the meaning of human love. She would silence the music if he ever killed again. The rules were set in stone.

He kept them.

A piano stood in the place where Da Vinci may once have had his easel. On the lid, a vase of pine-scented roses glowed red.

The sun was beginning to set, flaming the feathers of cloud, turning the Duomo molten copper, the campanile gold. Beyond the city, blue hills pocketed the remains of the day.

She opened the balcony doors, poured two glasses of Bellesol Shiraz and sat down to wait, an old song playing in her mind. When the moon floated like a golden balloon above the Duomo, he alighted on the balustrade and, twisting to catch the moon between his forefinger and thumb said, 'The first time I posed for Leonardo Da Vinci –' he dropped onto the balcony. 'Have I told you this already?'

Many times.

'No, my love.' She handed him a glass of wine. 'Tell me.'

'I stood where your piano is now, moonlight shining through my wings and robes. Da Vinci said my beauty would turn humanity's sights to heaven.' He sighed. 'They never looked up.'

'Patience. They will in time. Shall I play for you? Ease your soul.'

He caught her hand and kissed it. 'Play our song.'

He closed his eyes. Sat magnificently still. The scent of pine and roses sweetened the moonlit night while Mary's music wove the threads of life into a glorious tapestry of faith and light.

Everything was in its rightful place...just as should be.

FINI